BLOOD ORCHIDS

A LEI CRIME NOVEL

BLOOD ORCHIDS

A LEI CRIME NOVEL

TOBY NEAL

Proverbs 14:12:
There is a way that seems right to a (wo)man,
but in the end it leads to death.

Chapter 1

Drowning isn't pretty, even in paradise. The girl's features were bloated by water and nibbled on by wildlife. She lay half embedded in silty mud, naked as a seal carcass. Long hair that might have been blonde wrapped around her like seaweed, one sparkly hair tie still in place on the side of her head.

Leilani Texeira grimaced at the sulphurous smell of the mud as she stepped into it, shiny regulation shoes disappearing, and squatted to inspect the body. After three years on the force in Hawaii she'd seen several drowned corpses, and had learned to stay detached as she looked for any signs of violence. Still, she was thankful for the small mercy of the girl's closed eyes.

Her partner Pono's voice was a bass drone interspersed with static as he called in the discovery on the radio. Lei stayed on her haunches, her eyes slowly surveying the entire overgrown area of the small county park. Invasive christmasberry bushes and clumps of tall *pili* grass competed along the unkempt banks. Midmorning sun leached reluctantly from under cloud cover as she spotted what looked like a bobbing coconut a few yards out. Lei glanced around—no palm trees ringed the pond.

She pushed her pant legs up and splashed forward into murky water warm as blood, clots of yellowish algae dotting the surface.

"Hey!" Pono called. "What the hell are you doing?"

"Got another one," Lei said. The water reached her thighs. Any deeper and she'd have to go back and take off her bulky duty belt. She approached the body, floating face down. Female, small build, brown skinned and nude—Lei mentally composed the report. She extended her baton and poked the corpse, wondering if something might fall off if she touched it, but the flesh was hard. Still in rigor. These girls hadn't been dead long.

"Let the crime techs deal with it. You know you're not supposed to touch the body—I don't want you to get in trouble again." She ignored Pono, in the grip of a compulsion she couldn't put words to.

There was something familiar about this body.

She grabbed a handful of trailing black hair and gently pulled. There was bit of give, but the hair held and the body moved sluggishly at her tug. Lei steeled herself and, walking backward, slowly towed the body to shore in a parody of rescue. She backed up into the shallows, bringing the girl up onto the muddy bank, and rolled her by flipping the shoulder. The brunette landed on her back with a splash next to the blonde.

Lei sucked a breath and bit her lip, bile rising.

The eyes were open this time, and she recognized them.

Haunani Something-or-other—a sixteen year old kid with an attitude. Lei had busted her for possession at the high school a week ago. The girl's once-brown eyes were cloudy. Her open mouth was filled with water. Rigor kept the arms raised at an angle. Haunani looked as if she were waving for help, the motion frozen forever.

Off in the distance Lei heard sirens. She staggered out of the mud up onto the grass to stand beside Pono. Her stomach crawled back down her throat as she breathed in through her nose, out through her mouth and touched the tiny cowrie she kept in her pocket.

"I know her. I mean, I knew her."

"Who she stay?" Pono used pidgin, dialect of the Islands, when he was upset. He rubbed his mustache with a finger and she knew he wanted a cigarette.

"Remember a couple weeks ago? Drug bust at the high school? Her name's Haunani Pohakoa."

The last name came to her along with a memory of the girl's cocked hip and long shiny hair. Haunani had been vain about that hair, tossing it around like a pony flicking flies. Lei wished she could forget the slick feeling of the wet strands as her heart squeezed, remembering the fragile bravado Haunani had worn like armor—an armor they shared. She'd felt an immediate connection to the girl when she met her. Lei rubbed her hands briskly on soaked uniform slacks.

"Wish someone else could have found them," Pono muttered, pushing mirrored Oakleys up onto his buzz-cut head and folding bulky tattooed arms. "Simple patrol for vandalism down here and we gotta find this. Never going be done with the paperwork."

Lei didn't reply. She'd been partners with Pono long enough to know how much he hated dealing with dead bodies, a little superstitious about them since his daughter's birth two years ago. Fortunately they didn't come across many in sleepy Hilo.

Sirens announced the arrival of reinforcements. Lei looked up to see the new detective from L.A., Michael Stevens, striding toward them with a tall man's loose-limbed grace. His wiry Asian partner, Jeremy Ito, trotted in his wake. She'd seen the pair around the station but never worked with them before.

Blue eyes lasered her briefly from under black brows as Stevens scanned the scene and the bodies, hands on jeans-clad hips. Ito imitated Stevens' stance.

"Hey. What do we have?" Stevens was all business.

"We came out on a vandalism call. Someone had trashed the bathroom, done some tagging." Pono gestured to the dreary cinder block bunker mottled with graffiti beside their parked Crown Victoria. "We did a foot patrol around the pond and found the blonde first. Then Lei spotted the floater and towed her in."

Stevens and Ito both turned to look at Lei, incredulous. She felt a hot blush stain her cheeks, and her dripping slacks and squishy shoes screamed bad judgment. She extended a hand to Stevens.

"Lei Texeira. I've seen you around."

He shook it, a brief hard pump. "Michael Stevens. I assume you know you shouldn't have moved the body. Supposed to wait for the techs to get here, photograph it, all that."

"I thought she might be drowning." Lei's scalp prickled fiercely at the lie.

"With the other one right here, obviously gone?" Ito's soft voice had a hard edge as he narrowed eyes at her.

"I'm sorry. It seemed wrong to leave her out there." Closer to the truth, but still not the compelling need she'd had to bring the girl's body in, to turn it over and see her face.

"Well, what's done is done." Stevens squatted down to get a better look, leaning out over the mud. "The medical examiner's on his way. Why don't you two put up the tape before anyone else disturbs the scene."

"We know who the brunette is," Pono said. "Lei busted her with weed at school awhile back."

"Oh yeah?"

"Yeah. She's a Hilo High junior. Haunani Pohakoa." Lei shut her eyes against a flash of memory of sun on that shiny black hair—but when she closed them, she saw the girls' drowned faces, and between them her own: tilted almond eyes closed, wide mouth slack, olive skin so pale the cinnamon freckles across her nose stood out like paint spatters.

She recoiled, stepping back, and stumbled a little in the rough grass.

Ito's brows had come down in a frown as both detectives glanced at her. Pono gave her arm a tug.

"Let's go get the tape," he said. She followed him, fleeing toward their parked cruiser, her pant legs rasping and shoes squelching.

"I'll expect all the details on how you know the victim in your report," Stevens called after Lei as the M.E.'s van and the Lieutenant's cruiser pulled up, and the dismal little park filled with the organized chaos that follows death.

After combing over every inch of the banks of the small pond, Lieutenant Ohale ordered all available officers to search the two feeder streams for the original crime scene where the girls had gone into the water. Lei and Pono split from the others, taking the lower stream.

Pono trailed behind her, his eyes scanning the ground, as Lei chugged a bottle of water one of the crime techs had given her. Adrenaline from the initial discovery had worn off, leaving her shaky and exhausted—but the same compulsion that had driven her into the water to retrieve the body drove her on now.

Lei's damp uniform chafed and her duty belt, loaded with radio, sidearm, cuffs, pepper spray, ammo, evidence bags and more, caught on scratching branches as they moved along slowly, looking for any signs of human presence. Humidity caused her rebellious brown curls to frizz out of the tight ponytail she'd restrained them with. Sweat beaded on her forehead and she swiped it away, glad of physical discomfort that distracted her from drowned faces.

Once outside the immediate area of the park, their progress through underbrush along the creek was slow, impeded by tall christmasberry bushes.The invasive species from Brazil had become an islandwide problem, smothering native growth with its rapid spread. Dark green, glossy bushes peppered with clusters of red berries blanketed miles of open space, and almost choked the stream.

A real estate sign marked the edge of the park and abandoned cars filled with trash, a rusted Jeep and rotting Pontiac, had been pushed into the undergrowth from the nearby road.

"We might as well tag these abandoned cars for pickup." Pono, ever conscientious, took out his pad of orange removal stickers.

"I hate the way people dump their cars around here." Lei picked her way over boggy ground to the first vehicle by stepping on top of grass clumps. "But it doesn't help we don't have any recycling facilities on the island. Anyway, you tag 'em, I'm going to keep looking."

Pono was still writing his description of the Pontiac as she pushed through long grass, hearing the rushing of water beyond the overgrown bushes. She spotted an opening.

"Pono, looks like a break here. I'm gonna check it out."

"Right behind you." Pono peered in to look for the VIN number on the Jeep's dashboard.

Lei edged her way across the boggy ground, pushing through raking branches. On the other side of the wall of shrubbery, a stream flowed beside a clearing marked with a fire ring and a shelter made by tying a tarp to the bushes. A palm tree leaned out over ruffled water, fronds waving in the slight breeze.

Something about the setting oppressed Lei as she walked forward, surveying the area carefully. Perhaps it was the pile of discarded propane cans, soda bottles, and a dirty sleeping bag that testified to someone having camped there not long ago. Rocks made a handy access point to water otherwise choked by thick grass.

A white rag was caught in the vegetation, along with something shiny. Lei squatted on the rocks and fished the objects out of the water: a long strip ripped from a T-shirt and a cluster of iridescent ribbon attached to an elastic hair tie.

"Hey." Pono crashed through the bushes, muttering as he slipped on the mud. "Anything interesting?"

"These were caught in the stream." Lei held up the hair bow. "It looks familiar."

"Looks familiar to me too. That's a little girl's hair tie." Pono squatted beside her, examining the items.

An image burst across Lei's brain, indelible. Bluish closed eyes, straggling blonde hair on one side, and on the other . . . a pigtail with a sparkly ribbon cluster.

"Oh my God, Pono. I think we just found the primary crime scene."

Chapter 2

"Shit. We trampled all over the ground," Pono said. He hooked his radio off his belt and called it in. Lei let her eyes wander slowly over the lush scene, looking for anything out of place. She pictured a scenario: the girls coming out here, maybe to party, and then drugged and tied up. Raped? Maybe they knew their captor?

"Detectives are on their way. They want us to stay put, secure the scene."

"Okay," Lei said, standing at last. It was weird she'd found the crime scene so easily; almost like it was staged. This was one of those times Lei felt an electric tingle that signaled she was onto something, and that inner drive she'd followed hardened into resolve. She had to get assigned to the case—Haunani needed justice.

She turned to look at the shelter. They would have to take everything there into evidence, including the trash in the junked cars. Stevens, Ito and the crime scene techs arrived, groaning at the mud and the amount of garbage that they would have to sort through.

Lei helped empty the junked cars, putting garbage into heavy-duty evidence bags. Her uniform was hopeless by then, the legs of her pants soaked and muddy, mosquito bites peppering her arms. Replacements eventually arrived, sensibly dressed in boots and zip-front canvas overalls, with big portable lights to work into the night.

"Stevens." Lei addressed the tall detective as he sifted through the grass along the bank, latex gloves on his hands.

"Yeah?" He straightened up. "Funny how you keep finding things, Texeira."

"Just lucky. That's why I think I should be on this investigation, Detective. I really want to find whoever killed Haunani Pohakoa." She was surprised to feel tears stinging the backs of her eyes and blinked hard.

"No offense, but I need experienced detectives. I'm asking the other districts to send us some of their best people."

Lei felt slapped. "You'll find out for yourself how strapped for personnel Hilo District is. We're always fighting the budget battle."

"Yeah, well, I gotta try."

"Let me know if I can help. I feel like this case found me as much as I found it."

"You take initiative, I'll give you that." He made a gesture that took in her filthy uniform and bedraggled appearance. "I'll try and find something for you."

"Great. Hope you can use me." Lei didn't bother to suppress the sarcasm in her tone as she spun on a muddy heel and pushed back through the bushes to the cruiser.

* * *

Sunset gilded the surface of the creek as a full moon crested above a backdrop of swaying trees. Lush grass lined the bank where a single palm leaned out, leaves fluttering over two girls floating in light-streaked water. The creamy skin of one contrasted with the earth tones of the other as their hair swirled in the stream.

He adjusted the colors in Photoshop and tried black-and-white and sepia tones, eventually rejecting them. The final version enhanced the darkening blue of evening sky, fat pearl of moon and waning sunbeams caressing naked, face-down bodies. Blunt fingers rattled the keys as he titled the photo Orchids, and saved it to an external hard drive in a file filled with flowers.

Not that photos were ever enough—that was why he kept a few reminders.

He took a shiny new metal key ring out of his desk drawer, along with a Ziploc bag. Two long hanks of hair twined together in the bag—one silky blonde, the other a glossy raven-wing black. He eased the hair gently onto the desk, stroking and separating the colors, brushing them with a soft doll's brush.

Each piece was exactly twelve inches long. He savored the memory of measuring the hair on each sleeping girl's head, his fingers finding the barely noticeable spot where he cut it, two inches up from the tender dip where the skull joined the neck.

He doubled the blonde hank into a loop and tucked it in through the key ring, inserting the tail and tugging down so the hair hung secured by its own strands, and trimming it with surgical scissors so all the ends were aligned.

He lingered a bit over the black hair, brushing and remembering. It was too bad he'd had to get rid of Haunani, but when she'd showed up to their special spot with her friend, he just had to have them together. The photos brought his art to a whole new level, and he could remember his time with them anytime he wanted. He opened his drawer and looked in at the other key ring, lush with a rainbow of red, blonde, brunette and black hair.

That ring was full and the girls deserved their own—after all they'd given their lives.

He attached Haunani's hair to the new ring beside the blonde hank and leaned back in his chair, trailing the hair down his arms, across his chest. He stroked it beneath his nose where he could inhale their scent—grass, girl, and sunshine.

That scent took him straight to his afternoon with them faster than jewelry, clothing, or even the photographs. As the criminologists said, he was evolving. He chuckled at the irony of it all, and closed his eyes again.

Chapter 3

*L*ei pulled into the detached garage of her little cottage. It had been a long day. The single-walled wooden structure built in the 1960's—dark green with white trim—was characteristic of Hawaii plantation homes, right down to the galvanized tin roof that amplified the frequent Hilo rain to a percussion orchestra. Lei particularly loved the deep covered porch and the fenced yard where her Rottweiler could patrol during the day.

Keiki put her massive paws up on the chain-link gate and whuffled with joy. She'd bought the young, police-trained dog for security when she moved to Hilo two years ago, and in that time Keiki had become much more than a guard—she was someone to come home to.

"Hey, baby." Lei rubbed Keiki's ears. "Go around the back and I'll meet you for drinks." The big dog peeled off the gate and galloped around the side of the house as Lei unlocked the front door and let herself in, deactivating the alarm with a few keystrokes. Pono had teased her about her security measures since few people in Hilo locked their doors, let alone had an alarm system—but he'd backed off when she told her a little of her story. More than anything, she needed to feel safe in her home.

Keiki burst through the unlocked dog door. She skidded to a stop as Lei held up her hand. The dog plunked her hindquarters on the floor, grinning. Lei squatted in front of her and rubbed her wide chest.

"Good girl. Mama's home."

Keiki snorted, burying her nose in Lei's armpit.

"Yeah, I know I'm ripe," she said, getting up and dumping food into Keiki's bowl. "You pour the wine and I'll be out in a minute."

The dog buried her nose in the bowl. Lei had grabbed a burger on the way home—food was not something she liked to spend time on—just fuel for the body. She went into the linoleum-floored bathroom and took the cowry out of her pocket, setting it on the sink as she stripped the filthy uniform off her lean muscular body, dropping it into the laundry hamper.

She'd picked up the smooth little domed shell with its ridged base at the beach the last time Aunty Rosario visited, and rubbing it was one of the ways she'd learned to manage anxiety. She stepped into the shower, luxuriating in hot water pouring over her petite frame, washing away mud and aches as she mulled over what was being called the Mohuli'i case.

She'd asked around about Stevens, the lead detective. He had a solid reputation, and as a seasoned big-city cop his experience was going to be important on a double homicide that was looking complicated and inflammatory. His partner, Jeremy Ito, was a local boy whose biggest case prior to the girls was a homeless guy beaten to death in a park.

It was a good thing Stevens was there to take the lead— South Hilo Police Department seldom had homicides, let alone this kind of case.

Lei scrubbed mud off her legs and out from under her short, unpainted nails, trying to keep her mind from wandering back to images of the drowned girls. Her eyes lighted on the note thumbtacked to the peeling drywall above the shower surround: *Well-behaved women rarely make history. —Laurel Ulrich.*

Haunani Pohakoa hadn't been well behaved when Lei met her at the high school.

"I nevah going show you notting." Her dark eyes flashed defiantly as she spoke pidgin English—thick as burnt sugar in the cane fields that spawned it, the language of choice among 'locals' in Hawaii. The dialect had evolved as the many races brought over to work the plantations learned to communicate.

"Open up the backpack," Lei said. "Your principal called me and we already know you're carrying."

"Haunani, no give the officer hard time." The principal, Ms. Hayashi, wore a muumuu over athletic shoes with a jangling bunch of keys on a lanyard around her neck. The older woman shook her head and the keys rattled. Per protocol, Haunani had already been searched in the library conference room by the principal and a teacher before the police were called. No one had answered at the girl's parents' numbers.

"I don't have to," Haunani insisted. Lei rolled her eyes. The girl shoved the backpack over abruptly, refolding her arms across a shapely chest that spelled out **HOTTIE** in rhinestones.

Lei opened the backpack. Inside a rolled up pair of socks were a baggie of pot and a glass pipe.

She pulled a plastic evidence bag out of the snapped pouch on her duty belt and put the marijuana and pipe in, labeling them with a Sharpie marker.

Pono stuck his head in the door. "What's the story?"

"Got some *pakalolo* and a pipe here." Lei held the bag up.

"All right. Let's go." Pono gestured. "We'll try your parents again at the station."

For the first time, a ghost of fear stole across the girl's face. "I going be in so much trouble," she whispered.

Lei took her by an elbow and escorted her past staring and gossiping students to the cruiser and put her in the back. She

got in front and waited as Pono finished up paperwork with
Ms. Hayashi, glancing in the rearview mirror to see Haunani
curled up with her knees beneath her chin and tears tracking
down her cheeks through dark makeup.

She felt a pang for the girl. She'd been that miserable once.

"It's not going to be so bad," Lei said. "You're a juvenile
so you'll probably get community service or something."

"It's too late now," Haunani whispered. "He's going to be
so mad I got busted."

Lei knew what it was like to be abused—by a mother whose
drug use ruled her life, by a father who'd abandoned her when
he was incarcerated.

"We can help you."

"No you can't. Not that I want help from cops anyway."
More tears belied this statement but Lei couldn't get another
word out of her, and in the end no one answered at any of the
numbers they called. Pono and Lei would have sent Haunani
home with Child Welfare Services, but the worker said there
was nowhere to put her.

Lei remembered Haunani's stony stare as the teen walked
out of the police station, thumbing her phone to call someone.
It had seemed there was no one who cared about the girl—but
now, with shower water cooling around her, Lei wondered if
someone in Haunani's life had been angry enough to kill her.

Lei rubbed the scars on the inside of her arms with a
washcloth—thin silvery threads left from days when she'd
been desperate to express her pain. She was glad to have those
reminders of how far she'd come, and wished she could have
shared them with Haunani somehow. Maybe it would have
made a difference.

Later, Lei moved through the house, checking the sturdy
hasps on the windows. She locked the dog door and rechecked
the locks on the both entrances, arming the alarm. Even
without her duty belt, she knew she still walked like a cop,

energy coiled, arms away from her sides to keep them from catching on her sidearm.

Lei's bed was a king, with an old-fashioned, curly iron frame and a canopy draped in filmy voile. She dove in, dressed in her usual boxers and tank top, enjoying the silky sheets. She patted the ratty handmade quilt at the foot of her bed, and Keiki leapt up with a graceful lunge, turned in a circle, and stretched herself out with a doggy sigh of content.

But even physically exhausted, with her dog at her feet and the boxy black Glock on the bedstand, Lei didn't sleep well. Long black tendrils of hair tried to wrap around her and pull her under in dreams of clouded eyes.

Chapter 4

*T*oo early the next morning while brushing her teeth, Lei glanced at the mirror where she'd taped a 3x5 card: *Be the change you want to see in the world—Gandhi.* Across from the toilet, precariously stuck to the pebbled-glass shower door: *God has a plan for every living thing.*

The "affirmations" were part of the cognitive behavior therapy she'd done in California while doing her AA degree. They were meant to remind her of positive truths and be replacement thoughts when memories dragged her into a dark place. Still, it was hard to believe *God had a plan* when she'd spent the day looking for the crime scene where two young girls were drowned.

She'd been so tired last night she'd forgotten to get her mail. She put on her rubber slippers and tripped down the cement steps to the aluminum mailbox, listing on its steel pole. She took out the handful of bills and circulars and flipped through them as she headed back to the porch. An envelope caught her eye, **LEI TEXEIRA** printed on it.

She ripped it open and pulled out a piece of plain computer paper. Bold capitals spelled out:
YOU LOOK PRETTY WHEN YOU SMILE

I'M GOING TO MAKE YOU CRY.

She looked at the envelope again. No address, no postmark, no stamp. Someone had personally delivered it.

The hairs on her neck rose, along with a surge of adrenaline. Her head flew up as she scanned the empty sidewalk, heart kicking into overdrive. The row of modest homes on her street were deserted except for her neighbor at the end of the block. The guy had no life. He was always either working in his immaculate yard or washing his car. This morning it was washing his car.

She bounced down the steps and ran down the street to talk with him, rubber slippers slapping against her heels.

"Hey. I got this weird message," she said, waving the envelope. "Seen anybody messing with my mailbox?"

The man straightened, the big sponge in his hand dripping. He was younger than she'd assumed, with an angular, handsome Japanese face. The pale early-morning sun caught in glossy black hair.

"No. I haven't seen anyone but the paperboy."

"Well, it's a weird note, and someone hand-delivered it. Can you remember anything unusual?"

He stared at her, and she remembered she was in the thin tank top she slept in and tiny boxers. She crossed her arms over her chest, trying to look casual.

"Aren't you a police officer?" he asked.

"Yeah—maybe that's why I'm a target. Can you keep an eye out?"

He seemed to relent, tossing the sponge into the bucket and approaching her with his damp hand outstretched.

"Tom Watanabe," he said. "Water Department Inspector."

"Lei Texeira. Police officer," she said, with an awkward laugh. She shook his hand.

"I'll certainly keep a look out. When did you check your mail last?"

"Not since day before yesterday. I guess it could have been dropped off any time since then."

"Well, here's my number," he said, opening the car door and reaching inside. It was a new Acura, charcoal with a silver flake. He handed her his card.

"I should be the one giving you my card, but I just rushed over here . . . I was so hoping you had seen something."

"Nope, sorry. Drop your number by . . . I'll call you," he said, smiling.

"Sure will." She backed up, uncomfortable. Was he hitting on her? "See ya."

She turned and speed-walked back to her house, conscious of his eyes on her ass. She looked back as she went inside, and sure enough he was still staring, the hose pouring unnoticed from his hand. She gave a little wave and he jerked his chin upward in 'local style' acknowledgement.

She slammed the door, whistling for the dog. Keiki came skittering in and she re-alarmed the house. She was rattled by the creepy way Watanabe had checked her out and his anal-retentive habits didn't help. She stood there for a minute and did some relaxation breaths. Her eyes fell on one of her notes, stuck to the bottom of the living room lamp.

Courage is the price that life exacts for granting peace. —*Amelia Earheart.* She felt calm move up and over her. She could handle this, freaky as it was.

She put the stalker letter in a Ziploc bag in her freezer between the stacks of Hot Pockets, and that seemed to neutralize the threat of it.

She called Pono at home. His phone was off so she left a message, changed into shorts and a ratty old Hilo Police Department t-shirt. This time she put on a shoulder holster and loaded her Glock .40 into it under a thin nylon running jacket, clipped her cell phone onto her shorts. Keiki lunged and bounced ecstatically as they went down the cement steps.

Tom Watanabe and his charcoal Acura were gone, she noted with relief.

Her phone rang as they jogged through her neighborhood toward Hilo Bay. She stopped to answer it, stretching her hamstrings.

"Lei, what's up?" Pono asked.

She told her partner about the note.

"We should check it for prints."

"I have a feeling he didn't leave any, but I guess we should anyway when I come in."

"Keep your gun close until then."

"How'd you know?" she asked, patting the Glock.

"I know you. Just don't shoot anybody you don't have to."

"Aw, stealing all my fun. You're such an old lady." She shut the phone and slipped it in her pocket.

They picked up some real speed after that as Lei worked off the adrenaline the note had brought on. The sidewalk around the Bay was buckling, pushed upward by huge banyan tree roots. Coconut palms stood sentinel around the park, their arching fronds shimmering in the light breeze. Mynah birds hopped and chattered on the mowed grass. Keiki seemed to enjoy the briny scent of Hilo Bay, tossing her head and snorting.

Lei ran all out, the emptiness of total effort blocking out intrusive images of the dead girls brought up by the smell of the water. Keiki's ears flattened back as they thundered through the park and made their way through the town back to the cottage. She took Keiki into her small fenced backyard and hosed the dog off, then misted her collection of orchids.

A delicate purple blood orchid, a veined variety of phalaenopsis, was blooming. Raising orchids was a pastime she'd shared with Aunty Rosario, her guardian, and working with the plants never failed to comfort and calm her. She took the orchid inside and set it on the table.

Lei showered and did the beauty routine—a handful of gel in her hair to tame it and a swipe of gloss on her full mouth. She didn't know what accident of nature had landed her with the sprinkle of cinnamon freckles over her nose—a Portuguese, Hawaiian and Japanese heritage was full of genetic surprises. She buttoned into the stiff navy-blue uniform, buckled on her loaded duty belt, grabbed the stalker note out of the freezer and hurried out the door to her little white Honda Civic.

"Hey, babe," said Sam, the watch officer behind the front desk, as Lei pushed through the aging glass doors of the South Hilo Police Station.

"Hey babe, yourself."

Sam chuckled and went back to his crossword puzzle as she passed the second glass door into the bull pen and went straight back into the lab, where Pono waited at one of the workstations. She handed him the note and he sprayed it with ninhydrin.

"Gotta let it set for at least 12 hours, but usually something pops right away." He slid the paper under the portable arc lamp but nothing fluoresced. "No dice. Let's come back and check at the end of the day."

"I expected as much. Damn."

"Well, let's open a case for you. In case this isn't the last we hear from this kook."

"It better be."

Lei signed the complaint Pono had filled out under Harrassment/Stalking. They were late for the morning's briefing and hurried back to the conference room, where Stevens and Ito were clipping pictures of the girls from Mohuli`i Pond onto the whiteboard on the back wall. Lieutenant Ohale had already taken up a stance behind the battered lectern, his broad build dwarfing it. She and Pono slipped into empty molded plastic chairs, trying to be unobtrusive, but Lei felt Ito's stare-down from the corner of the room. The rest of the current shift officers were already seated.

"Today's priority is the Mohuli` case. We have a few more facts since yesterday." The Lieutenant shuffled through some notes. "The blonde girl is identified as Kelly Andrade, aged fifteen, the brunette is Haunani Pohakoa, aged sixteen. Approximate time of death is sometime late evening on Tuesday; the girls were discovered Wednesday 10:00 A.M. Preliminary tox screens came back positive for Rohypnol. There was sexual activity prior to drowning but little premortem bruising."

He looked up, his deep brown eyes intense, ridiculously tiny reading glasses perched on his wide nose. "I can't stand this sick shit happening in my town. Detectives Stevens and Ito are primary on the case; I'm requesting more backup from Hilo District. Stevens will be asking for additional support from you as it's needed. Detective Stevens?"

Stevens came up and took the lectern. "Our top priority is interviewing the girls' parents. In fact, early this morning we heard from Kelly Andrade's parents who called in to report her missing. Ito and I did a quick trip to the house to inform them. Mother was too upset to talk so we set up an interview for this afternoon." He looked down at his notes. "We haven't talked to Haunani's parents yet and we need a female officer. Texeira? Can you come do the interview with me?"

Lei went rigid, eagerness warring with apprehension, but her voice was steady as she answered.

"Of course."

Chapter 5

L ei and Stevens got into the unmarked Bronco he drove. Lei's stomach cramped around the granola bar she'd eaten on the way into the station, and with a panicky feeling she realized she'd forgotten the tiny cowrie shell. She'd only been on one death notification before and it honestly wasn't something she'd ever wanted to do again.

"So you wanted a female officer—why?"

Stevens' jaw bunched as he turned the key and the Bronco roared into life. The vehicle smelled of Mohuli`i Pond. Lei glanced into the backseat and saw muddy boots on a pile of plastic evidence bags from yesterday's crime scene.

"Kelly's mom, Stacie, did a lot of screaming, ran into the bathroom and took a big handful of sleeping pills. Not enough to send her to Emergency for stomach pumping, but I'm doubting she's going to make it into the station this afternoon for the interview. The stepdad, James Reynolds, was cool as a cucumber. Blamed us for upsetting her." He shook his head. "Ito's a good partner but he just froze up when it got emotional, left the room. I was thinking if you talked to Haunani's mom, you know, woman to woman, it might help us get a little more out of them."

"Not sure why you thought I'd be any better at this than Ito." Lei gave a short laugh.

"You said you wanted to help. This is all I got right now."

"Yeah, okay. Thanks for giving me a shot."

She looked out the mud-speckled window into morning light that failed to brighten the shabby low-income neighborhood they'd entered. Tiny tin-roofed cottages leaned into each other, draped in flapping laundry, lawns decorated with decrepit cars and scratching chickens.

Stevens peered over at the navigator bolted onto the dash. "This is it."

They pulled onto a scrap of grass in front of a dwelling made of multicolored plywood shaded by a rusting tin roof. A broken Big Wheel leaned against a cement stoop where a thin brown woman sat, wreathed in cigarette smoke that did little to soften the haggard planes of her face. A flagrantly blooming plumeria tree shaded the doorway above her, and as Lei got out, a single pinwheel blossom spiraled down and landed on long black hair that reminded her of Haunani like a punch to the gut.

She hung back as Stevens approached, holding his shield up.

"Hi there. Nani Pohakoa?" His tongue still tripped over the multiple vowels of the musical language.

"I'm Nani. Who you stay?" A smoker's voice, gravelly and suspicious.

"I'm Detective Stevens and this is Officer Texeira from South Hilo Police Department."

"What she done? Stupid girl gone two days now."

A long pause. Stevens glanced at Lei, signaling her. She stepped forward, lowered her voice. "We need to speak to you privately, Ms. Pohakoa. Can we come inside?"

Dark eyes peered at her through a rheumy film. The woman's bony arms gestured to a couple of frayed beach chairs leaning against the wall.

"We talk here. Nowhere for sit inside."

Lei and Stevens brought the chairs over, sat on them gingerly. The older woman dropped the cigarette butt into a jar of water at her feet, lit another one with hands that fumbled with the red Bic lighter. She took several drags and her eyes skittered away.

"Where's Haunani's father?"

Shrug. More drags on the cigarette. "Haven't seen the man in years."

"Well. I'm sorry fo' say we get bad news," Lei said. She steadied her voice. "Haunani stay *make*. She's dead."

No reaction. Nani looked blankly out into space, took another drag off the the cigarette, but now her hand shook as if with an ague. Lei reached over and captured the one holding the lighter in both of hers. Stevens shot her a quick glance.

"I'm sorry."

Nani's hand felt like a bundle of sticks. The woman's throat worked as she swallowed. "How?"

"She was drowned."

"I told her a hundred times never go swimming by the rivermouth but she never listen. She always get one hard head, that girl."

"It wasn't accidental." Stevens' low voice sawed across the tension.

Another long pause.

Moving faster than she could have believed, Nani brought the lit cigarette down on the back of Lei's hand, spitting into her face. Nani's black eyes were empty pits of wild as she clawed at Lei, screaming incoherent curses.

Lei recoiled with a cry, flying over backwards in the flimsy beach chair as Stevens surged up and grabbed the woman, spinning her around and putting her against the wall. He cuffed her as she continued to yell incomprehensible abuse.

Lei scrambled up and went to the Bronco, listening with one ear as Stevens tried to calm Nani down. She fumbled in the glove box for the first aid kit, hoping there wasn't HIV in the spit making its way into her eyes, down her cheek. She ripped open a Bactine-soaked wipe and scrubbed her face with it, rubbed another one on the blistering circular burn on the back of her hand, using the minutiae of attending the small wound to collect herself.

Stupid rookie move, getting close, touching the woman like that. She deserved to get burned.

Nani's invective had switched to a dry sobbing that sounded like branches rubbing in a high wind. Lei finally turned to face the tableau of Stevens beside the frail, hunched woman on the stoop, her hands cuffed behind her, skeins of black hair trailing.

"Do you want to press charges?" Stevens asked. She could tell by the timbre of his voice he didn't want her to, and Lei knew that would shut down any further communication they might get out of Nani. Lei shook her head—she couldn't seem to find her voice.

"I'm going to take these restraints off," Stevens said gently. "But I'll put them back on and take you down to the station if you try anything more."

A tiny nod among the terrible sounds coming from the slight form. Stevens took off the cuffs. "Who can we call for you?"

He needn't have asked, as doors had been opening along the row of dwellings and neighbors came out. A tall, wide woman in a muumuu and slippers approached.

"What you wen' do to Nani?"

"Her girl, she drowned," Lei said, coming forward.

"Oh the poor 'ting!" the neighbor exclaimed. It was unclear whether she meant Nani or her daughter, but she wedged her bulk between Stevens and Nani on the stoop, effectively squeezing him off as she looped a hamlike arm over the woman. "I going take care of you."

"Damn you, Ohia," Nani snarled, trying to get up, but Ohia just hoisted her closer.

"I take you inside, fix you something for eat. Bet you never wen' eat today," the neighbor went on, hauling Nani into the fetid interior. They disappeared, and the door slammed.

"That went well." Stevens gestured Lei over. "You okay?"

"Worried about HIV, but yeah." Lei put her hands in her uniform pockets, missing the cowry.

"Shit." He seemed at a loss, finally went on. "So much for the female officer breaking the news strategy. Let's canvass these neighbors since we're here, maybe she'll be calm enough to answer some questions later."

"Okay." She followed him as they went to the next house and worked their way down the street.

The neighbors were voluble on the subject of Nani, Haunani and the younger brother Alika, a high school freshman. Nani, a known drug addict, had been turned in to Social Services multiple times over the years and the neighbors had given up doing much besides feeding the kids when they came by. One witness alluded to Haunani being picked up and dropped off by someone in a "dark Toyota truck."

Stevens shut his notebook after the fifth house. "We've got some leads here. Let's head back to Nani's and see if she's ready to talk."

Chapter 6

S tevens' cell rang as they walked back through untrimmed grass along a cracking asphalt road that had never seen a sidewalk. Various barking dogs marked their progress.

"Yeah, come down," Lei heard him say. "We're heading back for another run at the mother. She didn't take the news well, got a little belligerent."

That was one word for it, Lei thought, looking at the band-aid on the back of her hand. She could still felt the shocking wet of spittle on her face. She put her hand back in her pocket. No cowry. She bent and picked up a kukui nut out of the grass, slipped it into her pocket with an immediate feeling of relief.

He slid the Blackberry back into a holder on his belt. "Jeremy's on his way with your partner; he's swinging by to pick you up after we talk to Nani."

Lei didn't answer. He gave her a sidelong glance, a quick blaze of blue that seemed to see more than she wanted him to.

"Stay back from her."

"I have more experience with her type than you think." She couldn't help the bitterness that crept into her voice. Her mother's face flashed into her mind's eye, dreamy as she pushed down the plunger of a syringe.

"She got you good with that cigarette. You may not be able to make this any better for her, but I appreciate that you tried."

They reached the stoop and Stevens banged on the plywood door. He had to bang twice before Ohia's face appeared, eyes like raisins pushed into rich brown dough.

"She lying down. She high."

"Let us in." Stevens pulled the door further open, and brushed by Ohia into a dim interior that smelled of mildew and rotting food. A living area furnished with futons on the floor and a TV with rabbit ears opened into a bedroom. Lei followed Stevens in and stood over a mattress on the floor.

Nani lay in the center of the bed on a quilt that had once been beautiful, handsewn in a traditional Hawaiian pattern. Her legs were together, her arms crossed on her chest. She laid perfectly straight, eyes closed. The glass pipe and red Bic were set on an upturned coffee can beside the mattress, along with an empty twist of foil.

"Nani. Can you answer some questions? We need to know anything we can about who Haunani was seeing, who might have done this to her."

No reply.

"Nani." He reached down, nudged her shoulder. Her body went loose then, wobbling with the force of his shaking, and her head dropped to the side, mouth falling open.

He put two fingers on her neck. "Still got a pulse, but she's too far gone right now. We'll have to come back."

Lei turned to Ohia, who stood behind them, a bulky shadow.

"Can you keep an eye on her? Maybe get some friends in to clean up a bit?"

"She nevah get any friends." Still the woman backed up, headed toward the sink piled with pots and pans.

"Thanks," Lei said. "We'll be back to talk to her again."

They pushed out into sunlight that felt blinding, air that tasted sweet. Lei rubbed the kukui nut. Its ridges were soothing under her fingers. The Crown Victoria, with Pono behind the wheel and Jeremy in the passenger seat, pulled up on the lawn in front of them. Stevens reached into his pocket, handed her his card.

"Call me if you think of anything else. Thanks for helping."

"You know I'd like to work on the case full time."

"I'm holding out for more detectives. I may still be able to use you though."

"Okay. I guess."

She headed for the Crown Vic and passed Jeremy, who deliberately avoided eye contact. He must resent her replacing him, however briefly, she thought as she got into the cruiser beside Pono. She glanced back at Stevens and Jeremy as they pulled away. They were looking at his notebook and discussing something. Stevens gestured to the houses they had already canvassed.

She turned her eyes away.

"How'd it go?" Pono had his Oakleys down but she could see concern in the deep line between his brows.

"Not well." She held up her hand with its band-aid and gave a brief summary. Pono rubbed his mustache, shook his head.

"Damn tweekers."

"She's still a mother whose child was killed." Lei wished she could forget the way Nani had arranged herself like an effigy on the bed.

They drove in morose silence on a beat of downtown Hilo, which Pono called his "hood." The cruiser rolled past the corner of a warehouse in the industrial section, and Lei spotted several teenage boys with paint cans tagging the side of a building.

Pono hit the siren and lights, and the Crown Vic roared forward. Lei snorted a laugh at the way the kids jumped about two feet in the air, dropped the cans, and ran. The squad car chased them down the alley until they scattered in different directions.

"Feel like running?" Pono asked.

"Oh yeah!" Adrenaline surged through her, the perfect antidote to angst, and she jumped out of the rolling vehicle to chase one of the miscreants. Pono continued after the others in the cruiser.

She charged after the teen until he ran into a chain-link fence, and grabbed the back of his shirt as he began to climb. She peeled him off the fence and slammed him down, her knee in the middle of his back as she cuffed him. He spat curses at her but shut up when she gave his arms an extra upward wrench. She walked him back toward the main road with a hand on the back of his neck, the buzz of adrenaline singing along her veins.

Pono had caught another of the kids and they took them down to the station and walked them in.

"You Chang boys getting in trouble again?" Sam at the watch desk frowned when he saw the teens. "I going call your grandma. She going give you lickins."

The kids hung their heads as he berated them, following them into the station. Lei spotted Stevens filling up a plastic water bottle from the water dispenser. She hurried across the bull pen toward him.

"Stevens—how'd it go after I left?"

"You look hot."

"Yeah." She brushed sweaty curls back from her forehead. "Chasing some taggers downtown."

"Get your man?"

"Of course." She gestured toward Pono and Sam at the booking desk with the boys. "So how did the canvassing go?"

"Didn't get much more than when you were there." He screwed the top back onto his water bottle. "We have some leads with Haunani's cell phone, which that neighbor Ohia found at the house. We also have a shitload of stuff to process from the campsite."

"What about talking to Kelly's parents today? Need any help?"

"No, Jeremy and I are handling that. You can get back to . . . whatever you do." He made a vague gesture that encompassed her sweaty hair, crumpled uniform and the hangdog teenagers at the booking desk.

"You know what? Forget it. Good luck with the investigation." Lei spun away, a hot prickle of rage sweeping up to her hairline, knowing she was over-reacting and no longer giving a damn. She stomped back over to Pono. "Let's go, Pono. I think we missed a few."

Pono ripped the boys' incident writeup off his pad, slapping it down on the desk.

"Yeah, okay. Sam, can you finish this up? My partner's out for justice."

Lei blew through the double doors and was in the Crown Vic revving the engine when Pono got in. She pulled out and laid down some rubber turning onto the busy avenue, roaring back toward town.

"What's up?"

"That jerk, Stevens."

"Turned you down for a date?"

"Turned me down for the investigation."

"Asshole," said Pono, rubbing his lips hard to suppress a grin. "So I guess you asked to be on the case."

"I have an interest," she said. "And a lot to offer. But whatever. He's a prick."

"For the record, did you for once think about how this would affect me if you got reassigned?"

"Hey, you get along with everybody. It'd only be temporary."

"Well . . . if you feel that strongly you should go to the Lieutenant and ask."

"Maybe I will."

After a long pause, Pono turned the radio to the Hawaiian station. Slack key guitar filled the Crown Vic with soft rhythms.

"Let it go a'ready. Otherwise you come stress out," he said, leaning back with his trademark mellow. "Seems like those Chang boys we picked up are following in their grandpa's footsteps."

"What do you mean?"

"Terry Chang. He was a real crime godfather around here. Got put away finally and some good citizen offed him in prison. Word is his wife is running things now. She's not going to be happy with those boys drawing attention by getting picked up."

"Looks like they wanted to get to work building their rap sheets," Lei said. She hit the steering wheel in frustration. "Those girls deserve more."

"Like what? You're not even a detective yet."

"Something about this case—it's like it found me. But whatever, it seems like you and Stevens are on the same page."

"I never said I agree with him, but I understand why he's trying to get the best. This is the biggest murder to happen in Hilo in forever."

Lei had no answer, no way to explain her need to help—because what he said was the truth. They drove back through the industrial area, but the taggers were long gone. They continued on their normal route as late afternoon turned into evening.

"There's more to this than meets the eye," Pono said eventually. "It could have gone down like people're saying, with the girls going to party with some nasty icehead or something. But I like Kelly's stepdad for this."

"Really?"

"He's squirrelly. Lawyered up for his interview today, and so far there's no reason to."

"How'd you hear this?"

"I have my sources." Pono knew everyone, and the station was full of his 'talk story' moles.

"Maybe he felt discriminated against," she said, elbowing him. "It's not easy being the white minority."

"He one stupid *haole*," Pono stated. 'Haole' meant Caucasian or newcomer, and the word wasn't always complimentary in a state where only a third of the population was white.

"Huh," Lei said. "Hey, it's trash day, early evening . . . maybe he put their trash out on the road already." She typed the stepfather's last name into the ToughBook computer screwed into the dash with her right hand while steering with her left. He lived in central Hilo, only a few miles away.

"No need we go look. They always saying, do your own job. You so nosy, you going get us fired," Pono lapsed into pidgin, cracking his big brown knuckles.

"Not nosy. Pro-active. If that trash is out there, it's in the open and fine for us to take it, and tomorrow morning it will be gone as an option. We'll turn anything we find over to the detectives. What are you so scared of? Extra work?"

"Shut up. I just know Stevens and Ito won't like it."

"So what? We're helping them. If we find anything, we'll give it to them, let them take the credit."

"It's a miracle we found the crime scene. Now, we're investigating. It's not our *kuleana*, our responsibility."

"I don't know about you, but I care about catching a killer. I care about what happened to those girls, and if you like the stepdad for it, that's a valid hunch. We're just looking for another miracle."

Pono subsided, moodily adjusting his side mirror.

"What's the baby up to these days?" she asked, to distract him.

"You don't really care."

She didn't, so she shut up and drove.

It didn't take long to get to the middle-class neighborhood where Kelly had lived. They rolled quietly along the street, lit tastefully by carriage-lamp streetlights. Lei passed the house, a modest ranch. The black plastic trash cans sat on the curb.

"They're out there. What do you think?" Lei tried to suppress the excitement in her voice.

"Since when did you listen to what I think? Let's just get this over with. Cruise back by, we'll dump the trash into the crime-scene bags," Pono said, his mouth tight.

The backseat held a box of heavy-duty transparent garbage bags from emptying the junked cars. Pono pulled on latex gloves as she turned the corner again and drove slowly toward the house. She pulled up and put the car in park, as Pono leapt out and headed for the first can. She was still pulling on latex gloves when he dumped the contents of the can into one of the plastic bags.

A dog began barking from inside the house as she helped him with the second can, holding the thick transparent plastic open so the garbage, fortunately already bagged, tumbled in.

"Shut up, goddamnit!" someone yelled at the dog, as they emptied the third one, threw the bags into the backseat, and jumped back in the cruiser. Lei put it in gear and they quietly picked up speed.

Pono sighed, leaning back and closing his eyes, rubbing his lips hard with his right hand.

"That imaginary cigarette taste pretty good?"

"You have no idea," he said, his eyes still closed.

"Let's pull over, have a quick look," Lei said. Her hands were actually itching to rip into the bags.

"No way. Pollute the chain of evidence? What if there is something there, you want to be able to give it to Stevens, don't you?"

That shut her up.

It only took a few more minutes to pull into the station, haul the bags in past the startled night watch officer and back to the evidence room. They logged the three bags in and locked the room.

"That's not going to smell so good tomorrow morning," Pono said.

"We could go through them now."

He just narrowed his eyes at her, gave her back a whack that made her stagger forward toward the door.

"Okay, okay. Tomorrow then."

* * *

He'd opened the Orchids file again. He couldn't resist looking at his handiwork, savoring the sequence, the tragic beauty of the girls in the water. He played with the key ring, smoothing the girls' hair through his fingers.

The newspaper article was such a wonderful contrast. He picked up the paper with its grainy, obligatory shot of twin white-shrouded gurneys, and in the background the tense-looking female officer who'd found the bodies. He read the snippet aloud.

"Officer Leilani Texeira and her partner Pono Kaihale were first on the scene of a possible double homicide at Mohuli`i Park." He tapped her face with its aureole of curly brown hair. "Officer Texeira. You look like you'd photograph well."

Chapter 7

Sam was at the watch desk again when she got to the station the next morning.

"Hey, do you know a seven-letter word for 'outrageous female pop star'?" he asked, pencil in hand.

"Try Madonna," she said, pushing through the glass interior door.

"It works!" He looked up. "We've been getting a lot of calls on those girls you found. Community's pretty upset. Even had to send a unit down to the high school to deal with the students."

"Bummer. Don't know why we aren't putting more people on the case; I'm trying to get on the investigation but Stevens is holding out for more detectives."

"Good luck with that." He went back to the crossword as the door swung shut behind her with a muffled clunk.

Lei picked up some coffee and headed for the back room with a box of various-sized evidence bags and a pair of latex gloves. Pono had sent her a text message that the baby kept him up all night and now they were all sick. He didn't like it when she took chances, so she wasn't surprised he'd left her holding the proverbial trash bag.

"You the one brung the rubbish in there last night?" Sherlyn, the veteran evidence clerk, was at her station outside the door. "It can't stay here. It's stinkin' up the place."

"I know, that's why I'm here early," Lei fumbled on the gloves. "I'll try to work fast."

"What case is this for?" Sherlyn shoved the sign-in sheet at Lei.

"Uhm . . . the Roosevelt case." Lei named the owner of the lot with the abandoned cars on it and filled it in on the check-in sheet.

"Never heard of it. You get that rubbish out of my evidence room today."

"I'm on it." Lei took the key from her and opened the door. She wrinkled her nose at the smell. "You're right, Sherlyn, it's nasty in here. I'm going to turn on the AC unit, air it out."

"Just turn it off when you finish." Sherlyn went back to her computer.

Lei closed the door behind her, facing the three bags of trash arranged in a row. Her heart picked up speed and she felt a bubble of excitement clogging her throat. Truth was, she was thrilled not to be slowed down by Pono's nit-picking or Stevens' patronizing.

She plunked her coffee mug down on the small steel table inside the door and turned on the outside-vented AC unit.

She dragged the first bag toward her, sat on the metal chair, ripped open the transparent evidence bag and tore into the black liner underneath, filling her gloved hands with garbage. She dumped it in carefully explored handfuls into the steel trash container by the table. Most of it was the usual: coffee grounds, ripped up bill envelopes, a pile of crumpled, stained schoolwork, orange peels, and globs of what looked like a tuna casserole.

She was just sorting through a browning bunch of carnations when the door swung open so hard it banged into the steel trash can. Lei started, dropping some of the carnations. She kept her eyes down, but could see that the man who'd come in was long legged, wore jeans, and his shoes were muddy. Michael Stevens. Damn.

"What are you doing?"

She looked up into blue eyes slanted into hard triangles.

"What do you mean?"

"You're investigating my crime."

"Stevens, this is just a little research."

"The Roosevelt case? I don't think so." He folded his arms. "Primary crime scene? Ring a bell? It should, you were there most of yesterday."

"Okay, yeah. This is not trash from that site." She threw the handful of carnations into the discard can.

"You got that right. If you want trash to sort, we've got plenty! What the hell are you up to?"

"I'm following a hunch." She stood up, but it didn't make her feel any taller. She glared back at him and refused to look away.

"What hunch?" he said, and she exhaled.

"Kelly Andrade's stepdad. This is his publicly discarded trash, right there for anyone to take."

"We interviewed him. Alibi seems solid."

"I don't know anything about that. I just decided to grab the trash while it was available and see what's there. I'll turn anything I find over to you."

"No way," he said. "You got company."

He hooked the other chair over with his foot and pulled a pair of latex gloves on from the box on the table. His cell phone bleeped, and he tersely told his partner to "keep at it" and that he was following a new lead.

Lei kept her head down, her hands carefully digging, as that bubble of excitement tightened her chest. A new lead! Maybe there was something off about the stepdad after all.

A few minutes went by. Still nothing of interest.

"Kinda sad. All her schoolwork," Stevens said, dropping a handful of crumpled, stained papers into the discard can.

"I know."

"So I know you want to move up. What are you doing to make detective?"

"Putting in the time, getting experience. I've been taking criminology classes at UH, working on my bachelor's in Criminal Justice."

"Well, you gotta be a team player," he said, shaking out a soggy coffee filter. "Tell people everything you're thinking."

"Like you'd listen to me."

"You found the bodies, the crime scene. Not bad. Not afraid to take initiative. Also not bad."

She blushed and hated it. She reached down into the last few bits at the bottom, and her hand wrapped around the hard steel circumference of an empty propane can.

"What do you think?" She held it up.

"There were a couple of those at the campsite, so I think you better try not to smear any fingerprints," he said, snapping open an evidence bag. She dropped the canister into the bag and he sealed it, filling out a label.

She was galvanized now, carefully sifting every bit at the bottom. He helped her open the next bag of trash. This one yielded some bondage porn magazines, which he wordlessly bagged. The last sack was mostly full of the dead girl's clothes.

"Doesn't this seem odd to you?" asked Lei, holding up a little spaghetti-string top. "I mean, dead less than a week and they throw her clothes out in the trash?"

"Not really. Most people give them to Goodwill or something, but I've seen people burn everything just to have it gone forever . . . grief takes people different ways." Stevens had gone out and gotten a camera, and he bent over, photographing the items they had spread on the floor.

"What's missing from this picture?" he frowned. They had laid the clothes out in neat rows.

"Her underwear," Lei said. Goosebumps erupted all over and she rubbed her arms, her gut clenching. "Wow, that AC unit really got going." She squinched her eyes shut against a memory of Kelly's naked body sunk into the mud.

"You look like you've had enough," he said, cocking his head to look at her. "Jeremy's coming anyway."

"I'm fine." She gazed blindly at the ruffled yellow skirt at her feet.

"Well, thanks for following your hunch. Call me on my cell with any more you have and I promise I'll listen."

"Okay." She picked up one of the discarded bags of trash and fumbled open the door handle.

"Hey," he said. She stopped, looking back. "Good job."

"Thanks."

Lei pushed through the steel door.

"I don't see enough bags of trash going out." Sherlyn looked up from her keyboard.

"Detective Stevens is finishing up some things in there and will dispose of them," she replied, swinging the bag up to her shoulder. Lei chucked the bag of trash including the gloves, and after a brief wash turned on her computer.

While it booted up, she fished Stevens' card out of her pocket. She slid the card into her desk drawer, shut it, then opened it again and put the card back into her pocket. She called Pono at home and briefed him on the case, then went on her assigned patrol route, still mulling over the encounter with Stevens.

Not her type. Still, those blue eyes were hard to forget. She wondered at the swings of emotion she felt around him, what they meant. She fingered the card in her pocket, trying not to remember Haunani's face, trying to make her boring patrol matter. It just didn't seem that important to catch speeders and call in loose dogs with the bodies of two dead teenagers lying in the morgue.

* * *

The dark truck he drove blended in with so many others, the ride of choice in that rural area. After finding her address it hadn't been hard to follow her to this regular destination, an evening class. His camera sat on the seat beside him, along with a pair of night vision binoculars.

He waited, and scrolled through the pictures on his phone—women he'd spotted and secretly photographed. Each of them had something special that had caught his artist's eye—a special curve to the ass, shiny long hair, a sweetly drawn mouth. He loved to capture that uniqueness at the moment it was surrendered to him. Beautiful women wanted to be discovered, captured, conquered. He did them a favor, fulfilling their secret fantasies as he acted out his own.

This next target was a police officer, holding back the crowd at an accident scene. Her navy-blue uniform hugged her body. This one would be a risk, but he was ready for a challenge. He'd titled each photo, and he brushed his thumb across the name on the slightly glowing surface of the cell phone.

Chapter 8

Saturday morning dawned grey and wet. Lei slept in, tired from being up late at Criminology class at University of Hawaii the night before, but got up when Keiki woke her to go out. They did their morning run, but Lei still felt restless and unsettled when they got back and decided to clean. She hung the rag rug from her living room on the chain link fence and was taking her frustration out on it with a broom when she heard a shout.

"Hey Lei!"

She turned, the broom raised, and her heart rate jumped.

"Stevens! What're you doing here?"

"I'd feel better if you put the broom down." He chuckled, his hands raised.

"Sorry." She laughed a little too, lowering it. "Spring cleaning."

"I was in your area and I thought I'd stop by to talk about the investigation. Turns out you were right. We aren't getting any other detectives from Hilo District, and I still need help, a lot more manpower than Jeremy and I."

"Okay. I won't say I told you so." She whacked the rug a few more times and thought of the stalker note. "How'd you get my address?"

"Irene gave it to me. She told me I needed to come talk to you." Irene Matsumoto was in charge of Dispatch, personnel records, and general morale. She also knew how much Lei wanted to make detective.

"Nobody crosses Irene. So does this mean you're putting me on the investigation?"

"I asked the Lieutenant if I could borrow you, yeah. He said okay. I'm still hoping for some more detectives since the community is making so much noise, but until then—" He shrugged. "We're it. I'm going to use Pono too."

"Let's go inside." Keiki began barking from inside the house, a deep snarling Cerberus boom. "Don't worry. She only eats assholes."

He laughed, but it was a little hollow. She opened the front door and signaled Keiki to sit.

"This is Stevens," she said in her 'friend' voice, making the hand signal.

"Michael," he said. "Call me Michael." Keiki sniffed him, a little leftover growl rumbling in her chest, but she moved aside and followed them in. Lei took him to the little Formica table with its delicate orchid plant.

"Coffee?" she asked.

"Yeah, please. Nice place."

"It's perfect for the two of us," she said, getting him a mug and filling it up with the strong morning brew.

"Oh. Where's your boyfriend?"

"No, I meant the two of us." She pointed to the dog. "Keiki and I."

"Right. Okay." He covered the awkwardness by taking a sip of his steaming coffee. She sat down after refilling her own mug. Keiki put her head on Lei's leg and eyed Stevens, her triangle ears pricked.

"We got some more details back from the autopsies," he said. "Looks like most of the girls' injuries appear to be postmortem. The lab matched blood on the rag to Haunani Pohakoa. It doesn't seem like there was much of a struggle, so hopefully they didn't suffer."

"I guess that's something." Her stomach churned at the images that flashed through her brain. She took a relaxation breath.

"I've seen a lot more of this kind of thing in LA. I told the DA my opinion on the case, which is that I don't think the murder part of it was premeditated. I think he had his fun, and then decided they could ID him and he put them in the stream so he wouldn't have to deal with it."

"What were they doing out at that campsite anyway?"

"Got a theory. The one girl, Haunani Pohakoa, had a pretty regular pot habit."

"I know. That's how I met her, picking her up for possession."

"Well we've started interviewing the kids she hung out with. Some of them said Haunani was getting Kelly into drugs. I think both girls were troubled, experimenting. But something fishy was going on with Kelly and her stepdad."

"How do you know?"

"He wouldn't say squat when we brought him in for another interview after you picked up the trash. He stonewalled with his lawyer, acted hinky. When we canvassed the neighbors they reported late-night fighting between Kelly and the parents, and Kelly ran away overnight more than once this last year. Before the mom married the new guy, Kelly used to be a happy, normal kid."

Lei struggled to focus on the present moment, taking a couple relaxation breaths, tightening her fist in her lap so the nails dug in, the pain anchoring her.

I need to pay attention, she told herself. *I need to stay with this.*

His words vibrated through her. She closed her eyes and it got worse: she saw the looming black of expanding pupils, felt herself slipping away to the place she went when things got bad.

Stevens was patting her shoulder and Keiki was growling, a distant thunder, as she blinked, the room regathering itself around her.

"What happened?" He frowned. "You okay?"

"Sorry, I got distracted," she said. She squeezed her fist. The pain answered, and her body was hers again.

"It was more than that. Did you hear what I said? You were totally out of it there for a minute."

"Sure," she said, racking her brain for what they'd been discussing. "Which part?"

"The part about the girls meeting some older guy to go out," Stevens prompted.

"Right," Lei said. She knew she was missing information. I can't remember what he said that made me black out. What if it was important to the case? Her brain skittered around, but it remained a blank from when he had said Haunani had a pot habit. She would just have to look for clues, managing and hiding the "lost" moment as she had for years

"Anyway, it looks like there's some substance to that idea," Stevens went on. "Haunani stopped buying from her regular dealer and started flashing some bling, a new cell phone, stuff like that. She told her friends she had a 'secret admirer' and he was taking care of everything she needed."

"Why would he need to drug her then? Was it for a threesome with Kelly?"

"I don't know. But there's that witness in her neighborhood who talked about her being dropped off from a Toyota truck, and a student who saw her get picked up after school one day in a black Toyota truck. That's the lead I want you to run down: possible sugar daddies with black Toyotas."

"Great," Lei groaned. "You know how many black Toyota trucks we have in Hilo?"

"Yeah, I know. Why do you think I'm here on a Saturday, eating crow and roping you in on this thing?"

"Okay," Lei said, not about to argue with this chance to help. "What else should I be looking for?"

"We've consulted Dr. Wilson, the police psychologist, for a profile on the type of guy Haunani would be with. She's thinking someone twenties- to mid-thirties, probably single, with a newer black Toyota, Tundra or Tacoma model. He lives in this area since he was able to carry on a relationship with the girl for a while."

"Sounds like most of the younger guys in Hilo. Okay, I'll get on it Monday."

"I got overtime authorized for you," he said sheepishly. "I was hoping you'd want to get started tomorrow."

She stared at him, laughed.

"Wow. What a turnaround. Okay, fine. Want to meet up?"

They set a time, and he keyed it into his Blackberry. She walked him to the door.

"See you tomorrow, Stevens."

"Call me Michael. Really."

"Doubtful," she said, smiling.

In the bath that evening, Lei leaned her head back against the cool porcelain, taking one of those deep breaths in through the nose and out through the mouth her therapist had recommended, hoping this time it would be different. This time she'd be able to reclaim one more thing he'd taken from her.

It was getting to be more and more important that she manage the weird memory loss and blackout moments she'd struggled with since she was nine. She thought back over the conversation with Stevens, and decided the moment that had triggered her was when he said "she'd been a happy, normal kid."

She saw Kelly's bloated, empty face again in her mind's eye and felt her heart squeeze.

At one time Lei had been a happy, normal kid too—but she'd already been messed up by her dad's arrest and her mother's lifestyle by the time Charlie Kwon got his hands on her.

These thoughts weren't helping her relax. She closed her eyes, but as soon as she did, she smelled the Stetson cologne Charlie always wore. She took another relaxation breath, blowing out the remembered scent. The next second Charlie was there, leaning over her, the soap in his hand.

"Let me wash you," he said. The pupils of his eyes were wide and black, swallowing her with their need.

Lei reared up, the water sloshing. Keiki, who'd been napping on the bath mat, lunged to her feet. Dripping suds, Lei reached out a trembling arm to pet the dog's wide chest.

"My guardian. It's okay, girl, I'm safe now."

Keiki subsided with a whuff, her ears still swiveling for possible danger. Lei's heart was still thudding, and she dried a shaking hand on a towel and thumbed open her phone, speed dialing Aunty Rosario at her restaurant in California.

"Baby girl!"

"Hey Aunty. How's the rat race treating you?"

"Not bad. Been getting some new customers from the ads my busboy put in the mailboxes."

"Still serving the *lilikoi* pie?"

"Of course. My regulars would mob me if I didn't. 'Sides, how else can I say I serve Hawaiian food?"

"What about those *poi* rolls you were doing?"

"Turns off the truck drivers. They won't eat anything purple. So what's new in Hilo?"

They chatted and when they hung up Lei was waterlogged and ready to get out, the flashback gone but not forgotten.

She wondered if she'd ever be able to take a bath without his appearance. Charlie'd had a way of getting to her, twisting everything he did to her into something she'd wanted. Most of her childhood memories remained mercifully elusive but she knew the bath had been bad.

The only thing she remembered for sure were his eyes.

That night she hung her holster from the bedstead and fell asleep with the matte black, boxy shape of the Glock only inches away.

Chapter 9

Lei took extra time in the mirror the next morning, whisking on a little mascara. She mashed in one last handful of CurlTamer, trying to get her hair to lie flat. It refused, as it usually did. When she realized what she was doing, she gave up and went to the station. She didn't care what she looked like, she told herself, and felt the lie stick like a chicken bone in her throat.

"Hey." Stevens met her at the coffeepot in the break room, dark hair damp and spiky and cheeks red with razor burn. He smelled like soap. "Ready to get started?"

"Of course." The station was quieter than normal—Sunday mornings being more about church and hangovers in Hilo, and staffing allocated accordingly. Lei plunked down her coffee and booted up a workstation in the computer lab. Stevens sat next to her on another machine.

"So what're you looking for?" she asked.

"I'm rolling through Haunani's cell phone calls. I want to see if I can find any connection with Kelly's stepdad or anyone else interesting. I think we're going to have to track down and interview everyone she has in her contacts."

"Oh." Lei keyed in her password and logged on to the server. She began searching under "black Toyota truck." The page loaded with entries. She opened each one and began screening the DMV information against the early-to-mid thirties male profile.

Stevens printed something, and then hopped up from the workstation.

"Gotta check something out." He snagged his black leather jacket off the back of the chair. She envied that as a detective he didn't have to wear a uniform. "Call me on my cell if you see anything likely."

"Like what?" She swiveled the chair around. "'Sugadady' on a license plate? How the hell are we going to investigate all these dudes anyway?"

"I have a witness from the high school who says she saw the guy in the black Toyota. If we can show her the license pictures, she might be able to pick him out."

"Nice. Thanks for sharing."

"Just find the guys who fit the profile, print their pictures and make me a folder." He shrugged into the jacket.

"For giving up my Sunday I expect to be at the interview," she said, giving him her best stare. *Arrogant asshole*, she thought—not for the first time.

"Fine. I'll check in later."

She watched him go, enjoying her tiny victory. It was a nice view, and she grinned as she spun her chair back around and got on with the boredom. A thought occurred—she opened another window and tapped in Kelly's stepdad's name and a second later, stared in astonishment.

James Reynolds drove a 2007 charcoal Toyota Tacoma. She hit PRINT and pulled the page out of the laser. Heavy brows and a receding hairline bracketed a square jaw; dark eyes looked truculently at her. She threw the page into the growing pile, then fished the dog-eared card out of her pocket and punched in the number.

"Stevens."

"Stevens, the stepdad drives a dark Tacoma!"

"I know. We're looking at him pretty hard. Alibi's holding up though."

"Why didn't you tell me? He doesn't fit the profile, too old."

"Sorry, I meant to. I've been pretty damn busy," Stevens said. "That's what I have you for now. Thanks for checking."

"I'm putting him in the pile with the others."

"Why don't you expand the search, add navy blue, charcoal? Maybe our witness was confused on the color. We'll be bringing Reynolds in again."

"What's the alibi?"

"Tell you later," he said, and rang off.

She snapped her phone shut, rubbed her chest briskly.

That's what I have you for now. The butterflies or bubbles or whatever they were that had flown up at those words were still there. They were enough to fuel the long day of poring over records, and at the end of it she had a folder of fifty-seven printed license photos, one of whom was James Reynolds. She set it on Stevens's desk, leaving a note on the front:

Looking forward to the interview.

Monday came too soon. She had Criminology class that night, and hadn't studied. She let Pono drive and she read factoids aloud to him from her textbook, one ear tuned for a call from Stevens to help with the case.

"Did you know seventy-nine percent of long-term prisoners have at least one diagnosed mental health disorder?"

"Maybe we should be spending a little more on treatment and less on punishment," Pono said.

"Now you're sounding like a Democrat. I don't give a shit why they do what they do—dysfunctional childhoods, economic challenges—whatever. Criminals should be locked up where they can't hurt anybody." The words came out more heated than she meant them to as she thought of her father, incarcerated for dealing. She hated him for what he'd done: first for being taken from her, and then for forgetting about her after he was gone.

"C'mon, you know better. Mostly victimless crime like drugs around here."

Even in Hawaii where they tried for a more rehabilitative approach with innovations like Drug Court where a defendant completed incarcerated rehab in lieu of a sentence, the jails were overflowing.

"You do the crime, you do the time." Lei flipped the page.

"I just wish the stats were better for Hawaiians," Pono said. "There's got to be a reason so many of our people end up in prison."

"It's the cycle of addiction, they call it."

"We need more things fo' the young people, so they no go into the game," Pono said. The topic was getting him down. He absently rubbed his lips with a forefinger.

"Hey, did I tell you Stevens came by? He roped me in to helping him on the case Sunday."

"Seriously? Did he kiss your ass to get you to do it?"

"Properly, thank you."

"Glad you're on the case. You wanted it bad enough."

Lei looked up. They were in Haunani's neighborhood, as if the discussion on drugs had led them there. Lei wondered if Stevens had ever got back to re-interview Haunani's mother.

"Slow down."

Pono did, and they rolled along the cracking road until they came to the plywood door in the shadow of an extravagant plumeria tree. Sure enough, Nani sat there, cigarette smoke curling upward in a ribbon around her head.

Lei held her hand up, the small circular burn on it suddenly itchy.

"I need a minute."

"Here we go again," Pono groaned, but pulled over. Lei got out, straightening her duty belt with its heavy accoutrements, and strode across the tufted grass. Without a word she took one of the beach chairs from its leaning position against the wall, flipped it open, and sat down next to Nani.

"How you stay?" she asked.

A shrug of the narrow shoulders, a heavy drag on the cigarette, but Nani's eyes looked clear if sunken.

"I'm sorry about your daughter."

Again the shrug.

"Did the detectives ever come back and talk to you?"

Slight shake of the head.

"We need to know anything we can about who might have done this. Who was Haunani seeing?"

"Someone she shouldn't have been." Nani's voice sounded like it came from the bottom of a rusty metal bucket. "She wouldn't tell me. Had that damn cell phone going all the time, got her pot for free and never gave me notting."

"What kind of vehicle did he drive?"

"Black Toyota truck." Another drag. This time she let the smoke curl up from her bottom lip, inhaling it into her nostrils. "I could tell he was too old for her, I told her not to see him, but I never could do notting with that girl. I told you, she get one hard head."

"So how old was he? Did you ever get a look at him?"

"Saw him one time, picking her up. Not too tall, dark hair. That's all."

Lei thought of Reynolds, who was 6'3" and on the bulky side. But, his hair was dark and it would be hard to judge height sitting down in the cab of a truck.

"Did she have any special jewelry or clothing on her the day she disappeared?"

"Nothing special. Just her gold ring—had an initial H on it. Her grandma gave it to her."

"Anyone else who might want to—hurt her? What about her father?"

"Haven't seen his sorry ass in ten years. Never gave me one dime of child support."

"So where is he?"

"I told you, ten years since he got popped."

Lei sat with that a minute. Another father incarcerated and gone from a child's life, abandoning her to a druggie mother. Too much of a theme. Well, so much for the theory of a vengeful father. That left the questionable boyfriend, mysterious enough to be a candidate.

"Well, thanks for talking with me. Detective Stevens may be back by to talk to you again."

"Probably won't be here." She dropped her butt into the cigarette-clogged water jar, stood up and went back into the house.

Lei got out of the chair and headed back to the cruiser, speed-dialing Stevens on her cell.

He hadn't been back to talk to Nani, and after grilling her for details, he thanked her.

"You're good at taking initiative. Just check with me first next time, okay?"

"Got it," Lei said. "We were just in the neighborhood, thought we'd just try, save you some time." She closed the phone, got in the cruiser and slammed the door, putting on her seatbelt.

"We?" Pono rolled his eyes, and dropped the Oakleys down over them. "'We nothing.'"

"Well it worked out okay, didn't it?"

"Just because she didn't get you with her cigarette this time?" He shook his head. "You got lucky she wasn't high at the moment, is all."

"Well, if I keep getting lucky, I might just catch this killer."

Chapter 10

Lei drove to the University of Hawaii campus at the end of the day, eating her favorite Whopper Junior in the car. She pulled in under the spreading African tulip tree next to the Social Sciences building and retrieved her book bag from the backseat, glad to have a distraction from her obsession with the Mohuli`i case. All day she'd been thinking about the trash, the stepdad, Kelly's clothes—in part to keep from remembering Haunani's empty white stare and the smoke curling up into Nani's nostrils. Driving around on patrol with Pono just didn't feel like she was doing enough, and Stevens hadn't called her back.

Once in class, she got caught up in the lecture on social control theory and the factors that tend to predict criminal behavior. Lei hadn't finished her reading, so she skimmed as the lecture progressed and took notes in the margins of her book. She couldn't help noticing she had most of the "risk factors" herself: child of parents with addictions, father incarcerated, victim of abuse and neglect. The only reason, according to the research, she wasn't a criminal herself was her Aunty Rosario taking her in and providing a stable home.

At the break, she got up and stretched. Her uniform was one of several in the room. Most of the criminal justice majors were law enforcement or parole officers. She headed over to say hi to her friend from Pahoa station.

"Hey, Mary."

Mary swiveled away from the guy she was talking to. She was a tall, shapely girl, her hair a black waterfall over her police uniform. Her big dark eyes glittered, mischievous.

"If it isn't Texeira! Lei, this is Ray Solomon."

"Howzit," Ray said, shaking her hand. He had the smooth brown skin of mixed, *hapa*, Hawaiian blood.

"Good to meet you," she said. His grip was solid, and she smiled up at him.

"My pleasure. I love women in uniform."

"What about out of uniform?" Mary teased, flicking her stiff navy lapel.

He laughed. "If I can get you there."

"This is too rich for me. Mary, I'll catch up with you later."

"Don't run off, shy girl," Mary teased, pulling one of Lei's curls. "Lei's a local but grew up on the Mainland. Kinda like you, Ray."

"Oh yeah? Where'd you end up?"

"San Rafael, California. From Oahu before that."

"I did my mainland time in Riverside," he said. "Solomon's a Kaua`i family. You know them?"

"No, sorry," Lei said. This was part of the ritual of meeting someone in the Islands—telling where you were from, who your people were.

"Lei was *hanai*'ed to her aunty in California," said Mary. Hanai was the informal adoption practice used by Hawaiian families—when a family had challenges or problems, children were raised by relatives in an open-ended but committed relationship.

"What you telling him my business for?" Lei punched Mary's arm.

"Well, Ray get same kind story," said Mary. "Family problems, the uncle wen' take him in . . ."

Ray's face seemed to shut down, his hazel eyes going opaque.

"Boring stuff," he said.

"She never stop running her mout,'" Lei said. "Come, I keep you out of trouble." She pulled Mary off to the side. "He's cute, but quit trying to set me up. Anyway, he seems pretty into you."

"I wouldn't mind a piece of that, but Roland and I are pretty serious," Mary said. "You're the one who needs some action. Why don't we all go out to Pahoa Music Club tonight, have a few beers, listen to some music?"

"I've got work and so do you. And Keiki's waiting for me."

Mary rolled her eyes as they went back to their seats. After class Ray fell into step beside Lei as she headed down the hall.

"More theories about what makes a criminal."

"I'm not buying it all. There's no excuse. People make choices."

"Texeira's Choice Theory," he said. "I'm sure it's out there. So, working on anything interesting?"

"Yeah, but you know I can't discuss an open investigation," she said, smiling to take the sting out of her words. He cocked his head, a glint of interest in his eyes.

"C'mon. I've got an application in to the academy myself. Maybe another perspective could crack open the case."

"Sorry, but good luck with your application. They should snap up a smart Hawaii boy like you."

"Maybe not," he said, still smiling, but his gold-hazel eyes had gone opaque again. How did he do that? "I got into a little trouble in my youth," he said.

"Didn't we all."

"Yeah. Well, I've got a record. I'm hoping the Criminal Justice degree will tip the balance."

"It's worth a try, if you really want it," she said. "You could always work for a law office, be a private investigator or something, if it doesn't."

"I guess," he said. They had arrived at her old Honda, and Ray lifted a hand in a wave as he headed across the parking lot.

After class, Lei drove home, preoccupied. She wished that for once in her life she could just go out with an attractive guy without getting all wound up and paranoid. Life was short—Kelly and Haunani reminded her of that, and maybe she owed it to them to learn to live a little. She glanced in her rearview mirror—the headlights behind her loomed uncomfortably close. She sped up. The tailgater sped up too, and finally pulled around her, cutting her off.

It was a black Toyota truck.

Adrenaline hit her bloodstream and her foot hit the gas, an automatic reaction. She accelerated, trying to get a look at the license plate. The two-lane road they were on was dim, and the truck surged ahead, streaking around a slower-moving Camry. Lei wished she had a cop light to put on her dash. It might be interesting to pull this jerk over.

She gunned the Honda and the elderly four-cylinder engine burped in protest.

"Come on," she urged, wishing for the roar of the Crown Vic. She made it around the Camry but the Toyota was really flying now, its taillights disappearing over a rise. She floored it and nothing much happened. Next order of business—get a car with some juice. She hit the steering wheel in frustration as the Toyota peeled off to the right. She made the turn without ever hitting the brakes, the whole car shuddering and tires squealing at the abuse.

They reached an open stretch of country road. They'd left the residential area behind, and the Toyota poured it on, surging ahead. Lei held the steering wheel with both hands as it vibrated, the needle creeping to 75, 80, 85. The pickup truck was still accelerating. It disappeared over another rise, and by the time the Honda careened over the hill, it was gone.

The road had forked, and as she got to the intersection, there was nothing left to see but the moon shining on an ocean of waving *pili* grass, glimmering off the empty black asphalt leading away in either direction. The Honda glided to a stop, thoroughly smoked. It seemed like she was always too little, too late.

Chapter 11

Lei was curled up on the couch later, eating her Hot Pocket, when her cell rang. She thumbed it open.

"Hello?"

"Lei? It's Michael."

"Hey Stevens," she said.

"Quit calling me that. I just wanted to check in with you, give you an update. Nice work on the folder."

"Thanks."

"We've been running down some calls on Reynolds's cell, re-canvassing the girls' neighborhoods, and setting up the interview with the witness. Doing it tomorrow—still want to come?"

"Of course. When and where?"

"I thought we'd try to be less intimidating, so it's at Hilo High School library at 10 A.M. Wear civvies."

"Okay. Hey, a little something I think you should know," she said, and told him about the car chase.

"Could be related, but it's a stretch. You probably freaked some poor guy out."

"In my old granny car? C'mon, he was laughing as he dusted me. I really need some decent wheels."

"Why don't you get some?"

"Right," she said, playing with Keiki's ear. "Ha, ha."

"No, really, I've got a friend who works at the dealership downtown . . . he'll find a good deal for you. Let's go tomorrow after the interview."

Lei felt that bubble again, something reckless and wild, something like joy.

"What the hell. Let him know we're coming," she said, and said goodbye. She turned to Keiki. "We're going car shopping, baby."

She had always been careful with money, going to community college in California, being thrifty, and making do. When she arrived in Hilo two years ago, it was with savings she had built up. She'd bought the 1989 Civic for $1500.00 cash and, other than her dog, had no major expenses.

I really can afford to get a new car, she thought, and grinned.

Suddenly Keiki barked in the living room, the full-throated baying that signaled a stranger.

"Keiki! Come!"

The big Rottweiler continued to bark, her ruff distended, the boom of the dog's voice almost shaking the walls. Lei grabbed her Glock out of the holster on the headboard, bolted up from her bed, and ran into the room, her gun out.

"Hello?" she called, but there was no answer except Keiki's snarling as the dog faced the front door. She signaled Keiki back and put her eye to the peephole.

There was no one on the little porch. She opened the door and saw the gleam of paper, and bent down to retrieve the note that had been slipped partially under the mat, carefully holding it by a corner.

"Patrol," she told Keiki, giving her a hand signal. The dog went silent and trotted around the house, sniffing at the windows, and finally whisked through the dog door to do her circuit outside. Lei knew she would bark if there was anything there. She retrieved a pair of gloves and snapped them on. She sat down at the table and slit the envelope with a steak knife. It was the same computer paper, folded twice around a single sentence:

I'M THINKING ABOUT YOU. IT BRINGS BACK MEMORIES.

What the hell did that mean? She battled the urge to crumple the paper and throw it as far away as she could. Instead she slipped it and the envelope into a Ziploc bag. Adrenaline buzzed through her. She hadn't become a cop so she could sit around waiting to be a victim again and she was sick of being too little, too late. Damn if I'm going to sit here and let him scare me. He must still be nearby.

She slipped on her running shoes, clipped her cell phone onto her waistband, shrugged into the shoulder holster and whistled for Keiki. The dog streaked back in, still silent. She slipped the choke chain over Keiki's head. All playfulness was gone as Keiki waited, her triangle ears pricked.

"Work," Lei said, giving her the hand signal. She turned off the lights, letting her eyes adjust. She armed the house, pulled the Glock, stepped outside with the dog at her side. How long since Keiki gave the first alarm? Her mind raced, calculating. No more than five minutes, max. The bastard couldn't have gotten far.

The street was quiet and deserted except for the blue glow of TVs behind living room windows and pools of yellow street lights here and there. She and Keiki speed-walked down the cracked sidewalk, looking for any sign of movement, straining their ears for anything unusual.

They got to Tom Watanabe's house at the end of the block. The Acura was parked in the driveway, the streetlight gilding its chrome. His windows were dark, shades down, no flicker of TV showing.

There was no sign of anyone up or down the street, and Lei felt a sudden hot rage. Bastard thought he could scare her in her home? She'd give him some memories. The stalker was going to learn the hard way she wasn't like other women. She'd never be a helpless victim again.

She knew it could put Keiki at risk, anyone out in the neighborhood at risk, but in a split-second she unclipped Keiki's leash. If he was still here, Keiki would find him.

"Go," she said. The dog shot away, silent as a black arrow, hurtling up the street. Lei ran after her, trying to keep up. She was halfway to the next block when a cacophony of barking started up ahead and she broke into an all out run.

Her heart sank as she saw one of her neighbors, a plump lady in a muumuu, backed up against her mailbox clutching her fuzzy Shih Tzu. Keiki faced them, growling, her hair on end and ears flat. Her teeth looked enormous as she broke into the fast-paced barking meant to herd and intimidate. It appeared to be working.

"Help! Oh my God!" The woman shrieked as the little white dog tried to claw its way onto her head. Lei grabbed Keiki's chain collar and yanked her back onto her haunches.

"Friend!" she yelled, holstering her gun and making the hand signal where the snarling dog could see it. Keiki was so agitated her hair was standing on end, spit flying from gnashing jaws. Lei gave her another yank and a smack on the haunches to get her attention. The dog finally sat, and Lei made her lie down and expose her belly in submission. Only then did she look up at her neighbor.

Up and down the street, lights were coming on and the woman's husband came roaring down the steps, a baseball bat in his hand.

The woman ran toward him screaming, "She has a gun!"

"I'm so sorry," Lei said. "I'm a police officer and I was chasing a suspect. My dog was looking for him."

"What the hell?" screamed the husband. "Are you crazy?"

"I called the police," yelled another neighbor from her porch. Lei recoiled. This was a nightmare.

"I'm a police officer," she repeated to the couple. "I was looking for an intruder . . . I really am sorry. She wouldn't have hurt you. She was 'holding' you for me."

The lady had dropped the Shih Tzu at some point and the dog had vanished. She sobbed hysterically as her enraged husband helped her into the house.

"Tell it to the cops, you crazy bitch! I'm going to tell them to shoot that dog!"

Lei heard the wailing of sirens in the distance. She sat down on the sidewalk and waited, Keiki flopped beside her, her tongue hanging out.

"I'm sorry, girl," she whispered, rubbing her dog's neck. "This is all my fault."

Chapter 12

L ei rocked a little in her bed, her arms around herself, her eyes shut under the sleep mask. She'd called in sick for the morning, dreading facing anyone in the department. Unfortunately, she still had to go meet Stevens and interview the kid at the high school, or miss out on the chance to help with that. She was sure he would've heard about the humiliating interview she'd had with Detectives Ross and Nagata. Bathed in flashing blue-and-red lights and surrounded by hostile neighbors, it had been hard to explain the patrol of her neighborhood that had ended so badly.

"At least the stalker will think twice about coming by on foot while I'm home," she said out loud, flinging off the sleep mask. Keiki raised her head to look at her from the foot of the bed. Lei rocked herself some more, but for once it brought no comfort as she thought of the stark terror in her neighbor's face, the outrage of the woman's husband, the trembling little white dog they'd found two blocks away.

I wonder if he was watching? If so he must be laughing his ass off, she thought, and squeezed her eyes shut again.

Her cell phone bleeped from the side table and she looked at the caller ID before she answered it.

"Pono. Hey."

"Called in sick, huh?"

"I don't feel so good," she said.

"You're the owner of one sick puppy, that's for sure." He chuckled, but there was an angry edge to it.

"Very funny. What did you hear?"

"You and your dog were running around the neighborhood, out for vigilante justice, scaring old ladies out of their wits and waving a gun around. The husband is trying to press charges on you for attempted assault with a deadly weapon and terroristic threatening."

"What? The worst I did is disturb the peace!"

"The dog. Says she's a deadly assault weapon and you knowingly unleashed her. She was the one doing the terroristic threatening."

"Oh my God." Lei sat up. "I know Keiki scared the crap out of them, but she wouldn't have attacked."

"You say that and, frankly, you're the only one who believes it. Anyway you shouldn't have run out there alone with your gun and your dog, Lei! What were you thinking?" His volume was steadily increasing. "You should have had backup. Why didn't you call me? I would've come and helped you!"

She put her hand over her face. Tears rushed up and stung her eyes like a thousand tiny bees. She tried to control her voice.

"I just wanted to get him. I'm not going to be a victim again! I didn't want to let him scare me."

"I'm the one scared. And your neighbors . . ." She heard him breathing hard, trying to get control.

"I'll call for backup next time," she said in a small voice. Keiki belly-crawled across the fluffy duvet and licked the tears off her face.

"I hear that damn dog slurping. Hope she doesn't get put down."

Lei clutched Keiki's neck as fresh tears welled. The enormity of the trouble she was in hit her and she let out a sob.

"Oh, God," Pono exclaimed in a tone of horror. "Are you crying?"

"They can't take my dog!"

"They probably won't, but only because she didn't actually bite anyone. I'm just saying, if she's being seen as a dangerous weapon in the hands of a reckless police officer . . . it's not good."

"I know." Lei wiped her face on Keiki's ruff.

"Did you give them the note?" he asked. She heard the clicking of his keyboard.

"I did. They said they'd investigate, but what is there to investigate? That's what I was doing last night!" Her voice ended in a cry of frustration.

"Okay, yeah. Ross and Nagata entered the note into evidence and they must have seen you had an open case started. I hope that helps, that you were following protocol about that at least."

"I can't believe things got this out of control. If only I hadn't taken the leash off her . . ."

"That's another thing. I think you should stick to the story that you went outside investigating, and she got away from you."

Lei battled with herself. It was pride in her well-trained dog that was taking the worst beating: Keiki would never run away from her and go after someone. It was disloyal to say otherwise. It just wasn't the truth.

"No," she said. "I took a risk letting her off the leash. I knew she could find him if he was out there, but that she would confront anyone she found. I shouldn't have taken that risk."

"It's your ass," he said. She could tell he was still mad, and they sat there in silence. "I'll go talk to the Lieutenant. Tell him you were being stalked, and weren't going to take it."

Lei shot out of the bed in agitation, the sheet tangling around her legs.

"No way. I'll handle it myself."

"Whatever. Just trying to help," he said, his voice short. "I'll call you if I hear anything." He clicked off. Lei sighed as she put the phone down. She had to get ready for the interview at the high school.

Chapter 13

A t 10 A.M. Lei pulled into the "Visitor" stall at Hilo High School. She'd put on jeans and a tank top and for once her hair was behaving. She hopped out of the car, slamming the door, and a chunk of rust fell out of the wheel well.

"Stupid granny car," she muttered. She kicked the tire and it dropped more rust, this time on her athletic shoe.

"Lei!" Stevens called. She looked up, enjoying the way his long legs ate up the ground as he walked toward her. "I see you remembered to wear your civvies."

"Hey," she said, moving to meet him. "Nice change for me. Where do we go?"

"Check in at the office first. How're you doing after your adventure last night?" Braced for teasing, she was almost undone by the concern in his voice. She blinked, slipping her hands into the tight pockets of her jeans. His card was still in there, and she let herself feel its fuzzy edges.

"Okay," she said. "But it was scary."

"You've got friends who will vouch for you at the station. I don't think those charges will stick. But the whole thing must have been bad."

"It was. I shouldn't have gone out alone after the guy, I know that now, but at the time it just seemed so important not to let him scare me . . ." Her voice trailed off. She looked at the ground.

He reached out and pulled her close, wrapping his arms around her. It was so sudden she stumbled forward. Her hands were pinned at her sides, and she stiffened instinctively. As he continued to hold her, close but gentle, she slowly relaxed. His chin rested on her head. She closed her eyes, breathing in the warm smell of his shirt. Finally, he stepped back, clearing his throat.

"Let's get going. I sent Jeremy to work on another lead since you were coming to this interview—don't want to intimidate our witness with too many people."

She nodded, wordless. His hug seemed to have melted something around her heart. She followed him into the school office.

They signed in and got visitor badges, and the vice principal showed them to a small study room off the main library area. Stevens got out his portable tape recorder, the file of photos, a notebook, and pen.

The vice principal returned a few minutes later with a petite Filipino girl. Her long, glossy black hair hung over her face and she peeked at them through the screen of her bangs. She flopped into the molded plastic chair with boneless grace.

"Hi again, Angela. Remember me, Detective Stevens? And this is Officer Texeira."

The girl nodded, dark doe eyes flicking over to Lei and returning to Stevens.

"Is it okay if we tape this interview?" he asked. "Your parents gave permission for me to interview you." She nodded, a shy bob of the head. Her earrings swung, a sparkle of silver.

"Okay. Last time we talked, you told me you had seen Haunani Pohakoa get in a black Toyota truck after school with an older man."

She nodded.

"Please state your response out loud," Stevens said, giving her an encouraging smile.

"Yes," Angela said softly, her eyes still on him. Lei couldn't help noticing how something about him made even a high school student respond with trust and confidence.

"When was this?"

"I don't know. A week or two before they found them."

"Did she say anything to you about this guy?"

"She called him her 'secret admirer.'"

"Was there any student gossip about him?"

"Everybody was calling him Haunani's sugar daddy," she said with a giggle. The spiteful edge to it made the hairs rise on Lei's neck.

"But nobody knew who he was?"

"No. That's why I wanted to get a look at him," Angela said. "I thought it must be someone other kids knew—somebody's uncle or brother or something." Was she really a friend of Haunani's? Or more of an enemy?

"Did he pick Haunani up regularly?"

"I only saw the truck a couple times."

"Did you ever see Kelly go with them?"

"No. Kelly and Haunani were just getting to be friends. I don't think Haunani wanted anyone else to meet him. She wanted to keep him all to herself." Again the silvery giggle. "So I walked across the street when he was picking her up so I could get a look at him, but he wasn't anybody I know."

Stevens slid the folder of photos over to her. Lei had folded the license information over so only the pictures were showing.

"Do you think you could pick out his picture?" he asked.

"Maybe." Angela leaned over the photos, the swath of hair a black silk curtain hiding her face. She slid each printout to the side as she rejected it. She took her time, but in the end she pushed them all aside.

"I don't see him." Her eyes glittered defiantly. Stevens reassembled the pictures into a grid.

"Look again." He set the photos before her, six on a side. She went through them again, shook her head.

"No."

"Are you sure?" he urged. Lei felt the glare of James Reynolds's eyes burning up at her from his photo on the top left. Angela cut her eyes to Stevens.

"He's not here."

"These are all the photos of men 25 to 45 who drive a dark Toyota truck with Hilo or outlying addresses. That's what you told us. So what did he look like?"

"I'm not sure how old he was. Dark hair. And I think the truck was black." A long pause. The only sound was Stevens breathing through his nose.

"What about dark blue or charcoal?" Lei asked, gesturing to the photos.

"I don't know," Angela repeated. "I thought it was black." She stood up, gossamer hair swinging back over her narrow shoulders. "I have to go. My friends are waiting for me."

Stevens put his hand on her arm, held her gaze.

"It's important that you try to remember. Anything, any details. You don't know what might be important. This man may have killed your friends." Angela looked down, fiddling with the gold-plated logo dangling from her purse.

"I know. But he's not here."

"Okay. I may see you again if I get anything else. Here's my card," Stevens said, slipping it into the side pocket of her purse. "Call me if anything else comes to mind."

She nodded and spun on kitten-heeled slippers to clip-clop out of the room. The door shut with a clang behind her. Stevens shuffled the pictures back into the folder and looked at Lei.

"Well? What do you think?"

"I believe her. She didn't recognize him. I was so sure she would pick Reynolds out, and he does have dark hair. It's too bad, would have made things easier. So, what is his supposedly airtight alibi?"

"Nothing too exciting. He was out with his wife, having a 'weekend away.' Left Kelly on her own at the house to take care of the dog. Kelly's mom confirms they went to a bed and breakfast for the night, and when they got back, the dog was still locked in the house and hadn't been fed or let out. They were worried something had happened to Kelly and started calling all her friends and the police."

"What do you think?"

"I can't believe a mother would choose her new husband over her daughter and cover for foul play. I know it happens, but I can't get my head around it. So yeah, I believe them."

"Believe it. It happens," Lei said flatly. "Check it out."

"Jeremy's following up on it."

They made their way back to the office, turned in the visitor badges. Stevens's hand touched her lower back as they pushed through the glass door, and she felt the simple gesture zing up her spine. He squinted at her in the midmorning sun outside.

"Well? Are we going car shopping?"

"I thought you'd given up on that with all the drama that's been going on. I know I did."

"I'm still game if you are."

"Sure, I guess." She played it cool.

"Follow me," he said, with a sweeping gesture.

Chapter 14

L ei turned the key, smiling at the snarl of the engine
turning over, the purr as it settled down. Her silver
Toyota Tacoma had that new car smell and sound. That
black truck can't outrun me in this, she thought. Keiki sat
majestically upright on the seat beside her. She'd bought the
extended cab so that in case she had a passenger, she could put
the dog behind them. There was plenty of room for the leash,
water bottles, and beach and bookbags she'd packed. Since
she'd already called in sick, she might as well try to relax,
have a little fun.

Lei pulled out and drove past Tom Watanabe's house. His
second car, a black Nissan Frontier, was in the driveway this
time. She continued on through her meandering neighborhood,
with its plantation-style homes, neat yards, and sagging
electric lines. Most of Hilo was older, built in the style
popular in Hawaii with extended roofs over porches to catch
the trade winds. Hilo had a downtown area with big box stores
and industrial buildings, but most of it was unpretentiously
residential. The plethora of hapu`u fern trees lining driveways
and exotic hibiscus, orchids and plumeria massed in gardens

was what set Hilo apart—that, and the volcano looming in the distance.

She took Stevens' card out of her pocket and rubbed it absently as she drove, thinking about Tom Watanabe. As a water inspector he would be familiar with all of the waterways going in and out of Hilo, and with his job, his tramping around a stream or culvert would never be questioned. The black truck, while not the right make, struck her as an odd coincidence.

She pulled out onto the highway that ran out of Hilo toward Punalu`u Beach Park. The shiny hood of the pickup caught the afternoon sun, dazzling her as she ran her hand around the ergonomically engineered steering wheel.

Tropical jungle lined the highway: gigantic fern trees battled with royal palms, and majestic albizia trees hung with trailing vines soared over it all. The road was a wide, straight black ribbon furling to the caldera of Kilauea, the epicenter of the national park, and on through past Honuapo to Kona.

Lei stomped down on the gas, and the engine roared back at her, leaping forward. She'd got a deal by buying the stick shift, and she whooped with glee as she put it in overdrive at ninety miles an hour. They whizzed by a few tourists and she smelled the hot stench of oil burning off the new engine and throttled it back to a sedate seventy-five.

She thumbed open her cell in a celebratory double traffic violation.

"Aunty!"

"*Ku`uipo*, sweetheart! Whatchu doing?"

"I'm blowing down the highway in my new truck," Lei said. "A silver Toyota Tacoma four-wheel drive."

"Oh my God, girl! Whatchu doing spending that kind money?"

"I have it, Aunty. I had plenty for the down payment, I got no credit cards and just the basic bills . . . I can afford it."

"Congratulations, then you deserve it. You work hard enough."

"Thank you, Aunty," Lei replied. Well-being filled her as she whipped around another tourist, passing with ease. Keiki swayed, her eyes glued on the road ahead, the stump of her tail twitching with excitement. They chatted a while longer and Lei snapped her phone shut. It was good to hear Aunty Rosario's voice, there for her whenever she needed her.

Almost like a mother.

She tried to shut out the flash of memory: her mother reading the note and screaming like she'd been mortally wounded. She'd grabbed a wire hanger and beat Lei with it until her rage was spent, shoving the girl down the steps into the garage and slamming the door. This in itself was not unusual.

What was different was that her mother never came to let her out.

Two days passed in which nine-year-old Lei ate cat food, drank from the utility sink, and defecated in the kitty litter, staying warm by burrowing into the laundry pile. Eventually she got up the courage to break the little window over the sink and wriggle her way out.

She'd found her mother Maylene Murakami Texeira slumped over the coffee table, the syringe beside her and tubing still around her arm. Her legs were askew from convulsions, her face blue, foam dried on her lips. Rigor had already gone, and when Lei shook her, she seemed to slither over onto her side.

Lei still ached from the beating, she was faint with hunger, but worse than that, terror filled her at the thought of going to a foster home. She had already spent plenty of time in them. She ran to the kitchen and called the emergency number Aunty Rosario in California had given her.

"Call 911, and tell them I am on my way." Her aunt had taken the next flight out of San Francisco to get her.

The best thing that ever happened to me was when Aunty took me to San Rafael to live, Lei thought. She pinched her arm to stop the memory and refocused herself on her current surroundings: another technique the therapist in California had taught her.

She pulled into Punalu`u Beach Park and parked next to Mary's red Mustang. It was good to be meeting a friend, clearing her head, going to the beach—another experience the girls would never have again. Guilt was becoming a familiar gnaw, and she found herself pinching her arm again—too hard this time.

It didn't help.

Lei ran across the burning black sand and dove into the ocean. The cool water shocked the breath out of her, and she surged to the surface with a gasp. She dove again, opening her eyes. The lava pebbles covering the ocean floor made it look depthless as a black-bottomed pool and she kicked down and scooped up a handful, bobbing back up with a shake of her curls.

Keiki swam toward her, big square head held high, paws churning. Lei tossed one of the pebbles.

"Get it, girl!"

The dog spun and splashed after the rock, ducking her head into the water and coming up snorting. Lei tossed another one further away. Keiki floundered after it.

"That's so mean!" Mary called from the beach. She sat forward in her beach chair, rubbing coconut oil onto her long brown legs. "It's sick the way you torture that poor dog."

"Kinda like how you torture Roland?" Lei strode up out of the surf, adjusting her tank suit top, wishing she had a little more to fill it out. She tossed one last pebble and Keiki switched directions and splashed after it.

"Roland loves it," Mary said. "I never make him do anything he doesn't want to do." She rubbed the scented oil into her waist.

"Same thing with Keiki," Lei said. "She loves that stupid rock-chasing game."

"My only problem with Roland—he stay jealous. Always wanting to see what I'm doing." Her cell phone chirped from the straw bag beside her. "See? He texting me, asking when I'm coming home." She frowned, working the phone with her thumbs.

Hawaiian guitar music tinkled from the little CD player parked on their blanket. Lei stretched out on the warm cloth with a sigh. She'd been single so long she wasn't sure she'd want to give up her independence—it didn't seem like a relationship was worth dealing with the demands.

Both women jumped and squealed as Keiki shook water all over them. The big dog flopped onto the blanket next to Lei, panting, and Lei shoved her off. Maybe she was in a relationship after all.

"You stink," she said. "Go take a shower."

In response Keiki rolled in the black sand, grunting with pleasure as she worked the large grains into her coat.

Mary and Lei hadn't been out to scenic Punalu`u Beach for a long time. Lei decided to come more often, taking in the sun-jeweled ocean and rugged palm-dotted coastline. Only yards away, several huge green sea turtles slept in the sand, their flippers spread and necks outstretched to soak up warmth from the sun.

Keiki finished with her roll and sprawled next to them. After a cursory sniff, she'd showed no interest in the turtles. Lei draped her arm across her eyes and dozed.

"So anything new on that stalker note you got?" Mary's voice woke her, and she sat up. She'd told Mary about the notes a few days ago at class.

"Pass me the oil."

Mary handed it over and Lei squirted a dollop into her palm, slicked it onto her lean body and toned legs. She was too late to head off the freckles that dotted her like a sprinkle of nutmeg.

"He came by last night, dropped another note under my door. I chased him but no joy." She told her friend about the debacle in the neighborhood with Keiki.

"Try solve your own problems and jus' get in trouble," Mary said. "I'm sorry. Like you don't get enough stress a'ready without that stalker shit."

"It's okay." Lei tried to smile.

"Pono won't let you go down if he can help it. Me neither. Lot of folks will stick up for you at the station."

"I meet with the Lieutenant tomorrow morning. I'm pretty damn nervous. It's like I'm cursed or something."

"What do you mean?"

"Shit happens to me. All my life. Something's wrong with me that makes things happen." The murmur of the surf and mellow slack key music failed to calm Lei's racing heart. She felt something important almost breaking through the memory fog that plagued her. She rubbed her temples where a headache threatened.

"What a load of crap. Shit happens to all of us. Listen, we better get going—Roland says we have plans tonight." They packed up and walked out to the parking lot.

"Oh my God, gorgeous!" Mary said, running her hand along the contoured wheel well of the new truck. The silver paint glowed opal. "Wish I could get one."

"You already have a nice ride," Lei said, gesturing to Mary's red Mustang, a former rental car bought for a song.

"Yeah, but this sweetheart has muscle. I like a nice truck." She put her hands on her hips. "Want to race 'em?"

"You brat," Lei said. "As if you didn't know I was *already* in trouble."

Mary laughed. "Bet I beat you," she said, jumping into the Mustang.

At home, Lei bounced up the steps of her little house, sorting her mail. Keiki barked from the back yard, eager to come in for dinner. She unlocked the door, deactivated the alarm, and noticed the envelope on the floor. Her pulse jumped. The stalker had pushed it under the door this time.

She went into the kitchen and got a fresh pair of gloves from under the sink, snapping them on as she returned. She picked the envelope up by the corner and took it to the cutting board, slitting the top with a knife to preserve any evidence trapped under the flap. She eased the trebly-folded note out and flipped it open.

A long hank of glossy black hair obscured the words on the page. Lei's vision swam and she clutched the counter, taking a couple of deep breaths. She looked back down and eased the hair out of the way with the point of the knife.

I'M GOING TO ENJOY YOU A LOT MORE.

Lei felt bile rise in her throat, hot and stinging. She gulped it back, took a few relaxation breaths.

He wasn't going to get to her in her own home. Her eyes fell on one of her orange notes tacked over the sink: *Courage is simply the willingness to be afraid and act anyway- Robert Anthony.*

I'll act anyway. She went to the dog door and unlocked it. Keiki streaked in and did a circuit of the house as she fished the cell phone out of her pocket.

"Pono," she said when he answered. "He's escalating. He might have a victim."

"What? Whatchu talking about?"

"There was another note," she said. "A big piece of black hair inside. No woman I know would let someone cut off a chunk of hair like this."

"I'm on my way."

She shut the phone and went back to the front door, putting the chain and deadbolt back on. Pono arrived shortly. He'd brought Jeremy Ito and Stevens with him. Lei introduced Jeremy to Keiki and led them back into the kitchen. Pono took a good look at her in the light, tipping her chin to look at her pale face.

"You need food, girl," he said, and went to her fridge, poking about inside. He held up a withered lemon and a bottle of ketchup. "Nothing in here."

Stevens examined the hair and the envelope at the kitchen table, putting on gloves Lei handed him. Jeremy looked on, his hands behind his back as though to keep them out of trouble, his lean young face intent. The kitchen light caught on their two bent heads, the rumpled dark of Stevens beside Jeremy's black.

"There's no evidence anyone has been hurt," Stevens said. "The hairs look like they were snipped off. It could be a clipping off the floor of a barbershop." He slipped everything into an evidence bag.

"I guess so," Lei said, unconvinced. "It's sure threatening though." She sat down in one of the chairs. "Anyone want something to drink? I have beer."

"Miller Lite," Pono scoffed.

"Still on the clock." Jeremy smiled, shaking his head. Pono flipped open his phone and speed-dialed the local Pizza Hut, ordering a large pepperoni with extra cheese.

"We were heading back to the station so we'll take this in," Stevens said. "Pono, you going to stay a while?"

"Got my pizza coming. You can come back by later."

"What the hell is this?" Lei said, mustering up some indignation. "I don't need a babysitter."

"What's new on the Mohuli`i girls?" Pono asked, ignoring her.

"Still got some leads to check out off the cell phones," Stevens said. "Lei, maybe you and Jeremy can run some of them down tomorrow. I have to do a conference call with the Oahu lab people analyzing what we sent over from the trash at the crime scene. I want to talk to all Haunani's contacts again, see if any of them remembered anything more about this mystery man of hers."

"Did you think anymore about the truck search?" Lei asked.

"Nah. If we get a hit on anyone else with that angle, we'll revisit our witness. Right now we need to shake the trees and see what falls. I'm hoping for the search warrant on James Reynolds's house today or tomorrow. I'll be back later to spell you, Pono."

"Bye," said Jeremy as he followed Stevens out.

Lei put the chain and deadbolt back on behind them, turning to Pono, who'd finally taken off his Oakleys and set them on the table. They'd begun to make dents above his ears.

He rubbed his bristly mustache. "I'm hungry. That pizza better get here soon."

"I don't need a babysitter," she repeated.

Pono shrugged. "This is how we look out for our own Big Island style. You think you're the only cop to be stalked?"

"I don't know—I guess not."

"Well you're not. One of ours gets threatened, we look out for each other. Even off the clock."

He went in and sat on the threadbare couch in her little living room, put his feet up on the trunk she used as a coffee table, hit the remote for the TV, and began scrolling through the channels.

Lei flopped next to him, giving up. It wasn't long before they were digging into the rich, stretchy goo of hot pizza. She hadn't realized how famished she was until she felt herself begin to relax as satiety worked its way through her system. She sat back and belched behind her hand.

"Feel better?"

"Yeah. I didn't know I was so hungry."

"Girl, you looked terrible. And to come home to this . . ." He rubbed a finger over his lips.

"Thanks for coming over. I hope Tiare doesn't mind."

"She wouldn't like me sleeping over. That's why I got Stevens doing the night shift." He leered, looking exactly like an ominous tiki god come to life. "Play it right, you might get more than a bodyguard."

"Shut up." Lei punched him in the arm. "I gotta go shower." She hauled herself off of the couch and went in to the bathroom. Keiki followed and flopped outside the door with a whuff.

Lei just stood for a long time under the falling water. It felt wonderful to wash off all the nervous sweat from the day, to feel safe with her partner downstairs . . . to know she had some friends. She got out and pulled on her favorite old sweats from high school hanging from a hook on the back of the door.

An hour later, Stevens rang the bell. Lei let him in. His hair was wet, and his eyes were dark with fatigue.

"Second shift," he said. He carried a small navy duffel.

"You don't have to do this." Lei trailed him into the living room. Keiki gave his pants a sniff as he passed.

"Good. I'm off home," Pono said, getting up. "Don't let her out."

"What do you think I'm here for? Gotta keep the vigilante locked up. Yeah, I dropped the letter and hair off and logged them in for your case," he said, turning to Lei. "Sure wish we could get some sort of break on it, but at first glance it's clean: no follicles on the hair, nothing caught under the flap, no fingerprints. Cheap plain envelope and computer paper you could get anywhere. It sucks, but there's nothing."

"Sick son of a bitch." Pono banged his beer bottle down.

"What's sick is that he's getting away with this and there's not a thing anybody can do about it," Lei burst out. She began tidying the pizza debris, blinking rapidly. "I'm a police officer, for godsake."

"Sometimes that's what makes you a target. I've seen contracts put out on officers in L.A."

"This isn't L.A. and I shouldn't have to put up with this shit, including you guys camping on my couch."

"Eh then, I going see you tomorrow," her partner said, giving her shoulder an awkward pat as he let himself out.

"Hey." Stevens sat on the couch. "It's okay to be mad. Come sit."

Lei hunkered down in the corner of the couch and honked her nose on a paper towel.

"Stalkers prey on your fear. Try not to let it get to you." He picked up the last piece of pizza and took a bite.

"It's a kind of torture," Lei said. "I try to make my home safe, and he slips things right in to it . . ." her voice trailed off and she hugged the couch cushion. He gazed at her, then reached out a finger and brushed a dangling curl off her forehead.

"We'll get him. I think this is about more than you, somehow."

"What? Going with your gut now?" Lei said. Immediately she felt bad, but clamped her lips shut on any apology.

Stevens got up and went into the kitchen, getting one of the beers and opening it. He took a long drink, and Lei couldn't help noticing the wide tanned muscles of his throat working as he swallowed. She made herself look away.

"I guess I am going with my gut," he said. "I deserved that." He sat back down beside her, rolling the beer bottle between his palms. "I should have brought my sax over. I could have distracted you with some tunes."

"I didn't know you played."

"Yeah. Not well but with enthusiasm, as they say." He chuckled a little, rubbed his eyes which looked red-rimmed and tired. "Coming and keeping an eye on you is a helluva lot more fun than picking my mom up from the drunk tank and bringing her home. I used to have to put her to bed, sleep over to make sure she didn't drown in her vomit or something."

"Shit. That why you came to Hawaii?"

"In a nutshell. I love the job, the life, the adrenaline hit when you get the call." He sat back, put his long legs up on the battered trunk. "But when a couple of times a week the call was to pick Mom up for drunk and disorderly, I got sick of it. She's gonna kill herself and I'm not going to watch her do it." He finished the beer and set it on the coffee table with a thunk. "Good thing I picked something up on the way over here. Pono didn't leave much."

"Yeah." She laughed, a little watery. She wasn't the only one who'd had a messed up mother, but she wasn't ready to tell him anything yet. "We were both starved. Listen, I'll make the couch up for you if that's okay."

"'Course. No hurry."

They sat quietly. The TV, muted, flashed luminescence over the comfortable silence. Finally, Lei sighed.

"It's been a long day." She unwound her arms from the pillow, starting to get up.

"Stay," he said, reaching a long arm out. "You look like you need a hug." He pulled her in beside him with one powerful scoop, and she laughed a little, falling into the sagging cushion beside him.

"Yeah," she said, relaxing against his side, his arm around her. Her cheek found the hollow between his shoulder and collarbone, and she felt her eyes drift shut as warmth and safety flowed over her.

Chapter 15

Tuesday morning Lei perched on the molded plastic chair in front of the Lieutenant's desk. Sweat prickled her palms—she rubbed them on her dark blue slacks. She heard the faint buzzing in her ears that signaled she might 'disappear' so she dug her thumb and forefinger into the fleshy web of her other hand, anchoring herself with the pain and making it look like her hands were folded neatly in her lap.

Her eyes wandered around the cluttered little office decorated with stacks of papers, a wall of criminology texts, some plaques erupting in rust from the humid Hilo air. She did some relaxation breathing as she looked anywhere but at the bulk of the Lieutenant, his buzz-cut head lowered to read the Incident Report in front of him.

Lei glanced out the window at a pair of mynah birds gossiping in loud chattering voices on the chain-link fence that surrounded the station. The sight calmed her and she glanced back at the top of Lieutenant Ohale's head as he leafed through her file: the stalker letters, photocopied; the police report for the incident; copies of her Performance Appraisals for the last couple of years.

He looked up at her and sat back, his chair creaking. He took off the tiny reading glasses.

"Relax. I've decided on the charges: disturbing the peace and letting a dog off leash in the city limits. Couple fines, a performance review, and mandatory counseling for consequences. Think you should be able to deal with that."

Lei let her breath out, not even aware she'd been holding it. "Thanks, Lieutenant."

"Might not hurt to bake your neighbors a few cookies if you do that kind of thing. In any case, that's the plan. You have a solid record up until now, and while I don't think you used good judgment, you learned your lesson and no one was hurt. Now, what's the situation with this stalker? Any suspects?"

"Nothing." Lei sat back, threw her hands up. "No clues. I can't think of anybody who this could be except maybe one of my neighbors. He kinda creeps me out but nothing solid to go on. He's a water inspector—Tom Watanabe."

The Lieutenant gave her a sharp look, put the glasses back on, and typed Tom's name into the database. They waited a few minutes for the aged system to process, then he swiveled the monitor so she could see.

"No priors. He's clean."

"I don't know what could have brought this on." Lei rubbed Stevens' card which she'd put in her pocket that morning. "I haven't even dated anybody since I moved here two years ago."

"I tell you what's weird, that a pretty girl like you hasn't been out in two years. Something wrong with that, fo' sure. Anyway, how's helping with the Mohuli`i case going?"

"Okay." Lei sat forward. "We got nowhere with the girl who ID'd the sugar daddy in the truck, but Stevens is running down some leads on the girls' cell phone records that might help us."

The Lieutenant pressed down the old-fashioned intercom button on his desk.

"Irene? Find Stevens and get him in here."

Her tinny voice echoed: "Yes, sir. He may be out in the field. I'll let you know."

The Lieutenant sat back, interlocking his fingers over his belly. He seemed to feel no need for small talk, and Lei slumped a bit in her hard chair. Relief was making her a little dizzy, and she remembered she had been too nervous to eat breakfast.

"Hey, Lieutenant." Pono stuck his head in, a worried crease between his brows. "Everything okay?"

"We got some consequences for the perp here," Lieutenant Ohale said, gesturing to Lei. Pono eased his muscular frame into the room.

"Like what?"

The Lieutenant gestured to Lei.

"Fines, a performance review, and mandatory counseling," Lei recited.

"Whatever it takes to get this girl some counseling," Pono said, his relief evident in the broad grin he gave them. "She one crazy-ass bitch and I'm not just talking about her dog."

Lei glared at Pono's retreating back. She'd get him later. Stevens came in and lowered himself into the other plastic chair in front of the Lieutenant's desk. She opened her mouth and Lieutenant Ohale cut her off.

"Stevens, report."

"Yes, sir." Stevens faced the Lieutenant. "Came up dry on the witness at the high school. May have to broaden the search parameters on that: other brands of trucks, other dark colors. I think she's a little too eager to rat out her dead friend. Ran down some of the cell phone numbers. Looks like there are some calls to one of our small-time dealers in town who may know something. I'm bringing him in tomorrow.

"Jeremy's running down the alibi on the stepdad and it still seems to be checking out, the B & B confirms they were there. I was thinking Lei and Jeremy could go interview some of

Haunani's contacts today while I try and get in with the DA to discuss the warrant for the Reynolds house. Nothing's really popping right now but we've got plenty of leads."

"Keep me posted," Ohale said. "Dismissed."

Lei stuck her head over the top of Jeremy and Stevens's cubicle a little later.

"Hey, Jeremy," she said. He looked up from his computer, serious, his eyes wary. She wondered why she put him so on edge. He didn't seem to like her, and it was something to do with Stevens but she couldn't figure out what.

"Hi. Come check out this list of addresses."

Lei sat in Stevens's cushy leather chair beside him.

"These are the people Stevens wants us to check out today," he said. "All the people Haunani Pohakoa called or received calls from in the last month. We're doing drop-bys for some of them and I called some. They're expecting us."

"Okay," she said, looking at the printed list and the driver's license photos printed next to the names and addresses. "Looks like kids, mostly."

"Yeah," he said. He seemed preoccupied. His short, square fingers flew over the keyboard.

"So, how come you got these nice chairs and we got those crappy old ones from the '70s?" Lei teased.

"Detectives have a few perks," he said, shutting down his computer.

"You're pretty young. How'd you get the promotion?"

"My work on the Kolehole Park case," he said. "I was able to track down the other homeless guy who beat the victim to death."

"Nice. Any tips for me on making detective?"

He collected his jacket, gun, and badge.

"Nope," he said. She followed him out, disappointed. He certainly wasn't a talker.

She thought back to that morning, coming down the hall in her old kimono robe, looking for Stevens. The couch had been empty, the crocheted afghan neatly folded. Stevens had left a note under the coffee maker, which was already full of hot brew:

Had to get back early. Check in with me later.

He wrote with a bold hand, denting the little notebook. He'd drawn a smiley face underneath, and she found herself tearing off the slip of paper and folding it into a wedge she put in her pocket. The dog-eared card he'd given her had finally fallen apart.

She slipped her hand into her pocket now as she followed Jeremy for a long day of interviewing. The triangle shape of the folded note touching her fingers felt hard and reassuring.

She and Jeremy dropped in on six of Haunani's contacts, all of whom had claimed not to have known who her "secret admirer" was, nor had any idea who might have had access to Rohypnol or wanted to harm her. A couple of them weren't home and they left messages with relatives.

Far from the banter and teasing she had with Pono, Jeremy spoke only when necessary, answering her questions with monosyllables. Eventually she gave up, reading her Criminology text between the stops. She found the silence unexpectedly relaxing.

They met Stevens for lunch at Local Grindz, a popular cop restaurant. Lei started on her Japanese *bento* box lunch as Stevens and Jeremy hashed over the fruitless interviews.

"These kids are really upset over the girls' murder. I think they'd tell us if they knew anything," Jeremy concluded. His reserve was gone, she noticed. She stirred chicken *katsu* into the rice and added a little *kim chee* on top before deftly scooping it up with her chopsticks.

"What do you think about the interviews so far?" Stevens asked, turning to her.

"Nothing's popping. Just a bunch of high school kids, and so far they're broken up when we start talking about Haunani. We haven't found anyone obvious she could have been getting drugs from."

They cleared their trays back onto the counter, and Stevens draped his arm over Lei's shoulders as they followed Jeremy out.

"My back hurts," he whispered in her ear. "Got anything more comfy for tonight?" Jeremy turned back to them and frowned as he pushed the door open. Stevens dropped his arm when Lei elbowed him hard.

"Forget it," she snapped. "You're not getting in my bed."

"Hey," he said, trying to sound injured. "I just meant a futon or something."

"I can work a phone if I need help. You guys are overreacting, seriously."

Jeremy had moved ahead of them and was already unlocking the car. She hurried after him and they got in and pulled away.

There was no mistaking the icy silence as they drove to their next interview. Lei was equally quiet. Jeremy was jealous. How ridiculous, she thought. Like she and Stevens were anything but colleagues, maybe friends. What the hell was wrong with the guy?

Somehow they completed the rest of the interviews without speaking to each other.

Chapter 16

He sat in his truck across the street from the bar in the waning light of evening. He'd been tracking her patterns, and today she usually finished her patrol shift and went in to eat and change before class. Sure enough, her vehicle roared around the corner and into the alley. She got out, pulling a rubber band out of her hair as she walked briskly, carrying a duffel bag, to the alley entrance into the bar.

He put the truck in gear and pulled across, parking just in front of her vehicle. He checked once again that he had everything he needed, and then slipped into the unlocked back alley door.

Inside, the hallway was empty, dimly lit by a bare, apathetic bulb. The battered door of the women's room was to his left. He heard splashing from inside. She'd taken her uniform off to change and was having a quick rinse at the sink. He imagined her as he'd seen her through the high louvered window on another day: washing her face, skin glowing pearl in the dim light, serviceable bra and panties only hinting at her unique treasures.

He put his ear against the door and heard rustling. She was getting clothes out of the duffel bag. He slid the wire through the crack of the door, catching the old fashioned latch and pushing it up and out of its metal loop. He gave the door a hard push and it swung wide.

She jerked upright, clutching a T-shirt against her breasts.

"Hey!" she said indignantly. He registered the swirl of loose hair, startled eyes, white cotton panties: then he shot her.

The prongs of the Taser flew out and smacked her in the chest. She crumpled to the ground, twitching.

He stepped inside, closing the door. He detached the prongs and retracted it. Moving quickly but with deliberation he cuffed her hands behind her back, stuffed a kerchief gag in her mouth. He took the syringe out of his pocket, uncapped it, and drove it into her hip. He dropped a pillowcase over her head, rolled her in the sheet he'd brought. He wrapped a long bungee cord around her a couple times to secure the sheet and pillowcase. He hefted her up, staggering a little, and checked outside the door: empty. Slipping down the hallway and out the back door of the bar, he opened the passenger door of his truck and threw her in. Her head bounced off the dashboard and she slid onto the floor as he folded her legs and shut the door.

He ran back into the restroom, let the water out of the sink, gathered her purse and uniform, and thrust them into the duffel bag. Then he hurried back to his truck. She was still, her head lying near his feet, her body an anonymous mummy. The prey, captured.

The heady power of it surged through his body, a high like no other. He couldn't resist putting his foot on her. Gave her a little kick, just a sample of what was to come. She didn't move. He threw the truck into gear and rolled out. Glancing back in the mirror at the red Mustang left in the alley, he smiled.

Chapter 17

L ei sat down at the rectangular table in her Criminology class. She put her soda cup beside her to save Mary's place. Tonight's lecture was on Criminal Rehabilitation and once again, she was behind on the reading. She opened her textbook, skimming the Chapter.

"Hey beautiful." Ray Solomon slipped into the chair next to her on the other side.

"Howzit, Ray?" She didn't want to keep being paranoid so she put on a big smile.

"Not bad. Small kine tired." His shoulder-length hair was glossy as an otter's pelt under the harsh fluorescent lights. He rubbed his shoulder. "I pulled something pounding nails today."

"Oh, that what you do?"

"Yeah, construction. For the moment," he said, with that flash of smile.

"Keeps you in shape," Lei said, her eyes flicking to his well-developed biceps. Am I flirting? That would be a yes. He grinned, making a muscle for her.

"Got all kinds of uses for these guns," he said.

The instructor came up to the lectern and class got underway. Mary never showed up, and afterward Ray lingered as she gathered her books.

"Like get something fo' eat?" he asked.

"Thanks, but I've got someone waiting at home."

"Sure, that's okay."

"It's my dog," she said. "I have to get straight home or she'll chew the wall down. It's a long day for her with no food or company when I have class."

"Sounds like you're pretty tied down." They walked down the hall.

"She's like family, so I don't mind," Lei said. "Hey, did Mary say anything to you about missing class today? She's always here."

"No," he said. They arrived at her truck and she hit the remote. The lights flashed as the door unlocked, and Lei couldn't help smiling—it felt like the truck was greeting her.

"Like my new ride?" she said, turning to him.

"Wow." Only his mouth smiled. "Nice." He stroked the muscular curve of the wheel well with both hands.

"I needed something with more juice," she said, slinging her book bag into the back. "I was sick of that granny car."

"Good. Well, see you." He walked away, and she stared after him. *He's not happy about the truck. Weird. Maybe he was jealous? Well, she was definitely not going out with him,* she decided. She got in and fired up the truck, and then called Mary's cell. It went immediately to voicemail.

"Mary. Where are you girl? Left me alone with Ray and he asked me out. It's all your fault." She shut the phone with a snap, but her smile faded.

She'd really been looking forward to seeing Mary after the day she'd had, she thought as she pulled into the driveway at home. She'd been deflated and tired as she went into her cubicle at the end of the interviews with Jeremy, around 3 P.M. Topping it off, on her desk had been a memo assigning her to

"Mandatory Counseling Session Number 1 of 6" the next day at 2 P.M.. Stapled to the back were two fine invoices for the charges the Lieutenant had authorized from the debacle with Keiki.

The last thing she needed right now was to stir up the past with counseling—it was hard enough pretending she had her shit together without talking about it. She pulled into the garage, letting the sectioned panel rumble shut as she got out of the truck. Keiki did her happy greeting bark.

"Hey baby. I hope you have dinner ready, I'm starving," she said to the dog, rubbing her ears through the chain link and stalling another moment. She hated what this guy was doing to her. She used to like picking up her mail.

Bracing herself, she went to the mailbox and opened it. There was nothing inside but a card, the kind that shows a package to pick up at the post office, with no indication of who the package was from.

Probably Aunty sending some poi rolls. She hoped.

Pono's deep purple lifted Ford F-250 pulled into her driveway. He was on his cell phone, the stereo blasting Bob Marley's *Buffalo Soldier.* She put her hands on her hips, trying to look annoyed as he hopped out of the cab in typical after-work garb, a pair of nylon athletic shorts and a University of Hawaii football jersey.

"Whatchu doing here?" Annoyance called for pidgin.

"Babysitting," he said, snapping his phone shut. "Get used to it."

She turned, unlocked the front door, stepped inside, and deactivated the alarm. Pono came in behind her. There was nothing on the floor. She frowned to hide her relief.

"I appreciate it, really, but this is crazy. You can't come over every night."

He ignored her, slipping past and going to the rear entrance where he unlocked the dog door. The big Rottweiler careened in, her toenails scrabbling. She barreled toward Pono, sitting at the last second, gazing at him in naked adoration. He squatted and patted her chest.

"Now this is a good dog," he said. "Eat anyone today, girl?" Keiki moaned in ecstasy, rolling on her back so he could rub her tummy. Lei went to the fridge. It was still empty.

"Damn. I forgot to get some food."

"No worries," Pono said. "Tiare sent some ono grinds." He went back out the front door and returned with tattooed arms wrapped around two bulging paper bags. He was unpacking various items as her cell phone rang.

"Hello?"

"Lei? It's Roland."

Mary's boyfriend? He never called her. Lei stuck her finger in her ear to block the sound of crunching foil as Pono unwrapped steaming *laulau*. The savory smell of the seasoned pork wrapped in taro leaves filled the air, distracting her. She went into the living room.

"What's up?" she asked.

"Do you know where Mary is?"

"No. Thought she'd be with you," Lei said. "She wasn't at class tonight."

"I'm looking for her. I don't know where she could be. She always calls me after class and she didn't. I went to her place and she wasn't there—no note or nothing."

"Was anything disturbed?"

"No. Nothing. The door was locked."

"Well like I said she wasn't at class. So something must have come up before then."

"Her captain—he told me call all her friends and family," Roland said. She heard the rough edge of terror in his voice. "I know it's too early to report her missing but I wanted to see if she was called in or something, and she wasn't."

"She's probably hanging out with a friend."

"She doesn't have that many friends, and her family don't know where she is. That's not like Mary."

"Then, you should call back and report her missing," Lei said. "Have them put out a "Be On Look Out" over the radio. They can't post it until she's gone twenty-four hours, but I bet she'll turn up, hung over and sorry."

"I hope you're right," he said, and clicked off.

Lei went back into the kitchen, buying time to collect her thoughts. Her heart had picked up speed and her stomach knotted. She'd known it wasn't like Mary to miss class and not call. She went to the cabinet and scooped dog chow into Keiki's bowl from the big Tupperware bin, grinding open the can of wet dog food and smooshing it in. Keiki dove into the bowl of food as Lei sat down.

Pono had dished up, adding scoops of white rice and lomi lomi salmon with tomatoes to their Hawaiian feast. He cracked open a couple of the Miller Lites and pushed her plate toward her.

"What's up?"

"You know Mary Gomes?"

"Yeah, went school with her."

"She's missing."

"She used to be a party girl in high school." Pono stirred the lau lau into the rice, scooped it up with his chopsticks. "She probably wen' spend the night somewhere." He sat back, took a swig of beer, rubbed his lip with his finger.

"Her boyfriend Roland says no. They are practically living together. He says she always calls, and she didn't. She wasn't at class tonight either."

"Twenty-four hours haven't passed."

"I just have a bad feeling." Lei pushed her plate away without taking a bite. She got up and paced the kitchen, opening cupboards.

"What you looking for?"

"Mary had a favorite club. She was always trying to get me to go there. I have their matchbook around here somewhere." She rummaged through her junk drawer, held it up, a black square with bold red letters spelling out PAHOA MUSIC CLUB. "Feel like going out for a drink?"

"Only if you finish your dinner," Pono said severely. "Tiare, she going be piss off if you no eat her food."

"Okay," Lei said, making herself take a bite. The lau lau were delicious, the lomi salmon salad tangy and tart, but her stomach hurt at the thought of Mary missing. What if the hair in the stalker note was hers? She tried to remember if the timeline could be right.

Someone knocked at the front door and Pono went to answer it, checking through the peephole before taking off the chain and deadbolt. Stevens came in, dropping his duffel beside the door.

Lei took her hand off the Glock in her shoulder holster. She wore it all all the time now, and hadn't even realized she had been touching the pebbled black stock. She kept eating, struggling to hide the fizzing emotions she felt: frustration at Stevens' presumption, relief that he was there.

"Hey bruddah," Pono said, slapping him on the back. Stevens lurched forward. "You still in time for some grinds."

"Nice," Stevens said, sniffing the air. "Tiare send something?"

"She trying for fatten her up," Pono said, indicating Lei with his head. He took a plate out of the cupboard and loaded it up for Stevens, set it down in front of him.

"Hey, Lei," Stevens said, sitting down. She ignored him.

"Stubborn, you." Pono said. "You should be saying thanks to us."

"Tell Tiare thanks," Lei replied. "You guys are exaggerating this thing. I can take care of myself." Stevens put his head down and addressed his food, but Pono got back up and piled the dishes in the sink.

"You never know when for quit," he grumbled. "Just shut up a'ready and let us look out for you."

Lei leaned back, flipping the matchbook back and forth between her fingers.

"So, Stevens. Want to get a drink after this?" she asked.

"Not particularly," he said. "And I told you not to call me that."

"My friend Mary's missing. She's a patrol officer with Pahoa PD. Her boyfriend called earlier. He's really worried. I thought we'd go look for her at her favorite bar in Pahoa, ask around."

Stevens went into cop mode, asking about Roland, how long Mary had been missing, did she have any enemies. Pono packed up the rest of the food and put it into the fridge.

"I'm outta here," he said. "Gotta get home to my girls now that Stevens can take you to Pahoa. See you tomorrow."

"Thanks so much, Pono," Lei said, getting up and giving him a hug, realizing she'd never hugged him before. He squeezed her tight, lifting her off the ground, and gave her wayward curls a tug.

"You like one sister to me," he said. "Watch your back out there in Pahoa and let me know what's happening."

"I will." She relocked the door, turning back to Stevens. "Okay. You done yet?"

"Chill," he said, forking up another mouthful. His chopsticks were abandoned beside the plate. She picked them up, twiddling them between her fingers.

"You'll never be a local until you get the hang of these."

"Fine by me," he said, finishing his dinner and taking a long drink from his water glass. She was struck by the powerful line of his throat, the light gilding the hairs on the back of his hand, the dark fan of lashes closed over those blue, blue eyes.

"What?" he asked, frowning at her. She started, dropping the chopsticks on the floor, and leaned over to pick them up, hoping to hide her blush.

"We need to get going. Hurry up."

They got in Stevens's unmarked police Bronco and rolled out of her neighborhood. He pointed to Tom Watanabe's house on the corner. The black truck was parked in the driveway and the lights were on, blinds down.

"That Watanabe's house?"

"Yeah."

"Seen him around anymore?"

"No, but when I do he's either working in his yard or washing one of his cars," she said. "He's a total neat freak."

"He's one to watch. He's close enough to be the stalker without much effort."

"I know." Lei flipped down the visor. Her hair, always difficult, was particularly crazy as it had been a long day without any gel. She twisted it back behind her head and anchored it with a rubber band in a frizzy wad. She saw his grin out of the corner of her eye.

"What?"

"Your hair. It's like . . . I don't know. It's like a pet or something."

She couldn't help laughing. "So frickin' true," she said. "But a gentleman wouldn't say so."

"Who said I was a gentleman?" he said with a wink. Lei looked out the window, a little rattled. They were on the road going out of town. Banks of high *pili* grass waved in the moonlight. It reminded her of the car chase after class. I hope I see him again, she thought, when I'm driving my truck.

Chapter 18

*P*ahoa was a rough town thirty minutes outside Hilo, near where the flows from Kilauea met the ocean. The town's economy had been depressed ever since the lava had taken out entire subdivisions in the area in the 1990s. Built like a western town, false-fronted old wooden buildings faced a single main street.

At 9 P.M., when most of the rest of the island was shut up tight for the evening, Pahoa was just warming up. The doors of the bars and restaurants were open to the streets, light and music spilling out, knots of people clustered smoking outside.

Stevens pulled the SUV into one of the side streets and parked on the shoulder. Lei got out and slammed the door, straightening her jean jacket and unobtrusively checking the Glock in its holster. Stevens waited at the bumper as she bent to touch up her wide mouth with sparkly gloss in the side mirror of the Bronco, running the wand over her lips. She pretended not to notice him watching, feeling his eyes on her like a touch. She straightened abruptly, snapped the wand into the tube and slid it into the pocket of her jacket.

"Pahoa Music Club was Mary's sort of home away from home," she said. "She liked to eat there between her shift and class. I hope they'll know something." They strode down the street, through the groups of people. Electric guitars wailed from inside the bar.

Stevens pushed one of the old-fashioned swinging half doors open and held it as Lei followed him in. The smell of sweat and beer hit her along with a wall of sound as a mediocre rock band banged out tunes from the battered stage. The postage stamp dance floor was crowded with people. Lei elbowed her way next to Stevens at the bar, hopped up on a stool. Stevens got the bartender's attention, ordered two beers, yelled above the din of the band.

"Have you seen Mary? Mary Gomes?"

The bartender flipped the tops off, pushed two green bottles of Heineken toward them.

"Yeah. Who wants to know?"

"We're friends of hers from the police department." Stevens showed his badge.

"She came in yesterday afternoon, ordered her usual. She must've got a call from someone and been picked up. She left her car in the alley." The bartender wiped the counter as he talked.

"Has that happened before?" Stevens asked.

"Sure. Not a lot but at least a couple other times I know of," the bartender said, polishing a glass. He moved off to wait on another customer. Stevens turned to Lei.

"Let's go check it out." She nodded, scooping up her beer. They went back out the front of the bar and around the corner of the building.

The Mustang gleamed in the dim light of the alley. They walked around the car, tried the handles. Locked. Guitar music leaked out of a door in the wall next to it.

"Mary would never just leave the Mustang here if she could help it." Lei pointed to the alley door. "Wonder where this goes?" She gave the handle a turn—it was unlocked.

They went into a run-down hallway. Clearly this was the back way into the Pahoa Music Club. Loud voices identified the kitchen on the left, and they could see the women's and men's bathrooms on the right. Lei stuck her head into the restrooms but there was nothing to see but the well-used facilities.

"So what do you think?" Stevens leaned against the wall, took a sip of his beer.

"Don't know. We should call her station, see if there were any emergency calls she might have had, though Roland said he checked on that. I think it's really weird she left the Mustang here. That car was her pride and joy."

"Yeah. But she could be meeting someone, someone she didn't want Roland to know about."

"That's what Pono thought too. But I know she would be careful to be back before Roland noticed. Now he's worried and upset. That's only going to draw attention, embarrass her. No, something must have happened. She might have been nabbed in the alley."

"Not too likely." Stevens said. "But if she doesn't turn up to claim the car, it looks like she's missing for sure."

"Do you think the hair the stalker sent me could be hers?" Lei put her fear into words. "I don't know how long she's been missing, I mean for sure yesterday, but I got the note the night before."

Stevens shrugged. She could tell he was trying to be casual but his mouth had drawn into a hard line and black brows lowered so she could hardly see his eyes in the dim light of the tired bulb.

"Let's find out," he said. They pushed off from the wall and went back outside. It wasn't long before they were on the road again.

"I'm starting to wonder if this is all connected somehow. The girls, the investigation, my stalker, Mary's disappearance. . ." Lei leaned her forehead on the cool glass of the window.

"How? What's the connection?" Stevens sounded serious.

"I don't know. I think Mary would have told me if someone was stalking her, and she never said anything. I don't know, I just feel it."

"At this point we have to follow the evidence, track down every lead we can. Every hour that goes by the trail gets colder. I'm open to anything right now if you can find a link. In the meantime I'm calling this in." Stevens picked up the handset radio and reported the abandoned car and their conversation with the bartender to the detective on duty at Pahoa PD. Stevens asked if there had been any emergency calls yesterday afternoon that Mary might have gone on. The dispatcher checked and said no, replied that a case was already open for Mary in Missing Persons.

"Looks like they're moving on it," he said, hanging up the handset and glancing at Lei. "I'm sorry."

She rolled down the window and stared out, lifting her face to the arc of night sky. A million stars circled far above, visible without the light pollution of Hilo. The cool evening air blew across her face, anchoring her in her body. She didn't let herself think about the Mohuli'i girls' drowned faces but they hovered at the edge of her mind, unforgettable.

* * *

He watched her wake up with the dawn, the drugs he'd given her slowly wearing off. They were in the special place he'd prepared, so remote she could scream all she wanted and no one would hear. A trackless jungle of tall ohia trees and gigantic ferns surrounded them. Her hands were cuffed behind her, and a heavy cable attached to the handcuffs fastened her to a nearby tree.

Terror and rage came into her eyes as Mary realized where she was, and she thrashed against her bonds. He sat on the plastic cooler and watched as she struggled, finally subsiding, sucking air through her nostrils above the gag.

"I don't have time for you now," he said. "I have to go to work." His voice was muffled by the ski mask he wore, his alter ego. He hadn't decided if he was going to kill her yet, and it kept his options open.

She glared at him and he could see her calculating whether or not she could take him.

Oh, this was good. He wanted it to last.

The first fingers of light pinkened the sky above the hidden grove where he had set up the shelter. He stood, looking down at her.

"You're going to enjoy what I have planned for you. Water's in the cooler." He leaned over, pinched her nipple. She writhed and heaved, trying to kick him, and he chuckled as he walked away, crunching through the dried ferns.

He smiled to himself, pulling the hot ski mask off his head with a pleasurable sense of anticipation. She was secure, but she would figure out how to get her hands in front because he'd left her cuffs loose enough. Eventually she'd get thirsty enough to drink the water. He was counting on it.

Chapter 19

Lei poured her first coffee of the morning and splashed in some half-and-half from the carton. She looked out the window over the sink at the spreading branches of the plumeria tree, spare graceful branches ending in clusters of creamy yellow-throated flowers, bouquets of tropical fragrance. A cardinal hopped in the branches, an unlikely spot of red.

Her head felt muzzy but she'd only had the one beer the night before in Pahoa. She looked over at Stevens. He'd put the cushions from the rump-sprung couch on the floor. They'd migrated during the night, leaving him sprawled on the floor, the crocheted afghan tangled around his legs.

She tried not to notice the contours of his back under the tank-style undershirt, the long ropy muscles of his arms relaxed in sleep. His rumpled dark hair made her hands itch to touch it. Keiki padded over to him and licked his ear, and he woke with a groan.

"Coffee," he intoned, sitting up and lurching like a zombie as he headed toward the pot, hoisting up sweatpants. His hair was spiky and eyes a dark, sleepy blue. She laughed, handed him a full mug. He took it, rubbing his lower back.

"Sleeping on the floor is making me feel like an old man."

"Quit whining. Pretty boys like you are such babies."

"Pretty boy? Did I detect a compliment in there somewhere?" He blew on the hot surface of the coffee. "Can't say I remember ever being called that before." He took a sip. She felt his proximity like a magnetic field, raising the tiny hairs on her arms with awareness.

"You're so vain, you just want me to say it again." Her face flamed. She dug in the utility drawer for Keiki's leash.

I'm so bad at this, she thought, but all thought stopped as his arms came around her from behind. He turned her and then, in slow motion, he leaned down, his lips brushing hers as gentle as a moth landing.

She went rigid, her lips closed, the reaction instinctive. He looked down at her, stepped back, let go. Turned away. Picked up his coffee and took a sip. She let her breath out with a shaky whoosh, turned away to rinse her mug at the sink. His voice, when he spoke, was deliberately casual.

"As far as today, I'm hoping the search warrant on the Reynolds house comes through. I could use some help on that if it does."

"Sure." Lei made certain her voice was as even as his. He'd almost kissed her—and freak that she was, she'd made him back off. She wished he'd try again, but now wasn't the time. "What do you think about Mary?"

"I think she's endangered missing, if she didn't turn up last night. Check in with the detective on her case. Dispatcher said his name is Lono Smith."

"Sounds like a plan. I can't stand to think something's happened to her."

"So far there's no sign of foul play. We just have to go through the steps. Try not to think the worst."

He put his mug in the sink, pulled on one of her corkscrew curls, stretching it out and watching it spring back, smiling at her somber face. Moving slowly, he put his fingers under her chin and rubbed the ball of his thumb across her lower lip. A tingle zipped down her spine, weakening her knees as he picked up his duffel and headed for the door. "I'll give you a call later."

"Okay." She followed him. "I want to get a hair sample of Mary's and compare it to what the stalker sent."

"Good idea." He turned. "Hey, get me a futon or something for tonight, would you?"

Lei opened her mouth to argue, and he put his fingers over it gently, leaning in close. There were tiny flecks of green in his blue eyes.

"Humor me," he said softly. "Please."

Struck dumb, she closed the door behind him.

Guilt smote her—how could she be thinking about kissing with her friend missing, and two girls dead?

Lei and Keiki did their run, and as she was buttoning into her uniform her cell rang.

"Come over to the Reynolds' house. The warrant came through. I'm bringing Pono in too." Stevens was all business.

"On my way," Lei said. She drove to the Reynolds' house with its elegant carriage lamps and manicured lawn. Stevens's SUV was in the driveway. Jeremy met her at the door.

"The parents left when we got here and served the warrant. It's a good thing. It's easier to work with them out of the way."

"How'd Reynolds take it?" Lei asked.

"Badly," Jeremy said, leading them into the living room where Stevens was lifting the cushions up on the couch, looking beneath them with a flashlight.

"Reynolds left pretty angry, said he was going to get his lawyer. I'd like to be out of here before they get back," Stevens said, pointing to a box of latex gloves.

Pono walked in as Lei snapped on a pair of gloves and helped herself to some evidence bags.

"What're we looking for?"

"Not sure," he said. "Anything to link him to the two girls, the campsite. I figure we'll know it when we see it."

Even with the four of them searching it was slow work. They went through every drawer, every closet, every box. Lei felt a stifling squeeze in her chest as she went into Kelly's room.

The pretty blonde teenager's presence had been erased. The bedroom had been stripped of her belongings and made over into a guest room. Lei lifted the tropical print coverlet, shook out the pillow shams, opened the closet. Pink plastic hangers rattled in the space. She pulled out the wardrobe drawers. Empty.

I know where her clothes went—in the trash. What a weird way to grieve—poor kid. She saw the girl's face again in her mind's eye, part of her nose gone, blue eyes shadows behind puffy lids. Lei pinched herself to stay in the present moment, sitting back on the bed.

Stevens came to the door. "Anything?"

"No. Totally cleaned out. Looks like they're making this into a guest room." She gestured to the faux rattan headboard and orchid-print drapes.

Just then Jeremy called, "Come see this!"

They went into the den, where Jeremy had been searching the computer. He swiveled the flat-screen monitor so they could see pictures of Kelly.

She was wearing the ruffled yellow skirt Lei remembered from the evidence room, sitting with her legs open. Jeremy clicked to the next photo. She was naked. Her flaxen hair was spread over small breasts, her hand over her mound. Her eyes shone with misery. More pictures, each progressively more seductive, and her eyes more glazed. The background was the oatmeal-colored couch in the living room.

The last picture was of Kelly and Haunani naked, lying facing each other in the green grass beside a stream. The composition was beautiful, the colors rich—and the subject matter haunting and terrible.

"Holy crap!" Pono exclaimed. "Bastard just had these pictures sitting on his desktop? He was asking to get busted!"

"I broke his encryption," Jeremy said. "It wasn't too complicated. This file is called 'baby photos' and I knew he never had any babies, so I checked it."

"I think we got him," Stevens said. Lei turned away and went back to Kelly's room. She felt dizzy. She turned on the special vacuum with its evidence collection bag, sucking any fibers out of the carpet. Bile seemed to be pressing up in her throat and she gulped it back, gripping the vacuum hard. Get a grip, she told herself, and felt hysterical laughter threaten.

Her cell rang. It was Irene at Dispatch.

"This is your reminder call. You have counseling today at two P.M., and it's one-forty-five. I thought you might forget. I know you guys are out searching the Reynolds place."

"Shit," Lei said, ripping the vacuum cord out of the wall. "This is not a good time!"

"When is it ever?" Irene said cheerfully. "Say thank you for the reminder, or I'll give you a graveyard shift."

"Thanks, Irene. Are you sure I can't reschedule?"

"Mandatory means mandatory. You ask me, you got off light so no mess with the Lieutenant on this."

"Shit," she said again. "Okay. Thanks." She clicked the phone closed. "Stevens, I need to go back to the station."

They were still clustered around the computer as she came back in, the vacuum bag in hand. Pono turned to her.

"What for? We're in the middle of something."

"That damn mandatory counseling."

"Bad timing," Stevens said. "I need you here."

"If you guys weren't just getting your jollies looking at the dead girls, we might be getting more done," she snapped. All three of them stared at her.

"Unplug the computer and we'll take the whole thing down to the station," Stevens said to Jeremy. He looked at Lei. "I think you better go get that counseling."

Fury and shame clogged her throat. She dropped the evidence bag and left, the screen door banging behind her.

It took her the whole drive to the station to calm down. She knew her response to the search was irrational, knew it had to do with her past. As usual, knowing didn't help. She took some deep breaths and put her hand in her pocket, feeling the triangular corner of Stevens's note. Asshole, she thought, glad they hadn't kissed but wishing they had. Wishing she could get the images of the girls out of her mind. Wishing she was normal.

She parked the Crown Vic and went into the industrial beige women's room, splashing water on her face and making sure her hair was under control. She touched up with lipgloss and brushed some lint off her uniform.

"I look fine," she said out loud. "Not remotely psycho."

Chapter 20

She went down the hall to Dr. Wilson's office. The police psychologist opened the door after her tentative knock. She was a diminutive woman, neatly dressed in khakis and a polo shirt. The bell of her smooth ash-blonde hair swung as she gestured Lei in.

"You must be Ms. Texeira. Come on in and get comfortable."

Lei took a seat in the corner. The room was furnished simply with a couch and several deep, cushy chairs. Amateurish paintings decorated the walls, and there was a low coffee table with a Japanese sand garden on it, complete with a tiny rake.

The psychologist took another chair across from Lei. She had a clipboard and a pen.

"Just a few housekeeping items before we get started," she said briskly. "You have six mandatory sessions. This one was scheduled, but we will set up the next one at a time we agree on. This time is completely confidential and I keep very few notes. However, at the end of your last session I have to fill out this assessment form." She held up the clipboard showing the form. "I have to give you a rating as to how engaged you were in the process and my opinion as to whether you are fit for duty. Needless to say that's a big axe to have hanging over your head, so I am going to remove it now."

She filled out the form. The 1-5 rating scale on engagement was circled at 4.5, and she printed "Fit for Duty" in the outcome area. She signed it, a bold Patrice Wilson, Ph.D., and held it up.

"I have never felt this was the way to treat people," she said. "Now we can put that behind us and just see what comes up."

She folded the paper and slipped it into an envelope, sealing the edge and writing "Lieutenant Ohale" on the front. She laid it on the coffee table and sat back comfortably.

"Isn't that unethical?" Lei frowned.

"Isn't it unethical to expect counseling to work with that kind of threat hanging over the process?"

"I don't know. I think this whole thing is bogus."

"So do I. But they still pay me."

Astonishingly, she snickered. It was such an undignified noise coming from such a polished, respectable-looking woman that Lei just stared.

"Want something to drink?" Dr. Wilson asked, getting up and going to a little mini fridge in the corner. Lei halfway expected her to hold up a booze bottle, the way things had been going, but she just held up a water. Lei took it, realizing she was parched from the busy day. Might as well shock this lady, she thought, draining the water bottle.

"I was raped when I was nine."

"Huh," said Dr. Wilson, sitting back down. "You'd be surprised how many police officers were."

Again Lei was off balance, flummoxed. Her other counselor had been warm, teasing the story out of her by inches, affirming her all the way.

"Female police officers, I should say," Dr. Wilson clarified. "Some guys get into the force because they like being aggressive. Got a lot of wife beaters around here."

"Huh," Lei said, mimicking her. "Well, it was my mom's boyfriend."

"What did you do about it?"

Again the unexpected response. Lei felt the heat of rage roar up her neck. "I took it. I was nine years old for chrissake. What the hell kind of counselor are you?"

Dr. Wilson said nothing. Lei felt the anger recede, felt the pressure of her secret easing. She settled back into the couch.

"I guess I didn't just take it. I got good with weapons. I decided no one was ever going to do that to me again."

Dr. Wilson inclined her head. "Nice," she said. "You're a fighter. How are your relationships with men? Do you have sex?"

"Not if I can help it," Lei said. "I'd like to, but I get all frozen."

"So are you gay?"

"What the hell? No, I'm not gay!"

"Okay. So have you been to counseling before?"

"Yeah. I went to my Aunty's when my mom died of an overdose. She sent me to a bunch of them."

"Was it helpful?"

"Some of them were. Mostly not. The one I went to in college helped me the most. She gave me some things to do when I . . . disappear."

"So you dissociate?"

"Is that what you call it? Yeah, I do sometimes. It's under control though. It doesn't interfere with the job." Not too much, I hope, she thought.

"Tell me about the last time you dissociated."

"Recently." Lei thought of the pictures on the Reynolds's computer. "Can I talk about a case?"

"Only if it's relevant . . . and, it's all relevant."

"Okay. The last time I almost checked out was this afternoon. We found some pictures of the girls who were murdered. I got a really sick feeling, kinda dizzy. I had things to do so I left the room, and when I came back in the other detectives were still looking at the pictures and I got super mad. I just wanted to kill them, and him most of all, the guy who did it."

"Go on."

"I know I just said it didn't interfere with the job but sometimes I think it does. Like today. And the thing that made me have to come in for counseling."

She took a deep breath and told Dr. Wilson about the stalker, how she thought the murder investigation and the stalker were connected somehow, though she hadn't yet found the link. She finished with how she'd gone after the stalker with her gun and dog.

"If I had been thinking clearly I wouldn't have done that."

"I don't know." Dr. Wilson shrugged. "If it had worked, it would have been awesome."

"Yeah. It would have." Lei broke into a grin. This was the first time anyone had said anything positive about her action. "I'll get him next time. Only, the guys are hovering around, taking turns keeping an eye on me. Detective Stevens has been sleeping over to guard me."

"One." Dr. Wilson held up her hand, folding down her fingers as she made her points. "The guys think the stalker is a real threat and you're in danger. Ergo, you should take it seriously too. Two: Stevens may have more than helping in mind when he stays over. Three: maybe these cases are connected and you could bust the stalker and find the murderer at the same time. Tell me again what makes you think they're connected?"

"I don't really know." Lei rubbed her hands up and down her slacks. "I just have a feeling. I'm also freaked out about Mary." She filled the psychologist in on her budding friendship with Mary, and the other woman's disappearance.

"It doesn't seem all that farfetched that this is all connected somehow," Dr. Wilson said. A tiny line had appeared between her smooth sandy brows. "How often do we have a case of unknown stalking, drowning, and disappearance in Hilo? I wouldn't be surprised if more comes out when Mary is found."

"That's what I'm afraid of."

"Well, your time's up. Let's get together next week, same time."

"Okay," Lei stood up, headed for the door, and then turned back. "This wasn't so bad. Thanks."

"Oh, music to my ears," Dr. Wilson said, laughing. "You did all the work and I get the credit. That's why I love my job."

Lei went straight to her desk. She knew she should go back to help with the search, but she hadn't had time to do anything about Mary. She sat down and called the Pahoa Police Department.

"I might have a lead on Mary Gomes," Lei said when she was transferred to the investigator on the case, Lono Smith. "I got delivered a piece of long black hair from someone who's been stalking me. I thought it might be Mary's. It was dropped off at my house with a threatening note."

"Do you have it logged in to evidence?" Lono asked. She could hear the clicking of his keyboard.

"Yes. If you want to compare Mary's hair and what the stalker left, it's here at South Hilo Station."

"On my way," Lono said. "We move fast for our own."

"Glad to hear it." Lei felt her throat close. She cleared it, blinking. "The hair has no follicles though—it will have to be a visual comparison."

"That's fine. I'll keep in touch." He rang off.

Lei sat back in her squeaking orange chair, did a few spins to discharge stress as she called Stevens.

"Still need me?" she asked when he picked up.

"Nope. We cleared out just ahead of Reynolds and his lawyer," he said. "I have the computer with me. We're going to do a more thorough search at the station. You can call it a day—I'll be by later."

She sat silently, thinking of what Dr. Wilson had said.
"Okay."

"What, you feeling all right? No arguing?"

"I've decided to rely on my senior officer's estimation of the situation."

He laughed. "Oh that's just great. Now I'm a senior. Just don't forget that futon." He clicked off.

She smiled, shutting down her workstation and feeling the triangle of Stevens' note as she left the building. She headed out to Wal-Mart and bought a set of twin sheets, a new pillow, and a futon. Who knows, I might need it for guests, she told herself, stowing it in the truck.

She remembered the package slip from the other night. She still had time to swing by the post office and pick it up, so she pulled into the crowded parking lot and redeemed the package—a thick bubble-padded manila envelope.

Her name and address were printed on it in block letters. There appeared to be a small box inside. There was no return address, and it was postmarked Hilo. She set it on the passenger seat.

She glanced over at it again and again as she drove home, torn between getting the suspense over with and opening it at home with Stevens or Pono. The sun dropped long red rays to the west ahead of her. She speed-dialed Mary's phone and it went to voicemail again. Time could be running out for her friend.

"Mary, where are you?" she cried into the phone and snapped it shut. She hit the steering wheel, but it didn't help—nothing did. Her friend was gone.

Chapter 21

*H*e brushed the ferns aside, making his way to the campsite in the dimming light of sunset. It was a good distance from where he hid the truck, and he'd had to use a wheelbarrow to carry her out there. The faint track of the barrow wheel showed in the dirt, and he dragged a branch behind him, roughing up the ground to erase it.

Just outside the scrim of trees that hid the shelter, he pulled on the ski mask.

He approached cautiously. It never paid to underestimate the prey. But Mary lay still beside the ice chest, the drugged water bottle empty beside her. Her cuffed hands were in front and she had taken off the gag.

He slipped off the backpack he'd brought with the essentials for tonight's activities.

He walked around her, making sure Mary was unconscious. Her breath had a noisy asthmatic rattle to it that couldn't be faked. Her skin was pale beneath her tan, greenish in the waning light as if she were underwater. Bruises braceleted her wrists from the cuffs and dappled her arms and face. She'd covered herself in the sheet he brought her in.

The tender bloom of bruising aroused him. He got his camera out and took his first picture. He knelt beside her, gently brushing black hair out of her face, and rolled her onto her side. He took his ruler and surgical scissors out of the backpack and snipped a swatch of that long shining hair from the spot two inches above the notch of her skull, and slipped it into a Ziploc.

She was limp, her eyelids fluttering. Reverently he folded the sheet down, his hand caressing down her breast, the smooth dip of her stomach. He set the camera on black and white to capture the contrast of her skin, hair, and bruises.

This was the way a woman should be. Soft and waiting, receptive. A memory from work crossed his mind—the woman strident, confrontational. *I would love to have that bitch in front of me like this,* he thought, bending over to tongue Mary's pale brown nipple. It peaked obligingly, and he smiled down at her.

"So beautiful," he said. "I'm going to treat you the way you deserve."

Much later, pleasantly exhausted, he opened a plastic box of baby wipes and tenderly rubbed her down with them. He cleaned her thoroughly, and then himself, discarding the used condoms and soiled baby wipes in a Ziploc bag to be disposed of later. Mary slept on, her eyelids fluttering, each breath the sound of cloth shredding.

She won't drink the water next time, he thought. *It's going to get harder to deal with her.* He settled beside her, covering them both with the sheet, spooned around her in a parody of love. He'd never taken off the ski mask—it was beginning to feel comfortable.

* * *

The package sat on the table, mocking Lei as she started dinner. Her cell rang, and she grabbed it, hoping it was Mary.

"Do you have food? Need me to bring anything?" Stevens. Her heart picked up. At least she wouldn't have to deal with the package alone.

"Some beer," she said. "I forgot to restock. You'll be happy to know I got the futon, so you can stop whining. Also—I think the stalker sent me something. I picked up a package today. No return address."

"Wait until I get there," he said, and hung up. Lei closed her phone. Somehow the brief exchange lifted her spirits. Her eyes fell on one of her favorite quotes, taped above the kitchen sink:

Only when we are no longer afraid do we begin to live.
—*Dorothy Thompson.*

In spite of everything—or maybe because of it—she was finally starting to live. Really feeling her feelings for the first time in years, all the range from rage to revulsion, joy to lust. It was exciting, terrifying, and entirely out of her control.

She was ready to stop being afraid for herself, if not for Mary.

She opened several cans of chili and heated them on the stove. It wasn't long before the doorbell rang. She checked the peephole and Stevens stood there, a duffel and grocery bag in his arms.

"Hey," she said, standing back to let him in. "Come have dinner. I've got chili and rice."

"I brought the beer," he said, following her into the kitchen. He took a six-pack of Heineken out of the bag. "Got an opener?"

She pointed to the drawer, taking out a pair of bowls and setting the table. He poured them each a beer into the plastic glasses he found in the cupboard. With a flair, she lit a fat white emergency candle and put it on the table. He smiled, watching her.

"If I didn't know better I would say this was Texeira being domestic."

She gave him a thwack with the dish towel.

"As long as the cooking involves a can opener, I'm golden."

She put the food on the table and they served it up, neither of them looking at the bulky envelope at the other end of the table.

"So did you find anything else on the computer?" she asked, sitting back with a sip of beer.

"Not at first glance. Jeremy's going to run a recovery program for any deleted files."

"How about the rest of the house?"

"Nothing obvious. Even if we pull prints from Haunani, that's not conclusive. The girls were friends. She could have gone over to visit. What's more interesting is that there is so little of Kelly in the house. You'd think at least her mother would want some mementos, but there was hardly anything left. We found one shoebox of photos in the mom's dresser. That was it. It's like they're trying to erase her." He forked up a mouthful of salad.

Lei closed her eyes, thinking of the empty hangers, the barren dresser, the tape marks where Kelly's posters had been.

"You said people grieve differently," she said. "Is what they did in the range of normal?"

"Who knows what's normal with a family like that?" They ate without speaking, the case casting a pall. With an effort, Stevens looked up, smiled at her.

"So how was the counseling?"

"Unexpected," Lei said. "That counselor is a piece of work."

"What do you mean? She has a good reputation."

"Not sure she takes me seriously or knows what she's doing, then I find myself spilling the beans," Lei said. "So I guess she does know what she's doing. Actually I felt better for it."

"Good thing too, you were . . . well, acting funny. Pretty bitchy."

"Screw you, Stevens. That search was upsetting and I'm not sorry for telling you guys to get your priorities straight."

"You notice I listened to you," Stevens said quietly. "We shut down the computer and took it to the station for the tech guy to hunt through."

They finished their food. Stevens leaned back, looked around the kitchen.

"I could get used to this."

"Don't," Lei said. She pointed at the package. She didn't want him imagining them as a couple. The thought terrified her, almost as much as the threat from the stalker sitting there in its anonymous bubble wrap.

"Yeah," he said, flatly. "The package. That's why I'm here."

He carried his bowl to the sink and she opened another beer, stroking Keiki's head since the dog had placed it in her lap, expressive eyes glancing up at Lei. Keiki always knew when she was upset.

Stevens wiped his hands on a dish towel and reached under the sink for the latex gloves, snapped on a pair. He got her kitchen scissors and came and sat down with some Ziploc bags. He pulled the package over and inspected it.

"Postmarked Hilo. No return address. Looks like it went out three days ago since it took you a day to go pick it up." She said nothing. She'd already noticed those things.

He took the kitchen scissors and snipped off the end of the package with its folded-over adhesive. He held it up to the light.

"No visible fibers or prints. We'll process and light it down at the station." He stuck the flap into one of the bags and reached into the package, pulling out a small square box. There was also a note, folded in thirds like the other three. He held it open so she could read it:

THINKING OF YOU EVERY DAY. YOU CAN HAVE THESE BACK NOW AND SHOW THEM TO ME ANOTHER TIME.

Lei found she was stroking Keiki's head too hard because the dog whimpered. She unclenched her jaw, took a few breaths in through her nose, out through her mouth as he set the note aside and opened the box. Inside was a pair of underwear, wadded in a ball.

Lei's face flushed, her scalp prickling as Stevens unfolded them, spreading them carefully on top of a Ziploc bag, his face blank and focused as he inspected them front and back, around the lace at the legs, the little swatch of extra fabric at the crotch.

They were her favorite underwear, black satin with tiny purple orchids on them. Aunty had given her three pairs of them this Christmas from Victoria's Secret, knowing how she loved orchids. They weren't particularly high-cut or sexy. The beautiful fabric was what made them special. Overwhelmed with tension, Lei snatched them out of his hand.

"How did he get these?" she cried.

"Give them back. They're evidence now. I don't see any fluids or anything, but we need to go over them back at the lab."

"Seriously, how did he get these?" she said again, reluctantly handing them back. He slid the underwear, along with the box, into the Ziploc bag. "You know how I lock everything up."

"Are you sure these are yours?"

"Yes. I have three pairs of them. In fact—" She jumped up again and ran into her bedroom, yanking open the top drawer of her bureau, digging through the contents in a frenzy.

Keiki barked in alarm as she flung underwear around looking, finally holding up a handful of black satin.

"Here they are! Three pairs of black orchid underwear. I guess those aren't mine after all!"

The relief was tremendous. He hadn't been in her house, touching her private things. She ran to Stevens, who had followed her to the doorway, and threw her arms around him.

"Oh my God! They aren't mine! He wasn't in here!"

He made a show of being knocked backward. She laughed, relief making her giddy, and turned her face up for the kiss she hoped would be there.

And it was, soft and teasing with a touch of urgency. She didn't know when she let go of the panties and filled her hands with his shirt, his back, his shoulders, the curling hair on his neck. He lifted her so their faces were at the same height, gave her a little spin, stumbling backward. He sat on the edge of the bed with her in his arms.

Sensations overwhelmed her: prickling heat in her belly, darkness behind her closed eyes punctuated by light spangles, the hunger of his mouth on hers.

"Damn, girl," he finally said, settling her further back down his thighs, brushing the curls back from her face with both hands. "Slow down. Be gentle with me."

She laughed. It felt like a triumph. He flopped back and picked up one of the pairs of underwear off the bed, twirled it around his finger.

"The stalker has good taste. These are hot."

She hopped up, putting her hands on her hips.

"That settles it," she said. "Men are pigs." She tried to look mad, and for a moment thought she was succeeding until he put the underwear over her head and gave it a yank. When they were done wrestling, they both had underwear on—Lei's was now around her neck, elastic sprung beyond redemption, and Stevens sported another pair on his head.

"I still think they're hot," he said plaintively, following her into the kitchen where she cracked open another beer for each of them.

Lei flopped in her chair, the feeling of menace gone as she looked at the underwear and box in the Ziploc bag. Must have been the kissing and rough-housing that did it, she thought.

"Okay, so he didn't get in here and steal it," she said. "How did he know about the underwear? Where did he find a matching pair? If I knew that I bet I could ID him."

"So put on your thinking cap." Stevens adjusted the panties down around his neck. "I'm not giving these back by the way. I'll wear them and think of you."

"Sicko," she said, taking a swig of beer. "I can't remember anything right now. Maybe it will come to me later. Anyway I've got to get some reading for class done. I set up your futon and the sheets should be done soon. Are you sure you want to stay over again?"

"I'm keeping an eye on you until this is resolved. Period. I let a friend down before in this situation by not taking it seriously, and I won't make that mistake again."

She opened her mouth to object and remembered Dr. Wilson's advice, instead getting up to clear the table. Stevens went to the dryer, got the sheets and made up the futon. He was sitting on it with his back against the couch when she came into the living room.

"Tell me about your security measures," he said.

"Okay." A little taken aback, she proceeded, sitting down on the corner of the couch. "I have an alarm system with automatic call to security as well as sound. It's on a movement sensor system. I spent some good money on it so it's pretty okay for a residential program. I also have locks on all the windows and triple locks on the doors. This is a rental or I would have reinforced glass and reinforced doors too. I also consider Keiki part of my security system."

Keiki pricked her ears at the sound of her name. She was sitting next to Stevens on the futon. He rubbed her broad chest and she swiped him with her tongue.

"She certainly qualifies. I think we need to plan for a bit of a long haul until we catch this guy." He stopped, took a breath, seeming to steel himself. "I'm your superior officer, at least on the murder investigation, and as such I'm not supposed to be having a relationship with you. I mean, the kind of relationship we seem to be heading toward."

Lei pulled her legs in on the couch, wrapped her arms around them.

"We aren't dating," she said.

"I know. Technically. But it would be wrong for me, as your colleague, to take advantage of you while I am voluntarily providing security. It's an emotional set-up, they tell us in the training manual." He smiled at her, but it was forced. "So, no more kissing until this is over."

Lei set her chin on her knees, thinking it through.

"You're awfully quiet. Are you okay?"

"It's complicated," she said. "I'm kinda relieved on the one hand because in case you haven't noticed, I have some pretty intense issues. But it's been fun and . . . I'll miss you."

He held his arm out. "Come over here."

She got off the couch and sat against him on one side, Keiki on the other. He put his arms over each of them, squeezing them at the same time. She felt that bubble again under her sternum, almost joy but something else. Keiki panted happily, leaning into him.

"This doesn't mean we can't be close," he said. "I want you to know, I'll still be here when this is all over and we can kiss all we want."

"You don't know what you're signing up for." She laughed, a sniffly chuckle. "I'm pretty messed up. You better deliver on that."

"That's just the kind of thing a guy likes to hear. Sends us dudes with commitment issues running for the hills."

"You think *you've* got commitment issues," she said. "What a pair."

"If you can work on trusting me, I can work on waiting."

"I guess so," she said. She and the dog snuggled against Stevens until they fell asleep in a pile on the futon. Lei didn't remember her reading until the next day.

Chapter 22

*H*e watched her for the second morning, this time sitting still behind a fern tree. He had that feeling again—anticipation. His favorite part of the hunt. Even though he'd had her already, she didn't know that. In a few minutes, she would.

She woke slowly, groggily, turning onto her side, moaning a little from her injuries. She sat up, realizing she was naked, and reached for the now-grubby sheet to cover herself, the handcuffs clinking. She scanned the clearing. He felt sure she would see him behind the scrim of fern, but she didn't.

She seemed to be taking inventory of her body, feeling her breasts, and then looking down at them. They were blotched with suck marks, and she gave a little cry of horror. The hair stood up on his neck. She felt lower, her stomach, her thighs, her vagina.

She closed her eyes. He saw the blood drain from her face, and in the pearly dawn light she collapsed, curling into a fetal ball, weeping. The sight was so arousing he felt himself getting hard, and reached down, unzipping his *pants and stroking, his eyes still on her. She cried and moaned, hugging herself.*

Suddenly she jumped up, swaying a little but standing, her legs spread wide. "Screw you!" she yelled. Her voice was like a cannon in the forest, silencing the birds, stilling his hand.

"Screw you, you coward! Come out and fight like a man! Look me in the eye when you rape me, you bastard!"

He sat paralyzed, shriveling. She threw back her head and screamed, again and again, roars of rage and pain. She kicked over the ice chest, bashed her cuffed hands against the poles of the shelter until it collapsed. She ran to the edge of the tie out cable, yanking at it, then back to the other end where it was padlocked to the tree, scrabbling at it until her hands were bloody.

Terror held him still. She'll kill me if she finds me or die trying, he thought. He waited until she finally sat on the fallen ice chest. He could see her trembling, and the asthma was back, muffling her voice as she cursed him.

It seemed like forever before she stood up, looking at the sun. She examined the contents of the ice chest, spilled on the ground. He had left a sandwich wrapped in plastic for her, and more water bottles. There was a bag of ice. She put the ice, food and water back in the chest, righted it. He could see her weighing where the drug might have come from, tearing a hole in the ice bag, taking a handful out and sucking it.

Good. He didn't want her drugged all the time, she could die too soon.

She propped the shelter poles back up. Her body was trembling all over now, and the asthma was strangling her. She saw the inhaler where he had left it for her to find, and she pounced on it. Then she paused, considering, her wheezing, constricted breath audible even where he crouched among the ferns.

She must think it's a trick, or drugged. He smiled in satisfaction. Gotta keep her guessing.

Finally she took two puffs of the inhaler and sat down, holding the vapor in her lungs as long as possible, sighing with relief as it took effect.

He moved away slowly, as one does when stalking something wild, careful not to make any noise. Eventually she would get hungry enough to eat, and the sandwich was fine. All of the water bottles were doctored, and he had a back up plan if she didn't drink any. Wouldn't it be funny if she deprived herself for nothing?

The thought was so satisfying he smiled, almost forgetting how terrified he had been of her—but not quite.

Chapter 23

Lei and Keiki pounded along Hilo Bay, past the hotels, under the massive banyans that buckled the sidewalk with their roots. It felt good to really stretch herself physically after the tension of the last few days, and she and the dog pushed their limits until Lei felt the knots inside loosening. By then they were at the park, jogging along the levee.

Weathered old fishermen dotted the canal with their bamboo poles, fishing for pan-fryer *papio* (jack) and *ama`ama* (mullet). Lei went into the center of the park under a big kamani tree and put her foot up on a cement bench, stretching. Keiki flopped in the damp grass.

Her cell rang and she dug it out of the nylon jacket pocket she wore to conceal her gun. It was Lono, the detective working Mary's case.

"The hair your stalker sent wasn't a match to Mary."

"Good," Lei said, still a little out of breath. "Do you have any leads?"

"We interviewed the bar guy. Just like you said, she ordered her usual beer and grilled cheese sandwich, went back to the bathroom to change and freshen up, and never came back. That had happened one other time when she got an emergency call, so the bartender didn't think much of it."

"What about the boyfriend?" Lei said, feeling guilty. Poor Roland. He'd seemed so distraught—but when a woman goes missing, it's usually her boyfriend or husband, she reminded herself.

"We've been looking at him but so far nothing there. He was at work during the time frame when she disappeared. We've also been looking at people she busted, like that. She wasn't working on anything interesting."

"Thanks," Lei said. "From all regular officers, everywhere."

"Well, you know. Nothing specific, nothing too intense," he said. "Anyway I'll keep you posted. We're searching her apartment tomorrow."

Lei clicked the phone shut, shocked that another police officer could just disappear in broad daylight and no one had a clue what might have happened. She scanned the park, her hand on the butt of her gun.

The exercise high vanished. Mary would have told her if she knew she was being stalked. Whose hair could it be? And how did he get the underwear? Thoughts whirled through her mind. She snapped Keiki's leash and the dog lunged to her feet, tongue lolling. Though it was still early, volcanic emissions from Kilauea Volcano that the locals called "vog" already blanketed the Bay. She turned back toward home and picked up her pace again, still puzzling over the situation.

"Hey," she heard. She turned her head. Tom Watanabe pulled alongside her, running easily, his Nike net shirt streaked with sweat.

"Hey yourself," she said, not slowing. Keiki flicked him a glance but kept up the pace. "I've never seen you run down here."

"Got an inspection, needed to get my run in early." He wasn't out of breath at all. They jogged along side by side.

"Any more weird notes?" he asked.

"Yeah, as a matter of fact."

"Like what?"

"I can't discuss it. Have you seen anybody around my house?"

"No, and I've been keeping an eye out."

I bet you have, she thought cynically. Suddenly it occurred to her that the stalker could have been watching her from outside and seen her underwear that way. She relied on her chain-link fence for security in the back yard, and the plumeria tree blocked her window, so she didn't always close her curtains. Someone might have been able to spy on her from a distance . . . including Tom.

"Well," he said. "You're in shape."

"I guess." He sure had a way with words.

"I was thinking . . . maybe we could go out sometime," he said.

This was an interesting twist. Lei slowed down, stopped. She bent over, touching her toes, buying time.

"Sounds fun," she said, with forced cheerfulness. He was attractive, and she didn't want to keep being paranoid. On the other hand, he was the easiest candidate to be the stalker. Take a chance, you might get him to reveal something. "What did you have in mind?"

"How about a run in the park and lunch at the Volcano House?" She looked at his face for the first time. He seemed nervous, and sweat popped out on his forehead. He swiped it away with his forearm.

"I'd like that," Lei said.

"How about Saturday?"

"Sure."

He nodded, smiling for the first time, a flash of white teeth. Damn, he's good looking, she thought. But this was just a fishing expedition. Stevens' skeptical look flashed into her mind—he wasn't going to like the idea.

"I'll pick you up at 9:30 or so," he said. "I'll drive. I've got room in my truck for your dog, if you want to bring her."

"Okay." More like, hell yes she was bringing Keiki.

He turned off at his house with a wave. "See you Saturday."

Later, she was on patrol with Pono when her cell rang. She dug it out of her pocket while steering the Crown Vic with her left hand.

"Hi, Stevens."

"Hey. Sorry I wasn't around when you woke up, I had to get going early this morning. The futon was a big improvement and my back thanks you."

"Least I could do. What's up?"

"I'm meeting with the lab techs who've been working on the crime scene trash. Can you come back to the station? After we find out the results we'll be planning strategy for the rest of the week."

"Sure." She clicked her phone shut. It wasn't the right time to tell him about her date with Tom Watanabe—especially with Pono sitting next to her, all ears.

"What's Loverboy up to?"

"Shut up. We're not like that."

"You wish you were," Pono said, taking the lid off his drink. He liked to slurp them and crunch the ice. He was just getting started on a Big Gulp from the 7-11 and he had to hold it with both hands as she cranked a U-turn, hitting the lights as she headed back to the station.

"Damn, girl," he grumbled. "Didn't know it was an emergency."

"I'm in no mood to be hassled."

"Whatever. You never answered my question."

"Stevens is meeting with the lab techs. Wants me to come down."

"Okay. So you didn't tell me about the package. I had to hear it from Sorenson in the lab. He was all hot and bothered over your panties."

"That's just great," Lei said. "Real professional. I love the thought of Sorenson pawing over my underwear with his little blue light and telling everyone about it."

"Hey, chill out. He told me because I'm your partner. My point is, *you* should have told me."

"God, you're so high maintenance." She elbowed him. His drink sloshed into his lap.

"Shit!" he exclaimed.

She laughed. "We're even now. So FYI, those weren't my actual underwear. Sorenson can keep them for all I care. But, they are the same kind as mine, which means the stalker got a look at them somehow and was able to get another pair to creep me out with. I just realized this morning he might have seen me through my window. I have to go outside and look for vantage points."

A flush made its way up Pono's brown neck. She glanced at him.

"This is why I don't want to talk about this with anybody. It's embarrassing."

"Sorry," Pono mumbled, dabbing at the spill with a paper napkin. "It sucks that this is happening. I like catch this guy so bad."

"Glad I'm not the only one."

Lei hurried into the conference room. District Attorney Hiro Harada, Lieutenant Ohale, Jeremy, Stevens, and two new detectives assigned from Hilo District sat around the big conference table with three lab techs from Oahu and an open box of Krispy Kremes.

One set of bad news followed the next. The trash in the abandoned cars only had prints that matched those of the vehicle owners, and the debris from the campsite had been through too much weather to yield much. Even the propane canister was frustrating, marked with smudges that were too degraded to make out. The moldering sleeping bag yielded some hairs that matched Haunani's, which seemed to confirm the theory that she had been meeting her boyfriend there. There were other hairs, but they remained unknown.

The canister Lei found in the trash at Kelly's house had Reynolds's prints on it. His story was that he had been using his propane stove for some beach barbequing, and when checked, the stove had sand in the folding legs. Nothing conclusive had been found at the Reynolds' house but the picture of the girls on the computer.

An elite team of technicians flown in from Oahu, a mountain of possible evidence, and nothing useful found. Lei felt a pang as she glanced over at Stevens, sitting with his hands folded on the table as the techs went over the reports, his head lowered. Jeremy held the same posture, his mouth tight.

At least they'd finally got more manpower.

When the reports were finished along with the thank-yous and better-luck-next-times, the techs departed for Hilo Airport leaving the group seated around the table. Lieutenant Ohale finally grabbed a Krispy Kreme and ate it in two bites, the savage way he tore the donut a little unsettling.

Harada, small and dapper in Brooks Brothers, spoke up. "I need blood, fibers, something from the crime scene. The picture on this computer's incriminating but defense will argue he doesn't have the camera to take it, there's no hard evidence, blah blah. I can't believe those Oahu techs couldn't make a connection for us with anything from his house or the campsite."

"So what do we know for sure?" Stevens got up and went to the white board, began listing key words. "The girls were raped by someone very careful. He drugged them and restrained them. He knew about forensic evidence because he cleaned up after himself to the point that we can't find anything. He chose his site carefully. He drives a dark Toyota truck, though we don't know that for sure. He may have cultivated a relationship with one of the girls, which shows planning and forethought." Stevens looked around at the rest of them for more facts, but no one said anything. "So what are we thinking about Reynolds? And where do we get more evidence?"

"You said he cultivated one of the girls," Lieutenant Ohale said. "Haunani's 'sugar daddy' drove a dark Toyota truck according to two witnesses. I think it could be Reynolds, and I say he cultivated both. You've all seen the pictures of Kelly." Nods went around the room.

"I like Reynolds for it," Jeremy seconded. "I think we should search his business next. Maybe he's got another porn stash somewhere, or a storage locker where he keeps his photography equipment."

Lei's stomach wouldn't let her take a donut though it growled with hunger; the talk had brought back memories of the girls. She rubbed her hands on her slacks under the table, feeling once again the slick wet strands of Haunani's hair.

Stevens nodded. "Let's put in for another warrant, expand the search of Reynolds' house to car and storage facility. Lei, I want you to do a database search for kidnap rapes with the same M.O. Maybe he's just begun killing his victims. Jeremy, you and I are going to re-interview Haunani's mother, if we can find her. She hasn't been at that house the last couple times we went by. Henderson and Na'ole, you guys can come and re-canvass the neighborhood with us. Gotta shake something loose."

The meeting broke up. Lei approached Stevens, feeling the frisson of awareness between them like static.

"I'm really worried about Mary. I think she might have been grabbed by this guy, or even be running away from Roland. He seemed pretty possessive."

"I know. I haven't forgotten about her either. But she's nothing like the girls—she's older, an experienced cop, not easy pickings. I think if you find a pattern of kidnap rapes that matches the M.O. of the girls, we'll know more about what kind of victims he chooses."

"Okay." She turned away, and felt his touch on her shoulder like a brand.

"Have a donut. You look like you need one."

She managed a smile, avoiding his eyes, and took the donut he handed her. She made herself choke it down as she headed for the computer lab, and dusted the sugar on her fingertips against her slacks. Somehow the tiny grittiness of it replaced that other feeling.

It didn't take her long on the computer to find his trail of destruction.

Chapter 24

Several hours later Lei hit print, put all the papers into a folder and called Stevens. The team had just finished a re-canvass of Haunani's neighborhood and upon hearing what she had to tell him, he sent the other detectives on to Kelly's neighborhood. Lei met him and Jeremy in the small conference room.

He'd brought her a fresh cup of inky coffee with chunks of melting powdered creamer in it and a red-striped swizzle stick. He set it down in front of her and leaned on an elbow. She wished he didn't look so tasty; the pull toward him felt like a betrayal. She shouldn't care about anything but the case. She pushed the folder over to him.

"You look like you need it." He pushed the coffee toward her with an index finger in exchange. Jeremy's eyes narrowed on her and Lei frowned back at him as Stevens opened the folder so both of them could scan the contents.

She blinked a few times, rubbed her eyes. Those old monitors weren't exactly easy for reading. She stirred the swizzle stick until the white chunks disappeared. The coffee was surprisingly good, a warm smoky mouthful of delicious.

"I can't believe no one has put these rapes together before. They're all listed as unsolved, different detectives on them, and no notes about them being connected." She sucked the end of the swizzle stick.

"Looks like we're onto something here," Stevens said, leafing through the printouts. "What did you use for search parameters?"

"I looked for kidnap rapes with use of drugs. There were a lot on Oahu that could have been him experimenting, getting his method down. Some girls drugged at parties, waking up in the bushes with no idea what happened. But I excluded date rapes and party situations. Just kept the ones where they were kidnapped, drugged, and held captive."

Stevens spread the photos on the table. "So it starts on Oahu four years ago. Melanie Costa, age 22. Brunette, brown eyes, mixed race. Kidnapped off University of Hawaii campus, drugged and raped at a campsite, dumped back on campus after a day. Lisa Holtzman, blonde and blue-eyed, age 19. Hit on the head at Longs Drugs late at night, drugged and raped at a remote area out in the woods, dumped at the beach after two days. Keani Taong, black hair, brown eyes, age 20. Drugged at a party. Wakes up 'somewhere in the jungle,' is drugged and raped." He looked up. "Doesn't appear to be one physical type he's into, except that these are all older than the Mohuli`i girls."

"There's a lot about the Mohuli`i case that's a little different. Like, they were bound with T-shirt strips and he used handcuffs on these others, if it is the same perpetrator," Jeremy ventured. Lei chewed the swizzle stick, realized what she was doing, and set it down.

"So then there are two here on the Big Island in the last few months," Stevens went on. "Jesika Vierra, age 21, waitress in Kona. Tased on the way to her car. Wakes up at a remote campsite, drugged, raped. She reports he wore a black ski mask the one time she saw him. Found on the side of the road in Ocean View. He just tossed her there like a piece of trash."

Lei's coffee burned her throat as she sipped it. Jeremy stared at the photos, his face colorless.

"Cassie Kealoha, age 18, going to her job at the family's restaurant. Tased, drugged, and raped somewhere in the fern forest, she thinks 'outside of Hilo.' She reports hazy memories of 'being posed and photographed by a guy in a ski mask.'" He arranged the victim photos in chronological order. They stared at them, looking for patterns.

"I'll tell you one thing," Stevens said, "this guy is a serious deviant who may kill in the future. What I'm not sold on is that he did the Mohuli'i girls."

"Maybe he has girlfriends as well," Lei said. "Maybe he also likes young girls. Sees them as weak, easily influenced and used. He may drug them when he's with them, I don't know. Anyway, he groomed Haunani, never intended to rape her—that's a side interest. One day she brings her friend Kelly to the campsite they've been using, and he gets carried away. Goes into his other mode, and he knows they can identify him and kills them to get rid of the problem."

"Let me work another angle." Stevens rolled his pen between his palms, his eyes on the ceiling. "I'm still liking Reynolds for it, and while he could be the rapist also, I'm betting he's not." He tipped his chair back reflectively. "So, he is already molesting Kelly. He becomes Haunani's 'sugar daddy' and one day goes too far, getting both the girls together. He thinks they'll finally blow the whistle and he drowns them."

"I think it was Reynolds," Jeremy said. "He's fitting the profile for both the rapes and the girls."

"The problem is, we're not making it stick to Reynolds," Lei said. "I think it's got enough in common with the Campsite Rapist's M.O. to be him."

"I can't see Reynolds as the Campsite Rapist because of his size," Stevens said, tipping his pen to her in acknowledgement of the moniker. "But, don't forget the photography angle."

They looked at Cassie's photo. Big dark eyes stared back at them from an oval face with creamy brown skin and full lips with a curl to them as if she were always smiling—a classically lovely Hawaiian girl.

"They're all beautiful," Lei whispered. "Maybe that's the link."

"Only Cassie reported the photography thing. That does link her to Reynolds, with his pictures of Kelly and that one of the girls together. Can you tell if they were missing any personal items? Often these sickos take trophies."

They scanned the reports again for a while.

"No mention of it. He could have taken anything because they were all dumped naked, missing their jewelry."

"Let's assume he takes pictures of them," Stevens said. "When Jesika Vierra saw him, he wore a black ski mask. She reported him as five-ten or five-eleven, lean build, athletic. That does not match Reynolds. He's six-three and on the big side, as I said."

"We could have a couple of predators operating," Jeremy said.

"Not likely. Sex crimes like this are rare here in Hawaii. No, I think there's one Campsite Rapist. He wears a ski mask to make sure the women don't identify him. And then there's Reynolds, who did the Mohuli`i girls."

"Okay. We need more on him then." Lei set her coffee down.

"And therein lies the rub."

Lei reached over and picked up Cassie's picture. "I'd like to interview her, see what she can remember about being photographed. She's the only one who had anything to say about the photography angle, and that could be something linking her to Reynolds."

"Good idea. Let's interview all our Big Island victims, see if anything new pops. I'll set it up."

Jeremy put the materials back in the folder and handed it to Stevens, who tucked it under his arm as they stood.

"Good job," he said. He seemed to be waiting for something, or reluctant to leave.

"How are the new guys working out?"

"Good. They're getting up to speed pretty quick. In fact, Jeremy, I'd like you to work with them tomorrow while Texeira and I do the rape victim interviews." Jeremy nodded, expressionless, as Stevens hooked up his jacket off the back of the chair. "I wish we had even more people working the case, but I'm glad Captain Brown sent them over. I'll see you later." He turned abruptly.

Lei watched their retreating backs, sighed, and went to find Pono out on patrol.

Much later, class was finally over. Lei packed up her books, sliding them into her bag. Ray Solomon handed her the last one. He'd come in late, sliding into the seat beside her with an unrepentant wink.

"Mary's still not here," he said, frowning.

"Yeah," Lei said. What the hell. Maybe he knows something. "Mary's officially missing. She disappeared Tuesday afternoon and no one's seen her since. Got any ideas?"

Ray's hazel eyes went wide.

"Holy shit. Not a frickin' clue. I can't believe a police officer can just disappear like that."

"Anyone can," Lei said, biting off her words. "Mary's a good cop but there are ways to disable even the best. We don't know that there has been foul play, but her boyfriend insists something bad has happened to her and I believe him."

"Wow," Ray said, shaking his head. "She was so sassy, so full of life."

"She's not dead," Lei said, hefting her book bag. "Don't even think it." She set off for her truck, striding fast. When she glanced back, Ray was staring after her.

She beeped open the truck and hopped in, throwing the book bag behind the seat and turning the key. The growl of the engine sounded like a welcome. She locked the doors, and then rested her head on the steering wheel for a moment.

She pulled her cell phone out and speed-dialed Mary's number, only to hear it go to voicemail yet again. It must be turned off, or destroyed. The thought made her stomach clench. Maybe she'd just run away from Roland, taken a quick trip to the Mainland . . . but Lono would have found her by now. Lei put the truck in gear, pulling out of the lot onto the main road and deliberately turning her mind to the events of the day.

Snapping her out of the reverie, a black Toyota truck swerved into her lane, cutting her off as it accelerated. She was sure it was the same truck she had chased before. Adrenaline surged as she hit the gas, following its speeding trajectory.

The black truck careened down the two-lane highway. He's not getting away from me this time, she thought, feeling a reckless grin bare her teeth. She shifted gears with a satisfying roar as she followed the truck out of town, tires holding around the turn that had nearly sent her old Honda off the road.

She veered around another car, its horn blaring in protest. The road opened up after that, a glimmering ribbon in the moonlight. The jungle flowed by, a trackless wilderness of dense black on either side of the highway.

Lei floored it. Her new vehicle answered with a surge of power that flung her back against the contoured seat. She was gaining and began pulling alongside, laying on the horn.

In answer the other truck pulled ahead, weaving to keep her behind. It cranked a left turn, gravel flying, onto a dirt side road, headlights bouncing crazily. Lei followed, frowning as they both had to slow down, bucking through potholes.

The black truck rained gravel and dirt on her shiny new hood as her high beams danced over the landscape. What the hell was she doing? Was this chase another bad move like letting Keiki off her leash? Self-doubt assailed her as Lei hit a particularly deep rut and banged her head on the roof as she levitated off the seat.

Still, it was the only lead she had . . .

The dirt road wound down into a steep canyon bisected by a stream. Water flowed across a low, rutted cement causeway. The black truck hit the stream, water arching up and raining down on Lei's windshield, blinding her. As they hit the water her Toyota hydroplaned, fishtailing and spinning sideways. It stalled, facing upstream, one of the front tires dropping off the edge of the cement into deeper water.

"Dammit!" Lei screamed. She turned the key—her truck roared back to life and she put it in four-wheel drive, easing backward on the slippery causeway until all four tires were back on the surface. Then with a careful turn, she headed out of the stream and onto the dirt track. By the time she got to the top of the canyon, the black Toyota had disappeared without even a dust cloud to mark its trail.

Chapter 25

She pulled into her garage, snapping shut her phone from calling Stevens to let him know about the chase. Her vehicle dripped from the car wash, fortunately no worse for its first off road adventure. She returned Keiki's happy cries of welcome with an ear rub through the fence and was unlocking the house when Stevens' unmarked Bronco pulled up at the curb.

"Good thing I was already on my way over." He strode to the porch. Lei switched on all the exterior lights. She really needed to replace that sensor light on the side of the house, she thought as Stevens followed her inside.

Reaction was setting in, and trembling in her hands had progressed to waves of shivering. She suddenly wondered what she'd have done if the black Toyota had pulled over and let her approach. She had her Glock, but no creds or handcuffs with her, not to mention any grounds for an arrest.

Maybe it was a good thing the chase had ended the way it had.

"I'm cold." She went into her room, pulling the fluffy comforter off her bed and wrapping herself in it, collapsing on the couch. Stevens went to the fridge and pulled out two of the Heinekens, uncapped them and handed her one.

Lei took a long drink, burped, sighed. Stevens sat on the battered coffee table facing her, elbows on his knees, blue eyes intent.

"So you chased him," he said. "Let's start there."

"I don't know it was him, not really. I just had a feeling." She took another sip of beer, scrunching the comforter tighter. "Anyway on my way home from class he came out of nowhere, that same black Toyota truck. I followed him out of town, tried to get him to pull over. He turned off on a cane road. My truck spun out on the causeway and I lost him. End of story."

Stevens got up, went to where the futon was folded next to the couch, pushed the coffee table out of the way, laid it on the floor. The sheets were folded inside, and without a word he spread them, straightened them, banged his pillow into shape and lay down, his arms folded behind his head as he stared up at the ceiling.

"Someone's driving a black Toyota truck that you've chased twice. And you have no idea if this is the guy, really."

"Basically."

It did sound ridiculous when put that way. "My gut tells me it's him, though." She yawned, going to the fridge. "If I weren't so hungry I'd fall asleep."

They ended up eating bowls of Cheerios at the kitchen table, and Lei said, "I gotta tell you something I keep forgetting to let you know. I'm going out with Tom on Saturday."

"What? Are you kidding me?"

"He ran into me in the park, asked me out. I thought I might be able to get some information out of him."

"There's a lot we don't know about this situation. I don't think it's safe to assume anything. This guy has the means and opportunity to be the stalker. He could have another pickup somewhere."

"I thought I'd take a chance on it. You know, keep your friends close and your enemies closer."

"Stupid idea—lotta people have died trying that one."

"Maybe I just want to go out with him. He's kinda hot." She peeked up at him from under her lashes.

"I'll show you hot."

He reached over and hooked an arm around her neck, pulling her over. She squeaked in surprise as he kissed her, a thorough exploration that made yesterday's kiss seem like kindergarten. Lei blinked when they finally came up for air, touching swollen lips with her fingers.

"Thought we weren't supposed to do that."

"You were trying to make me jealous, and it worked. Damn your womanly wiles." He spanked her on the butt and gave her a gentle shove toward the doorway. "Off to bed with you before I get into even more trouble."

* * *

Dawn was bleeding up into the sky as he hefted Mary up out of the bed of the pickup truck. He carried her over his shoulder across the damp grass of the deserted park, shadowed by tall ironwood trees and steep cliffs. The occasional car whizzed by on the bridge far overhead. Her cuffed hands, dangling limply, banged into the back of his thighs.

He walked to the edge of the rushing stream, where the exposed black bones of the earth jutted up, a jumble of lava rocks. He dropped Mary there, her head bouncing off the stones, her body a white-wrapped mummy. He leaned down, hearing a faint whistle of breath slip past her lips. She was still alive, but barely. That asthma was a bitch.

He'd had to Taser her last night, and then drug her for their activities. Couldn't afford to keep her any longer.

The roiling brown water was only feet away. He unwrapped her and threw the sheet far out into the stream. He arranged her long black hair over her body, scraped under her battered fingernails one more time with a toothpick to remove any remaining evidence, and took a last picture, taking care with the composition. He pinched her nipple with a gloved finger.

"Bye, Mary."

He nudged her with his foot, and she slid off the rocks and rolled facedown into the stream with only a small splash. He put his camera on multi-frame and clicked off half a dozen shots as the current caught her and carried her out to sea, her hair a dark flag behind her.

She never once lifted her head for a breath.

Chapter 26

L ei pushed through the doors into the station. Her hair was still damp from her run and a few handfuls of CurlTamer, and there was a spring to her walk. Stevens had been gone when she got up, but she still felt a little bubble of happy when she thought of the coffee he'd started and the neatly folded bedding and futon.

Sam looked up from his crossword.

"Hey girl. You looking sassy."

"Feeling sassy, thank you," she said, as she gave his collar a tug. "How's the crossword?"

"It's a tough one this week. I'm thinking of switching to Sudoku."

"I won't be able to help you with that. Bad with numbers." She pushed through the second set of doors to the bull pen, got her cup of inky coffee, and booted up her aging IBM. Pono eventually rolled in.

"Hey," she said, looking up from the endless departmental E-mail. "You look tired."

"Baby's got something again," he said, sneezing.

"Sounds like you do too," she said. "I think I might have chased the stalker last night, and since you wanted me to keep you informed . . ."

"Fill me in," he said, flopping into his rump-sprung office chair. She did.

"Man. You starting a whole new crime-fighting day when you get off work," he said. "I getting tired just hearing about it."

"Me too. It seems like it's escalating."

"No kidding. He went from a note, to a note with evidence, to sending you a package . . . I think he's going to try to make face-to-face contact soon. We gotta be prepared."

Lei's cell rang. She dug it out of her backpack.

"Hello?"

"Lono Smith from Pahoa PD. A woman matching Mary's description has been found washed up in Uli`i Park. I'm heading down to the morgue to see about making an ID."

"Oh my God. No!" Lei said, as her heart hammered and stomach dropped. "What's happened to her?"

"Drowned."

"I can identify her. I'm coming down," she stated, and shut her phone. Detachment dropped over her like a cloak.

"We need to go to the morgue," she said to Pono. "Mary might've been found." Her lips felt numb as her mouth formed the words.

"Oh shit."

They hurried out the front door, Pono telling Dispatch where they were headed. Lei fired up the Crown Vic and they roared onto the main road. Her hands felt greasy on the wheel and there was a tunnel quality to her vision.

"Maybe it's not her. I have to go see." Lei reached down to pinch her leg, hard, through her regulation slacks. The pain helped, and her vision expanded again.

"I should be driving," Pono grabbed for the dash as Lei whipped around another vehicle, hitting the siren and lights.

It was no time before they pulled into the emergency area of Hilo Hospital. Lei double-parked the Crown Victoria and they jogged into the lobby, where Lono Smith had already arrived with his partner, a lean *haole* guy he introduced them to as Brett Samuels.

They walked down the echoing linoleum hall to the elevator and Lono pressed G for the basement. In the long empty moment of watching the elevator lights and listening to the *bing* of them changing, Lei focused on her breathing, not allowing herself to think. Her heart roared and her stomach heaved, but by holding the pressure point in the web of her hand and taking one small slow breath after another, she was able to get off the elevator and walk down the hall to the morgue.

They pushed through the swinging doors into the pistachio green tile-lined room with its steel tables, deep sinks, and shiny row of refrigerator boxes. Morgues have a unique smell, and this one smelt of powerful, nose-tickling lemon cleaner with a decomp chaser that clung to the back of Lei's throat.

"We thought we'd have you guys identify her first," the morgue assistant said. "We'd like to spare the family looking at the wrong body if possible."

"What happened to her?" Lei asked as the assistant unlatched one of the refrigerator box doors with a vacuum-seal pop. Her nerves felt exposed, as if her skin was peeled off. She curled her hand into a fist, the nails cutting into her palm.

"Looks like drowning though we haven't done the autopsy yet."

He pulled the sliding rack out and the detectives clustered around as he lifted the drape off the shape he'd revealed.

Mary's dark skin was grayish and her lips were deep purple. Her eyes were a little open, her eyelashes cartoonishly long. There was a little brown mole beside her mouth Lei had never noticed before.

"It's her," Lono said. "I'm the detective on the case, so you can uncover the body."

Please don't, Lei thought desperately, but of course he did.

Mary's body told the story of her struggle, from bruises braceleting her wrists to the shadowy marks of hands on her hips and vivid welts from the Taser. Lei felt the blood leave her head and she swayed, grabbing the edge of the steel table and accidentally, unforgettably touching the marble-cold flesh of Mary's arm.

Pono's voice came from a long way away. "Her friend," she thought he said, before his warm bulk hoisted her against his side and he supported her down the hall, choked and blinded by grief and horror.

Chapter 27

Saturday dawned overcast and drizzly, as it often was in Hilo. Lei misted her orchids on their plastic shelving under the mango tree, Keiki panting contentedly beside her. It was almost time to bring one of the phalaenopsis inside. Two butterfly-like blooms had opened on its graceful stem, with a row of buds promising more. Delicate purple tracery marked the 'veins' of the blood orchid, a rare variety.

There were apparently still beautiful things in the world.

She'd gone home and cried her eyes dry, then gone to bed. She was barely aware of Stevens coming over, and he'd wisely left her alone. This morning's emotional hangover was the worst she ever remembered.

Lei wondered again what it was about her that brought such bad luck. She remembered telling Mary that, and the way her friend had dismissed it. Now all those possibilities, including their friendship, would never happen for a beautiful, brave, fun-loving woman named Mary who should've had her whole life ahead. At the thought Lei's eyes filled again and she blinked rapidly.

"Good morning."

She turned, mister in hand, every movement feeling heavy and slow. Stevens was leaning in the back doorway, a cup of coffee in his hand, holding another out to her. His hair was rumpled, his blue eyes dark and sleepy, and he hadn't put on a shirt. His jeans rode low on his lean hips and looked like they were going to fall off. This would have interested her on a different day, she thought with the muffled objectivity that cloaked her.

"Thanks," she said, walking over and taking the mug.

"Are you okay?" His voice was husky. He reached out a long finger and pushed a curl out of her eyes. She could only imagine how unsightly she looked.

"I don't know." She brushed past him and went into the house. "I guess so. I have a date with Tom Watanabe to get ready for."

"I'm so sorry about your friend."

"You keep saying that. I actually didn't know her that well." Lei heard how wooden, how stilted and wrong this sounded and couldn't seem to make it any different. She stood by the sink and looked out the window as she sipped the coffee.

"Well, she's got some good people on her case, I hear." He sat in one of the kitchen chairs and turned his coffee mug in his hands. "I don't want you to go out with Watanabe. It's a bad idea, especially today."

She picked up his shirt—draped over the back of a chair—and tossed it at his head. "And I think you should put this on."

She sat down as he pulled on the shirt and combed his dark hair with his fingers. She took a big swig of coffee.

"I actually can't believe I'm going on a date with this guy," she finally said. "What was I thinking?"

"You can always call and cancel."

"I guess I better. I'm just not up to it today."

Lei went to the coffeepot, pouring herself a refill for something to do. The muffled, insulated feeling was dissipating, replaced by an exquisite oversensitivity. The tiny hairs on her body seemed to stand on end, colors were suddenly too bright and her ears rang with every nuance of sound.

She must be going crazy.

Before she could change her mind she opened her phone, called the number on the card Tom had given her, and told him she was sick and couldn't go.

"How about dinner then? Next couple days, whenever you feel better. No big deal, I'll make one of my grandmother's recipes, you can just walk down the block."

"Okay," Lei said. Easier to say yes than keep arguing with Stevens across the table from her, listening. "I'll call you."

She snapped the phone shut.

"I got interviews set up with the two rape victims. Feel up for a road trip? Maybe it would be good to get your mind off Mary by doing something for the investigation."

"Absolutely," Lei said. "Let me just do something about my hair." No one was saying it yet, but Lei was sure whoever killed the Mohuli`i girls had also murdered her friend. She walked into the bathroom and whispered to her ghostly-pale, puffy face in the mirror.

"Interviewing rape victims. Great. Well, Mary, at least I'll be doing something for you."

Chapter 28

S he and Stevens drove to Kona first, knocking on the door of young Jesika Vierra's house. Her mother answered the door, brought them into the living room reluctantly. Jesika had little to add beside what was in the report.

The girl was pale, hair unkempt and eyes hollow, still traumatized by an attack she could hardly remember. The halting monotone of her story caused Lei's head to swim. Battling the familiar vertigo, she'd muddled through the interview with Stevens taking the lead. The only new clue they came away with was Jesika's impression that he was fastidious, for she'd found herself waking thoroughly clean and smelling of baby wipes.

"The smell makes me vomit now," she said, chewing her thumbnail. It was down to a nub.

"Definitely the same M.O. as Mary Gomes," Stevens said, starting up the SUV as they departed. "Even with the seawater they found traces of propylene glycol, the ingredient in baby wipes, on her."

"Yeah," Lei said. They drove in silence, headed for the other side of the island where Cassie Kealoha lived. Lei stared out the window at the sunshine on the ocean, remembering her trips to the beach with Mary. It was better to think of that than Mary's cold dead skin under her hand.

Cassie's family had a large tract of land on the Hamakua Coast, widely regarded as one of the most beautiful areas on the Big Island. They turned off the highway and wove their way into a lush valley ringed by jungled mountains. Tall *pili* grass waved in the breeze and a row of coconut trees, edging the driveway, led to the large plantation-style home.

Several trucks were parked on the grass and a huge pit bull heaved at his chain from a stake beside the porch. The dog's venomous barking brought the father to the door.

"What you like?" The tall Hawaiian crossed tattooed arms over a barrel chest as he eyed the police SUV.

"I'm Detective Stevens and this is Officer Texeira," Stevens said. "We're investigating the assault on your daughter and we're here to ask her some questions."

The man glowered from the top step of the porch, and the dog continued barking.

"She no like talk about it," he said. "She sick today." The mother, equally physically imposing, came to the screen door.

"You folks nevah tell us nothing about what stay going on," she yelled over the dog's snarling. "This the first time anybody even come talk to Cassie since when she went hospital."

"I'm sorry no one has been in touch," Stevens said. He took his card out, held it toward the father, but even that simple movement caused the pit bull to go into a frenzy, heaving its brindled body against the chain. Finally the man shushed it, gestured them to come up onto the porch. The mother held the screen door ajar and they went into the living room.

Several couches lined the walls, and an older couple was sitting on one of them, watching a ballgame. The father went over and turned off the TV, and the old man got up and shuffled out, leaving his elderly wife crocheting. She scarcely looked up at them. Cassie's father gestured to the couches.

"Sit," he said.

They sat.

"Thanks for talking to us," Stevens said. "The reason no one's contacted you is that there haven't been any solid leads on your daughter's attacker."

A long moment passed as they digested this.

"I'm Lehua Kealoha, and this my husband, Kenny," said Cassie's mother finally.

"We looking for him ourselves," Kenny said. He stood up and paced, waving his powerful arms. Tribal patterned tattoos wrapped around his shoulders and calves. "We know plenny people, and we going find the one who wrecked our baby girl."

"I don't blame you for wanting justice," Stevens said. "But please, let the authorities deal with him if you get any leads."

Kenny frowned and stabbed a finger at Lei.

"You related to the Texeiras up Kona side?"

"No. My family from Oahu."

"What is one girl doing investigating a crime like this?" Lehua said, her lips pinched disapprovingly. Her hand brushed a large gold cross that hung in the graceful neckline of her tropical-print muumuu.

"My friend was attacked too," Lei said. "I want to get the guy who did it as bad as you do."

Lehua seemed to consider this, studying Lei. She finally got up.

"Okay then. I'll go get her. Cassie lying down."

The grandma continued to crochet, and Kenny said, "You like something for drink?"

They were sipping cans of guava juice when Lehua came back, Cassie in her wake. She was tall like her father, a river of thick, shining black hair grazing the backs of her thighs. Her mother prodded her, and she came around the side of the couch and sat facing them, her parents on either side. She held her head high with unconscious pride, but her eyes stayed on the floor.

"Hi, Cassie," Stevens said, and introduced himself and Lei. Cassie glanced at them briefly, a flick of diamond-dark eyes. Lei put her elbows on her knees as she leaned toward the girl.

"Cassie, I know this has been a terrible thing. It's going to take awhile to get back to normal, and if you want to talk to someone, counseling can be helpful. I know from experience."

Lei felt Stevens go still beside her, but she knew she needed to make some kind of connection with Cassie. The girl glanced at her again, a little longer this time.

"We read the report about the attack. Is there anything you've remembered since then that might help us find who did it?"

"No," she whispered.

"Speak up, girl," her father rumbled. "These folks stay trying fo' help you."

"I told them everything." Cassie looked up, pushed her hair behind her ears. "At the hospital."

"Mr. and Mrs. Kealoha, this might be easier for Cassie if you left the room," Lei said gently. The parents looked at each other for a long moment, and then Kenny got up and touched the grandma on the shoulder.

"Tutu, come." The two of them left, but Lehua put her arm around her daughter. She wasn't going anywhere. Lei went on.

"It's hard to think about, I know. But if there's anything more you can remember, it's important. I'm wondering if you might remember anything about being 'posed and photographed.'"

"It was just . . . like a dream. He moved me around like a doll, and I saw flashes of light and heard clicking. When I was awake I thought it might be that he took pictures of me. It was like when you kinda remember something, but aren't sure."

"Anything else?"

"Yeah. I felt stuff like . . . silky stuff." She darted her eyes sideways to her mother, took a breath and went on. "I felt like . . . silky things. On my body. He also put something on my feet. I know that because when I woke up I had strap marks. I felt something wet and chilly on my skin. I must have opened my eyes sometimes, 'cause I can remember the blue color of the tarp overhead, and the light flashes . . . I know I was trying to wake up, but also not, because I think I knew what he was doing to me and I kinda didn't want to know, either. I feel guilty I nevah try harder to wake up, get away . . ." Her voice trailed and she hung her head, the curtain of hair sliding down around her.

"You never did nothing wrong." Her mother rubbed the girl's back in little circles. "You alive today and that what counts. Maybe he would have killed you if you seen him, if you fought him."

"That's right," Stevens said. "This man is very dangerous. I can't say anything more right now."

Lehua looked up at them, her eyes blazing with emotion. "Get him. Find this monster who hurt my baby."

Chapter 29

*L*ei went into Dr. Wilson's office for her session late that day.

"Hey," she said. The psychologist sat behind the sleek modern desk in the corner, poring over some papers.

"Hey to you too," Dr. Wilson said, pulling reading glasses off, laying them aside. She came around the desk and reached out as if to hug her. Lei stood stiffly. Dr. Wilson backed away.

"Sorry, I forgot," the psychologist said.

"Forgot what?"

"You don't like to be touched."

"I never said that."

"I can tell you don't like to be touched. Especially when you don't initiate it."

"If you say so," Lei said. She put her hands, clenched into fists, on the coffee table in front of her, and then consciously spread her fingers. "See how irritated you make me? I was having a good day until I got here." Except for the interviews, and the ache of sorrow that felt like cancer in her bones . . .

"Hmm. I thought things were going better between us than this. Could be some transference going on."

"What's that?"

"It's when the client projects their relationship issues onto the therapist. Do I remind you of someone?"

"Every stupid *haole* bitch who tried to help me growing up. None of you could do shit for me back then, and you can't help me now either." Lei surprised herself with the anger behind her statement.

"Too true," Dr. Wilson said comfortably. She settled back in her overstuffed lounger, pulling the lever on the side that reclined the seat. She opened the throw blanket draped over the arm and spread it over her lap. She folded her hands, closed her eyes. Lei stared at her.

"What are you doing?"

"Taking a nap. Let me know when the session's over."

Lei frowned, fidgeted. "I actually was going to tell you something, but obviously you don't care."

Dr. Wilson opened her eyes. They were a clear, commanding blue.

"You just told me a minute ago I couldn't help you. I'm tired. I might as well take a nap as listen to you make me the bad guy—first for trying to help, now for not trying." She closed her eyes again.

Lei looked down at her hands. They'd clenched into fists again. She wanted to get up and leave, but she knew she had to stay the hour. She'd wait it out. She sat back, rubbed her sweaty palms against the stiff blue of her uniform slacks.

The silence was broken by the ticking of the old-fashioned clock on Dr. Wilson's desk. Lei reached into her pocket to rub the well-worn triangle of the note Stevens had left her the first night he slept over. She got up, paced. Tension still crawled along her nerves.

"I'm ready to talk now."

Nothing from Dr. Wilson. Was that a snore? Like, a little, ladylike snore?

"I'm sorry. I was rude."

"Did you say something?" Dr. Wilson's eyes opened a crack.

"Sorry. That wasn't fair, what I said."

"You were right. No one can help you. I bet you know the answer why."

"I have to want help?"

"Bingo. And then, you have to help yourself. I'm just a sounding board."

"Sounding 'bored' is more like it," Lei said.

"Good one." Dr. Wilson chuckled. She didn't retract her chair though, still looking like she might fall asleep any minute.

"A lot happened this week," Lei said. "I chased someone I think might be my stalker. And my friend was kidnapped and murdered."

"Oh my God. Mary Gomes? She was your friend?"

"Yes," Lei said, and her eyes filled for about the hundredth time.

"I'm so sorry. It's a huge loss."

Lei nodded, unable to speak, and yanked a couple of handfuls of tissue out of the box beside her on the couch. She honked her nose.

"What really sucks is that there are no leads. It's like the Mohuli'i girls all over again. In fact, I think it's the same doer."

"So it's easier to focus on the investigation. Are you a part of it?"

"For the girls. Not Mary's investigation. What else can I do?"

"Grieve."

Lei got up, paced. Rubbed her hands up and down on her legs. "I don't want to grieve," she said. "I want justice."

Dr. Wilson inclined her head in silent acknowledgement. Lei went on.

"This is why I became a cop and not a nurse or a social worker. Justice is what I want, not tears."

"Can't there be both?"

"Not and do the job."

"So you hide it. Like you hide the dissociation episodes."

"I have to. I was so afraid I was losing my mind, I always tried to pretend it wasn't happening. I guess it's good to know I am not going crazy, but . . . how do I make it stop?"

Dr. Wilson retracted the chair and sat forward, brushing the lap blanket out of the way.

"Girl, here we are at the crux of the matter. You have to want to tackle this badass beast that is your past. You have to be in a place in your life where you feel strong enough to remember terrible things that were done to you by people who should have protected and loved you. I won't kid you. It may get worse before it gets better if you go down this road, because what brings healing is the integration of the past with the strong healthy person you are now. And it may take longer than your mandatory six sessions."

Lei sat back down. She slid her sweaty palms up and down her thighs. "What's the alternative?"

"I don't know. I guess you keep doing what you're doing. Maybe you'll get better on your own, maybe you'll get worse. What I've seen is that children who were abused and traumatized often hit a wall. Something sets them off, such as a major relationship, or having their own child, and they begin to decompensate. If they don't work through it with support, they often end up doing self-destructive things to themselves and those around them."

"Great. As if it wasn't bad enough with my mom dead and my dad in jail . . . I gotta be screwed up the rest of my life too? Goddamn it!" Angry tears filled her eyes. She jumped up, paced. "Every time I bust someone I feel like I'm getting them back, just a little bit. The best thing I ever did was become a cop, and now this shit is trying to take that away from me, make me act crazy, make me miss things. I almost lost it in the morgue seeing Mary's body. I can't afford to be like this."

"Can't afford to be human? Come on," Dr. Wilson said. "And anger is good. It's fuel. But don't stay there. That fuel can burn you up."

The psychologist reached out, picked up the little brass rake and brushed it through the silvery sand of the Japanese sand garden on the coffee table. Back and forth, back and forth. Lei slowed her pacing, sat on the couch to watch. Back and forth went the rake.

"You are safe here." Dr. Wilson held the rake out to Lei. "You were a helpless child then, but you are a strong, capable woman now, who can make her life what she dreams it to be."

Lei took the rake. She took a deep breath, letting it out in a whoosh, feeling the rage subside. She drew designs in the sand: arcs, swirls, waves.

"I am making my dreams come true already," she said, the ring of truth filling her words. "And I don't want to let the past steal one more minute of my future."

"Sounds like you've made your decision," Dr. Wilson said, watching the swirling pattern Lei created and re-created. "I think that's enough for today. I guess I didn't really need a nap."

"There's always the next happy customer," Lei said, standing up, brushing a few grains of sand off her slacks. "You certainly have a unique approach."

"It's taken years for me to learn to trust my gut," Dr. Wilson said. "That's what seems to work best for me and my clients."

She walked Lei to the door, and staggered a little, off balance, as Lei turned and impulsively hugged her.

"I'm learning to trust my gut too," Lei said, and hurried away down the linoleum hall.

Chapter 30

He sat in his chair, uploading the pictures of Mary. He scrolled slowly through the whole sequence, savoring them: the first shots when he brought her to the camp, tousled and glaring. The poses of her beckoning him with her helpless, waiting beauty. The shot of her sprawled on the rocks, the ripple of brown floodwaters inches away. Then, the final one—her body caught in the swollen current, only the top of her shiny black head visible. "You shouldn't have pissed me off like that, or I might have let you live," he said aloud.

He made a new folder, titled it Blood Orchid and stashed it in a folder with just the date he'd dumped her. Done saving, he unplugged the hard drive and pulled up the rug, stashing it in the floorboard cache he'd built.

Savoring the moment, he took the key ring with the black and blonde hair on it out of the drawer. He knew he should hide it with the photos, but he needed it close. He took the hank of Mary's hair out of the Ziploc bag and secured it to the ring on the other side of Kelly's hair. There was a symmetry there that was pleasing to his eye.

He got his phone out and slowly scrolled with his thumb through the photos he'd saved there, trailing the key ring's hair back and forth across his chest, down his arms, a feeling like the tenderest of touches. Faces of young women filled the small screen.

He paused at the one he was looking for.

He studied Leilani Texeira's face caught in a rare smile, her warm brown eyes alight. "You're next. I was right—you do photograph well."

He put the key ring away and got up, going out to the garage. He went to a large wooden cabinet, opened the combination lock, reached inside to a concealed back panel, opened it. He took out his kit, setting it on the work table nearby.

It was a black backpack with everything tidy and in its place: the ski mask, a couple of shiny new pairs of handcuffs, the Taser, a clear glass bottle of the drug, a sealed plastic pack of hypodermics, a roll of duct tape, a couple of freshly laundered handkerchiefs, the tie out cable, the pillowcase and neatly folded top sheet. He mentally rehearsed the capture as he touched each item.

He wasn't planning to be gentle with this one.

Chapter 31

Lei sat in the conference room with Stevens, Jeremy, Lieutenant Ohale, the two new detectives, and Hiro Harada the following morning. Across the table sat Pahoa station's commanding officer, Captain Brown, Lono Smith, and his partner Brett Samuels. Stevens had called the meeting to request that they combine the Mohuli`i investigation with Mary Gomes' homicide. A box of malasadas, round Portuguese donuts dusted with sugar, sat waiting to clog arteries.

"Okay." Stevens continued with his summarization of the main points, looking down at his notes. He'd asked her to keep track of the discussion, so Lei got up, uncapping a marker to make notes on the whiteboard. "We think these cases are the same doer for several reasons. One: the method. All three women were drowned. Two: all three victims were drugged with Rohypnol. Three: they were restrained. Four: all of them had evidence of sexual activity. Five: they all had trace evidence of baby wipes on their bodies, showing careful attention to cleanup." Lei wrote fast, wishing she could see the expressions on the faces of the other investigators, and feeling conscious of eyes on her ass.

"Now for the differences," Lono said, taking over. Lei drew a quick line dividing the board and began another list. "One: the method of restraint. The girls were bound with t-shirt strips. Mary Gomes was restrained with handcuffs. Two: Gomes was kidnapped and raped over days. The girls weren't identified as missing prior to their bodies washing up, indicating they weren't held captive like Gomes was. Three: the girls had very little evidence of violence other than sexual activity pre-mortem, while Gomes was pretty banged up."

Lei took a relaxation breath in through her nose, out through her mouth, the chemical smell of the marker bracing as smelling salts against memories of drowned faces flashing through her mind as she wrote.

"Four: the victim profiles are different," Lono went on. "The girls were young, easy pickings for a sexual predator. Mary Gomes was mature, a law enforcement officer, experienced in self defense, and armed."

Stevens picked up the rhythm. "Our main suspect so far in the Mohuli'i case, Kelly Andrade's stepfather James Reynolds, has a solid alibi for the time frame when Mary disappeared." He gestured to Jeremy.

"He was at work, witnessed by a dozen people. The wife says he was never gone at night during the time frame Gomes was missing," Jeremy filled in.

"He's got a helluva defense lawyer, and what we have on him is thin, namely a motive for the girls and an incriminating photo of them," Harada chimed in. "I didn't have enough to even issue an arrest warrant."

"Then there's what Lei turned up that could be practicing on the part of our perp. She found two kidnap rapes within the last six months that look like the same M.O. as Mary Gomes, only without the drowning."

"Yeah." Lei turned around and confirmed. "Stevens and I re-interviewed these two rape victims and filled in a little more information."

Lieutenant Ohale's slight nod indicating she go on gave her confidence. "The victims remembered being cleaned up with baby wipes. Handcuffs and Rohypnol by injection were used on them. Cassie Kealoha remembers being posed and photographed; she said she thought he dressed her because she had strap marks on her feet. She also saw a black ski mask."

The group seemed to be digesting this.

"Possible Reynolds did the girls, and the Campsite Rapist did Mary Gomes?" Jeremy used Lei's moniker.

"Campsite Rapist," Captain Brown said thoughtfully, reaching over to pluck a malasada off the pile. The brass on his uniform gleamed in the overhead lights, and Lei thought he'd left his hat on to add height to his short, fireplug build. He was Captain over the entire Hilo District, and Ohale's commanding officer as well as Pahoa's. "The media better not get wind of this. That nickname has a catchy ring to it."

"So far they don't seem to have put the two crimes together," Stevens said. "I hope we can keep it that way. We don't want this guy knowing we're lining up the dots."

"So are we in agreement there's enough in common with these crimes to indicate the same doer?" Lono asked.

Nods around the room and finally Captain Brown said, "Possibly. At this point we have to pursue all leads. Considering how much possible evidence we could have, hardly anything is turning up—Gomes' dump site, Uli`i Park, is coming up dry for trace, so is her body. So even though Reynolds isn't fitting with the Gomes murder, and technically his alibi is holding up for the girls, with that photo he's our best suspect."

"I think we all agree these rapes were a warm-up for the Gomes murder," Lono said. Lei noticed somewhere along the way Mary's first name had been dropped—getting some distance from the vic, she thought with a pang. "What's not really fitting for me are the Mohuli`i girls."

"Nothing to do but get out there and do some police work," Ohale said. Captain Brown stood, and everyone else did as well.

"Get to it, people. These women need justice." Brown spun and marched out of the room, a tugboat setting the course.

"We'll focus on Gomes. Keep us posted on any developments," Lono said, following Captain Brown out.

"You got it." Ohale sat back down, looked around at his team. "Okay. What's next?"

"I got the warrant on Reynolds' CPA office and he has a storage facility as well. Pretty interested to see what we turn up there." Stevens wolfed down a malasada. "Damn, these are good. What are they, donut holes?"

Portuguese food. They do good with fried stuff but watch out for the month-old pickled eggs," Harada said, gathering his papers into a leather portfolio. "Find me some physical evidence and I'm happy to sign Reynolds' arrest warrant."

"Let's get to it," Stevens said. "Jeremy and Lei, you're with me and we'll take the storage facility. Pono, you and the guys do the business office. Let's bring it in, people."

Lei capped the marker and set it in the tray, following Stevens' broad shoulders with her eyes as he left the room.

Jeremy stood up and moved into her space, his eyes hard on her face.

"Don't mess around with my partner." His voice was a hiss.

"I'm not," Lei stammered.

"He doesn't need some bitch ruining his concentration. If something goes wrong with this investigation you're going down for it."

Before she could respond he was moving away with a swift athleticism she'd never really noticed before. Cheeks burning, she followed him out, still groping for a comeback.

Stevens waved the warrant at her above the cubicle wall.

"Step it up, Texeira, we got evidence to gather."

Chapter 32

The storage container was hot and unventilated. She, Jeremy, and Stevens, particle masks and latex gloves on, spent hours in the stifling metal room sorting through boxes of old fishing gear, outdated college textbooks, clothes that should have gone to Goodwill, and some furniture in a heavy baroque style that looked too expensive to give away and too ugly to sell—probably inherited. After the first hour they didn't say much, simply shaking, sorting, and reshuffling.

"What exactly are we looking for?" Lei asked at one point, after dislodging a nest of cockroaches from a box of Kelly's old stuffed animals.

"Photography equipment. Bondage stuff. I don't know, we'll know it when we see it." They didn't see it.

Jeremy yanked the drawers out of an ornate desk against the far wall, one of the few areas where a clear pathway existed from the door of the unit. He dumped the contents of the drawers at Stevens' feet. Postit notes, highlighter pens, boxes of paper clips, a pile of floppy disks, and a jangle of metal spilled onto the floor.

"Hey!" Stevens cried, as Jeremy tossed the drawer aside and reached for another one.

Lei looked up from her box of old cassette tapes as Stevens stooped and, using a pencil, hooked up the tangle of gleaming metal. He held it up to the light. Lei scrambled up and Jeremy came forward to look. Threaded onto a key ring were a traditional gold Hawaiian bangle bracelet, a necklace with a locket, and a delicate gold signet-type ring.

"That desk is a weird place to store jewelry." Stevens used his gloved finger to part the items. "This bracelet says Kealoha. Isn't that our rape vic Cassie's last name?" He gently pried open the locket. Inside was a photo of a small blonde girl. Finally he poked the ring, and the Gothic letter *H* picked out in black enamel caught the light.

"That looks like it could be the ring Haunani's grandmother gave her!" Lei exclaimed. The three of them looked up and Stevens' teeth gleamed through smudges of grime as he grinned.

"I think we finally got Reynolds with this physical evidence." With that Stevens stepped outside to call Harada.

Lei and Jeremy followed him out, eager for some fresh air, and waited in awkward silence in the shade of the building as Stevens made the call.

"Good news. Harada signed the arrest warrant. Jeremy, let's go pick him up. Lei, I'll send Pono over here to help you finish up. I'll see you later tonight for surveillance."

"No need for that. Got a dinner date and haven't heard from the stalker in days," Lei said, shaking out a box filled with yarn balls. They bounced across the concrete floor and she groaned.

"Who?" Even strapping his weapon back on in preparation to leave, she got the intensity of his full attention.

"Tom Watanabe. No big deal, I got out of the thing the other day, but I still need to check him out closer and I guess . . . he wants to check me out too."

"I'll see you later, about 8:00 P.M.," he said, and strode out. Apparently he still thought she needed a babysitter.

Jeremy glared at her over his shoulder as he followed Stevens, and Lei flipped him off behind his back. Bastard got to be in on the Reynolds bust, and had the nerve to give her 'stink-eye' while she was stuck in this toaster oven of a storage unit.

Pono showed up and they spent the rest of the day in fruitless sweaty searching while the detectives arrested Reynolds and interviewed him. Lei would have given her right arm to be in on it.

Evening cast long shadows when she walked up onto Tom Watanabe's porch. She'd taken a brief moment at home to strip off her filthy uniform, splash her face and wind her hair up and pin it with a chopstick, throw on a tank top and jeans. She still felt far from date-worthy—good thing she was just trying to get information out of him. Ambivalence rose up yet again but it was too late; she'd already reached his house and tapped on the door.

He opened it, an oven mitt on his hand.

"Hey," she said, pointing at the mitt. "I like a man in proper gear." He laughed, embarrassed, whipping it off.

"Come in," he said. "I was just giving up on you."

"Yeah, sorry I'm late. We had a lot going on today with work."

"It's okay. The shoyu chicken was just getting a little dry and I pulled it out of the oven." She followed him through the house. Gleaming dark wood floors enhanced spare décor: a black leather couch, low enameled coffee table, and a flat-screen TV mounted above an obsidian Buddha. A framed obi, the wide traditional belt used to close kimono, was centered over the couch.

She pointed at it. "Your grandmother's?"

"Yes. It's over a hundred years old."

Lei went over, folding her hands behind her back, leaning close. The wide fabric belt was intricately worked silk, tiny coiling dragons curling around the edge.

"Beautiful," she said. "It must be nice to have this history."

"Not always." Tom led her into the remodeled kitchen, all chrome and grey granite. "Comes with a lot of expectations." He opened the fridge and took out a bottle of white wine. "Something to drink?"

"Sure."

"Why don't we check out the orchids while the food cools down?" He handed her a glass of the chilled wine.

"Okay." She followed him out the back door. The greenhouse was a sturdy little glass and wood structure, neatly painted and maintained as everything was. They stepped inside and Lei caught her breath in wonder.

Sprays of vibrant dendrobium tangled with the fragile moth shapes of phalaenopsis. Huge, lacey cattleyas thrust showy blossoms forward, spilling delicate fragrance. She leaned close to one, a glowing fuschia.

"I've never been able to get these to bloom," she said, touching the ruffled cup with a finger.

"The secret," he said, holding a mister aloft, "is liquid fertilizer sprayed on once a week and the right climate conditions. Now I've told you, I might have to kill you."

"You threatening a police officer?" She cocked her head, narrowing her eyes.

"I was just trying to be funny." He laughed, that nervous chuckle.

"Whatever," she said, reaching for the door handle. The charm of the greenhouse was lost.

"Wait!" He went down the aisle and plucked an orchid plant off the shelf. "This is a new variety. It reminded me of you."

She took it. The phalaenopsis's stem arched up from a base of dark leaves, three perfect butterfly blossoms perched on it.

They were creamy white with chocolate edges, a spatter of fawn freckles across the petals. She couldn't help smiling.

"This is sweet. Thanks."

He rubbed his hands on his jeans.

"Let's go have some dinner."

They sat in the bamboo-floored dining area at a traditional, sunken Japanese table and ate the shoyu chicken, rice, and fresh green beans he'd kept crisp and flavorful.

"Mm. I always overcook green beans," Lei said.

"Just drop them in boiling water for two or three minutes, strain them out," he said. "Now tell me about yourself."

"Not much to tell. I was born on Oahu and ended up here. I love what I do, and I'm working on making detective." Lei belatedly remembered she wanted to pump him for information. "So what's involved with your job?"

"Nothing as interesting as yours. I'm in charge of monitoring the diversion facilities, making sure our water pressure's good. We have some of the heaviest rainfall in the Islands, and we send a lot of our water to Kona side because it's so dry. All those ditches require a lot of monitoring." He took another bite. "Keeps me busy."

It would be easy for him to know about a remote but accessible area like the stream where Kelly and Haunani were drowned. Lei took another bite, reminding herself her stalker wasn't connected with the murders, though the black truck seemed to cross into both cases.

"You're quiet."

"Just tired." She put her chopsticks down abruptly. "Why'd you ask me out?"

He shrugged, did that awkward laugh. "You're single and cute. You live down the street. I like you. What else should I say?"

"Nothing. I'm sorry. I've just gotten used to interrogating people, being suspicious."

She felt panicky suddenly, claustrophobic. She swiveled to the side, stood up as gracefully as she could in the sunken bench, climbed out. "Listen, this has been nice but I need to go. Thanks for dinner."

"Wow, okay." He tossed down his napkin and followed her through the house. "Let's get together again sometime."

"Sure," Lei said. "Thanks again."

She fled out the front door, her heart thundering. Halfway down the block, with a pang of regret Lei realized she'd left the spotted orchid behind. She was such a freak, he was probably never going to speak to her again let alone give her that orchid.

Keiki flung herself against the fence in an ecstasy of doggy welcome. Lei checked the mail, barely able to keep from running into the house, her skin clammy and heart pounding. Still nothing from the stalker—nothing since she'd chased the truck days ago. Thank God. Maybe it was over.

It felt wonderful to deactivate the alarm, let the dog in, reset it, and take a shower—knowing she was safe at last.

She tried to think about why she'd freaked out at Tom's but her mind wouldn't go there. She just didn't know—but it felt like a classic panic attack. She thought over the whole evening and he hadn't said or done anything really suspicious. He just seemed like a lonely, awkward guy that liked to grow orchids and keep a very clean house and yard. That in itself was strange, for a guy . . .

She let herself smile at that as hot water pounded down on her shoulders, loosening the knots of tension that remained from the day. Maybe the panic attack wasn't about Tom at all. Mary's still face appeared in her mind, bringing grief like a wave of nausea.

The shower water had cooled, and she got out, wrapping in a big white towel. The doorbell rang just as she'd climbed into her PJs and pulled her old cotton kimono over them. She went to the door and put her eye to it, then opened it for Stevens. He held out the fawn-spotted orchid to her.

"This was sitting on your mat. Something nice from the stalker?"

"No." Lei took the delicate plant, let the way into the house. "Tom Watanabe gave it to me." She felt bad again for running out on him, but there was still something off about the guy.

"How was dinner with Watanabe?"

"Good food, lousy conversation. How was picking up Reynolds?"

"Guy's pissed as hell, says he's being framed. Almost got to Tase him." Stevens broke into a grin. "It would have been great but he settled right down when I got my weapon out, alas. He clammed up tight, though, so the interview was a waste of time."

"Speaking of waste of time—finishing the storage unit qualified."

"Sorry about that. I picked it because I thought it a more likely hiding place."

"Yeah, I figured. You hungry?"

"I know better than to expect anything when I come over, but some water to replace the liquids I lost today would be nice."

Lei got a bottle out of the fridge and handed it to him. She was so tired it was hard to think clearly. An awkward silence descended.

"I told you, you didn't need to come over. This really has to stop." Lei pushed her damp hair back with both hands, blew out a breath.

"What do you mean?"

"You spending the night. The stalker's stopped bothering me ever since the truck chase. It's over, and he never did anything dangerous in the first place. I feel so stupid about putting you and Pono out. It's really time for it to end."

"You said not to make it your fault." Stevens sighed, rubbed his bottle back and forth across his flat stomach. "It's not your fault. The stalker might not have attacked, but he could be a real threat."

"It's just . . . this whole thing. It's hard because it reminds me how unsafe I am. You know why I have all these locks and the alarm?"

"I wondered."

"Because I was molested when I was a kid. It messed me up." She'd decided to tell him, but it wasn't making her feel better. Instead, her stomach clenched.

"Hell isn't good enough for scum who do things to kids. I'm sorry that happened to you. I wondered if something did, all your security measures."

"My mom had a drug problem. My dad got her hooked before he went to prison for dealing. Her boyfriend was the one who worked me over, and when he broke up with her she overdosed. I was nine."

A long pause as he digested this, his eyes blue shadows. She couldn't tell what he was thinking. Then he smiled a lopsided smile that twisted her heart.

"Cheers." He held his plastic bottle out, she clinked her water glass against it. "Your dead-ass mom tops my drunk-ass mom."

They drank, the ironic toast of children of substance abusers. He went on.

"I told you I had a friend I let down before by not taking a situation like this seriously, and I won't let it happen again."

"Who was she?"

"My best friend growing up. She had a nasty boyfriend in college. He stalked her after they broke up and she kept telling me about it. I thought she was exaggerating, told her she was making drama. He killed her. That's when I changed my major to Criminal Justice and joined the force."

"I appreciate you telling me that, but I'm not that friend. In fact, I don't want to just be your friend," she said. She held his gaze. Dark blue eyes, intense and wary, met hers. She leaned over to kiss him, a tentative brush of the lips.

"Damn," he said, reaching over to pull her into his arms. "I don't want to be your friend either." He kissed her, pent-up hunger making their teeth click. Lei pulled away eventually, covering her mouth with her hand.

"Ouch. Smooth move."

"You're right about one thing." He stood up. "This can't go on."

"Finally." Lei picked up the empty water bottle and glass, took them to the sink. "Let's wrap up this investigation and go on a date like two sane adults."

"Are you asking me out?"

"Or we could just sleep together," she said. He stood speechless, and then reached for her again. She dodged, laughing, leading him to the door. This flirting thing was getting easier. Maybe she'd just needed some practice. She handed him his duffel, discarded by the entrance.

"See you at the station, Detective Stevens."

"Okay, but call me if you need anything. I mean anything." He wiggled his brows and she laughed. "Sleep well. Keep your phone on."

She let him out, locked the door, armed the alarm. *I doubt either of us will sleep well,* she thought. She leaned against the door, closing her eyes, savoring the faint bruising of her lips, the razor burn of his face still tingling her skin. She sighed and signaled Keiki for their evening lockup routine.

* * *

Across the street he lowered the miniature binoculars he'd been using to observe the house. Her light was finally out. She was in bed. He pictured her there, her lean athletic body curved in sleep, her nipples punctuating the thin fabric of the undershirt she wore to bed.

Sleeping. Waiting for him, for just the right moment. Soon.

Chapter 33

*L*ei walked up the old fashioned church aisle in her dress blues with her offering, an orchid plant in a turtle-shaped ceramic pot. She set it at the base of a three-foot picture of Mary's smiling face set on an easel, with a basket of round black pebbles from Punalu`u Beach beside it. Lei picked one up and put it in her pocket.

She turned and made her way to one of the wooden pews, sliding in to sit beside Pono and his little family. Pono reached out to give her a side hug and Maile, the toddler, dimpled around the finger that plugged her mouth. Statuesque Tiare had her hands full with baby Ikaika, but reached over to pat Lei's shoulder.

Lei took the surroundings in, tilting her head to see the arched ribs of the graceful nave, stained glass windows dropping coins of colored light across the polished floor. Massed arrangements of gardenia, Mary's favorite flower, filled in the air with scent. The church was standing room only for the memorial, filled with police, friends and family. Mary had been well loved, and outrage over her death felt palpable in the hushed tension of voices.

Lei sat, huddled inside crisp dark uniform armor, with a sense as if the event were a movie in which she had little part. An ukulele and guitar band had already begun playing 'Amazing Grace' when Michael Stevens slipped into the pew beside her. He leaned over next to her ear and whispered, "You okay?"

His warm breath tickling the hair beside her ear was the first thing she'd felt in her own body all morning. She nodded, holding the song sheet, her voice reedy and choked. Jeremy Ito slipped into the pew beside Stevens. He'd brought a digital camera.

"Got to get shots of all the guests. He may be here, watching."

Stevens nodded, and Jeremy took up an unobtrusive post behind a pillar on the side. Lei felt the eye of his lens on her and hated the necessity that put him there, watching for a killer.

She didn't cry through the poems, and speeches, and even the releasing of a dozen white doves outside the church, a heartrending touch Mary's boyfriend Roland performed in honor of the moment he'd planned for their wedding. She was able to stay in that bubble of disconnect all the way home, but when it was time to change out of her dress blues and go to work, she found herself getting out the emergency vodka bottle and calling in sick.

She threw back shots standing at the sink until her vision went blurry, then staggered to bed and fell into a black well.

Lei's senses slowly booted up, one at a time. She opened her eyes. She was looking up at the familiar net canopy of her bed at home. Her head throbbed.

Thank God for medication, she thought, lifting herself up enough to throw some extra-strength Advil into her mouth from the side drawer and swish them down with bottled water she'd left out. Keiki lifted her head and watched Lei as she subsided with a groan.

The door creaked open.

"Hey, you're up," Pono said.

"Not sure about 'up.' I'm still deciding if I'm alive."

"Here, Keiki," Pono called, and the big dog leapt off the bed. "Lieutenant told me to come look in on you when you called in. You forgot to lock your house or turn on the alarm. You look like shit, by the way."

"Sssshhhhhhh," Lei whispered. "I'm waiting for the Advil to work so I can go back to sleep."

"Oh no. It's almost 11 A.M., and I made the call last night. She's going to be here in only a couple hours."

"What? Who?"

"Your Aunty Rosario."

"Oh my God!" Lei sat up too fast and fell back, her head spinning.

"I'll get you some coffee."

Lei sat up slowly and carefully this time, swinging her legs off the bed. She tottered to the bathroom. One of her old notes was still dangling from the corner of the mirror. She pulled it off and dropped it into the rubbish and brushed her teeth carefully.

"Now what's this about Aunty Rosario?" she asked, reaching for the steaming mug of coffee Pono held out to her in the kitchen.

"I found your phone last night and called her," Pono said, sitting down. "I told her you been being stalked, your friend was murdered, and you needed some TLC."

"I didn't want her to know," Lei said, frowning. "She has a lot on her plate and she'll be upset."

"She's your family. She get one right to know you need her. She told me she was getting someone to cover the restaurant and catching the next plane out."

Lei sat back, looked into the milky coffee. Weaker than I usually make it, she thought grumpily. She took another sip.

"Great," she muttered. She felt vulnerable, thin in her own skin, brittle somehow. Keiki put her big square head on her leg and it was the only thing that felt good in the world.

Lei pulled the truck up to the sidewalk outside of the baggage claim. Her aunt waited, a sturdy brown woman in a muumuu with a thick curly braid hanging past her waist. She held a little suitcase, the kind of "overnight bag" they made out of vinyl and cardboard back in the 50s. A big white cooler on wheels also sat on the sidewalk. Aunty dropped the suitcase with a cry at the sight of Lei.

Lei hurried around the front of the big truck and threw her arms around her aunt. She buried her face in Rosario's neck, inhaling the smell of talcum powder and *pikake* perfume that had always meant safety and love.

"Aunty," she whispered.

"Why didn't you call me?" Aunty Rosario stroked the tangled curls back as she searched Lei's face.

"We're making a scene, Aunty. Let's go already." Lei slung the little bag into the back passenger seat and hefted the cooler into the bed of the pickup. Keiki wriggled with joy at the sight of the other woman. Aunty fended off slobbery kisses as Lei started up the truck.

"When you goin' teach this dog some manners?" Aunty scolded as Keiki nudged her with her big square head, her tongue lolling in a happy grin.

"She's actually very well-trained," Lei said, snapping her fingers. Keiki withdrew her head from between the seats and settled into the backseat with a sigh.

"So tell me what the hell has been going on," Aunty said, pinning Lei with her fierce black eyes. "Why I gotta hear from a stranger my baby girl being stalked?"

"I'm sorry," Lei said, keeping her eyes on the road. "I didn't want to worry you."

"What? Who raised you to talk crazy like that? Oh yeah, that crack whore momma of yours. That's why I should expec' this kine thing." She folded her arms and stared out the window. They drove in silence for some minutes, Aunty letting the full weight of her displeasure settle over the cab. Finally Lei put her hand on her aunt's arm.

"I'm sorry," she said again. "I'll call you next time I have a problem, I promise."

"That's what family is for," Aunty said, slightly mollified. "I guess I should expec' I gotta teach you that. Now tell me ever't'ing."

"I nevah like talk about it," Lei said.

"You goin' to," Aunty said. "I need fo' know."

Aunty never took her eyes off Lei as she filled her in on what had happened with the stalker and Mary.

"I want you to come back to San Rafael with me," her aunt said with a note of finality. "Take some vacation time. Momi and I will take care of you." Momi Pauhale was her aunt's longtime partner in the restaurant and like a second aunt to Lei.

"No," Lei said. "I have to see this through. I want to catch these guys—the one who killed Mary and the girls, and the one who's stalking me."

"Sometimes you gotta let other people take care of you," Aunty said, an eerie echo of fifteen years ago when she'd picked up a battered child of nine from Social Services.

"And sometimes you have to be the one who takes care of business." Lei pulled into her driveway, going through the motions of opening the house, showing her aunt where to stow her things, giving her the bedroom and getting out the futon for herself.

Rosario had brought a lot of food from the restaurant in the white cooler, and she put it away, keeping up a stream of gossip about mutual friends and relatives as she thawed some kalbi ribs and warmed up poi rolls for their dinner.

"Business has been pretty good. I still surprised how many Hawaii people drive for miles to find us. Momi and I are training some new waitresses; we lost Kailani when she went back school. The best one is our new girl Anela Ka`awai. She's related to the Ka`awais from Kaua`i and she a hard worker. Momi talking about making her assistant manager . . ."

Lei sat at the little table, and let the words wash over her.

She squinched her eyes shut, trying to shut out the memory of Mary's dusky face. Funny how she'd never noticed that little mole by her mouth before.

"Lei." Aunty touched her shoulder and she looked up.

"What?"

"I brought something. Something I've been meaning to talk to you about for a long time." She came and sat back down beside Lei. She was holding a thick packet of letters bound with rubber bands. She set them in front of Lei. "From your father."

Chapter 34

"What are these, Aunty?" Her heart accelerating, she picked the stack up, slid the rubber band off. She turned over the topmost letter, looking at the return address.

Wayne Texeira, Federal Correctional Center Lompoc, Lompoc, California.

Wayne Texeira. Her father—the man whose incarceration had led to such devastation for her and her mother. Her blood seemed to roar in her ears as she shuffled through the letters, postmarked all the way back through the years to the first one, written in 1989.

I was five years old, she thought. I thought he forgot all about me. She looked at the address they had been sent to:

Lei Texeira, c/o Rosario Texeira, 300 D. Street, San Rafael, California.

"He sent them to me. At first I'd lost track of you, couldn't get them to you. Then, it seemed like it would upset you too much to give them to you." Aunty got up, banged some pots around. Lei looked at her small, sturdy form, shoulders hunched as she flipped the ribs on the cookie sheet with her back turned.

"Why now?" Lei turned the packet over in her hands. Her chest felt constricted, that panicky feeling returning. She wanted to get up and run, run, run.

"I don't know. It just seemed time, and like maybe you needed something else to think about."

"You shouldn't have kept them from me." Lei stood, went into the bedroom and got the Glock in its holster, strapped it on. Picked up her backpack, slid the letters into it. Her voice trembled with the effort of self control. "I'm going out. Keep the door locked."

Her aunt nodded without turning around.

Lei hooked the light nylon parka shell off the back of the door and slipped into it to cover her gun, grabbed her keys and went back out to the truck. She drove to a nearby espresso bar and sat at her favorite spot in the corner, where the sun cut a sharp, bright lance across the table. She ordered a coffee of the day, and sipping it out of the thick, white mug, she pulled the letters out of the backpack.

She arranged them into chronological order. Interesting Aunty never read them, she thought, examining the intact flap of the very first one, dated November of 1989.He had been arrested in October of that year.

She'd been asleep in her little bed, and still remembered the boom of the front door breaking open, waking her up. Even at five, Lei knew it was smartest to hide, so she'd slid out and crawled under the bed, clutching her favorite stuffed kitty. She remembered her father's voice, raised in argument, her mom yelling, the glare of the lights, flashing blue and red . . . and eventually silence.

Lei crawled out and went into their bedroom, climbing into the wide bed, still dented with the shape of her father's body. She'd snuggled into his still-warm pillow beside her weeping mother, a fatalistic sorrow taking up residence in her bones.

Lei refocused on the letter in front of her. She realized she didn't know his handwriting, an unfamiliar hieroglyphic of deeply pressed block letters. She traced the dents on the paper with the tips of her fingers.

November 4, 1989

Dear Lei-girl,

I hope you are okay, and not missing me too much. I sure miss you, though. I wish so many things could be different. I hope you and your mom are staying with your Aunty Rosario. I told your mom to go there because I think you will do better there with her to look out for you both.

I am so sorry, honey. I never wanted you to know about any of this. Truth is, I always meant it to be temporary, just until I could get enough money together for something better, but I waited a little too long. I hope you aren't too ashamed of your old man. I always wanted you to be proud of me . . .

Love, your Daddy

Lei refolded the letter and put it back into the envelope. Her eyes prickled with unshed tears but she blinked them away. She went on to the next. His tone grew frantic, wondering why he never heard from them, then fatalistic as Rosario must have told him what was happening with Maylene's addiction. He expressed his helplessness, worry, sorrow, loneliness and, above all, love for her again and again. At some point, he seemed to realize she was not getting the letters, but he continued to write them every six months or so, telling little stories of his life.

Finally finished, Lei restacked the letters, slipped the old rubber bands back over them, put them back in the backpack. She checked the time on her phone. Aunty would be waiting. Her coffee had gone cold, a milky clot forming on the surface.

People sat at the little tables, reading the paper. The bell over the door dinged with each customer's entrance or exit. The smell of coffee, the periodic roar of the blender, the bubbling hiss of the espresso machine were all the same as they had been when she came in. But inside Lei something had profoundly shifted.

I thought he forgot me. I thought he never cared. All along he loved me. All along he was missing me, thinking of me. The truth of it pressed on her heart, a message written in deep block print.

She slipped the backpack on, waved distractedly at the barista, and pushed out through the glass door with a ding of the bell. A few minutes later she pulled back into the garage, letting the exterior door rumble down behind her as she went out the side door. The front door was unlocked—and she'd told her aunt to close up. She relocked it and put the chain and deadbolt on.

"Aunty?" she called, heading for her room. She slung the backpack onto the bed, patted it with affection as her aunt called from the kitchen:

"In here, *Ku'uipo.*" She went in. Her aunt was washing dishes at the sink. She'd always called her "sweetheart" in Hawaiian.

"Why was the front door unlocked?"

"Someone knocked. I opened it and there was a letter there for you on the mat." She indicated a plain white envelope on the counter, **LEI TEXEIRA** printed on it. "I hope it's okay."

Lei's heart picked up speed. She'd so hoped the stalking was over, *and now he'd come when her aunt was home alone.*

"Dammit, Aunty, it was the stalker!" she exclaimed. "There was a reason I told you to keep the door locked."

"No talk sassy to me, girl." Rosario dried her hands on the dish towel as Lei went and got a pair of gloves, snapped them on. Got a steak knife, slit the top, took out the trebly folded note, and opened it.

I THINK OF YOU EVERY TIME I TAKE A BATH.
Lei's stomach dropped and her vision swam. Aunty Rosario reached over her shoulder and snatched the paper up. Her color drained as she read it, hand coming up to cover her mouth. Her eyes were huge looking over her fingers at Lei.

"This must be the guy who did those things to you, Lei! Charlie Kwon!"

Lei got up, fetched a Ziploc bag, slid the letter into it, put it in the freezer between the frozen dinners.

"I don't know," she said woodenly. "How could he find me?"

"I don't know either! This is terrible! He should go to jail for what he did."

"Believe me Aunty, I'd send him there if I could find him." Lei sat back down. "Dinner ready? I need something to settle my stomach."

Her aunt went back to the stove, dished up the ribs and rice. "Aren't you going to call that Pono or something?"

"No. I just got them to stop staying over here for protection; we're fine in the house and I'll take the letter in in the morning. It does seem like it must have something to do with Kwon though. He's the only one beside us who might know that thing about . . ." Her voice trailed off. She couldn't finish the sentence.

Aunty set the plate in front of her with a purple poi roll. Her clenched stomach suddenly translated into hunger. The food was hot and savory, and took her straight back to being safe as a child. She ate quickly and wiped the plate with the tender roll.

"Delicious, Aunty."

"Thanks, *Ku`uipo*. I'm thinking about anyone who knew what happened to you. I only told the social worker at Child Welfare, and Momi of course. I don't know if Momi might have told anybody but I don't know why she would."

Momi was her aunt's partner in the restaurant business, a friend closer than family. Child Welfare was supposed to have confidential records.

"Well the stalker's finally said something I can follow up on. I'll work on trying to track Kwon down. Now can we talk about those letters from my dad?"

Her aunt looked down at her weathered hands, folded in her lap.

"*Ku`uipo*, I didn't want him to hurt you, let you down anymore. When he was arrested I tried fo' get your mother to come to the Mainland, stay with me like he wanted, but she wouldn't. I lost you—Maylene moved around so much. Finally I found you and gave you my number in case you needed me . . . and I was angry with them both. They'd screwed up their lives with drugs and they didn't deserve to have a little girl, when I would have loved you so much . . ."

"They were my parents." Lei put her hand on her aunt's shoulder. "But you were my mama."

Aunty threw her arms around Lei and tucked her head against Lei's shoulder. Lei folded her aunt against her, stroking the long, thick braid of her hair. A kaleidoscope of feelings swirled through her, but she just pressed her cheek against her aunt's head, realizing she was taller, realizing she was stronger too. She had never known that before.

Her aunt pulled away, tore a paper towel off the roll on the wall, honked her nose loudly.

"I'm sorry," Aunty said. "I kept those first letters because I didn't know where your mother had taken you, then because I didn't want you to be upset by hearing from him. I didn't think he deserved you. And later, I didn't know how to tell you I'd been keeping them all these years."

"It's okay," Lei said. "It's just that it would have made a difference. It would have helped me, to know he was thinking of me, that he loved me."

"I couldn't be sure what was in there. I was trying to protect you."

"You could have read them."

Aunty Rosario sat back, drew herself upright. "That would be wrong."

"Aunty, listen to yourself! It's wrong to open someone else's mail but not wrong to keep it from them?"

"It's complicated," Aunty said. "Anyway, what's done is done. What you going do now, is the question."

"I'm going to visit him," Lei said. She clapped her hand over her mouth as if to take back the words, but then slowly lowered it as she realized, yes, this was what she wanted to do.

Her aunt looked at her. Sighed. Picked up the sponge and wiped the table.

"I'm not surprised. Wayne always had a way with words."

Chapter 35

The bus bound for Halawa Prison on Oahu was a huge Greyhound, and Lei felt like she was in an ocean liner, gliding and swaying far above mere mortals fighting traffic in the narrow double lanes below. She snuggled into her comfortable seat, looking out the window as steep jungled slopes streamed by. She'd got going early that morning, flying out of the Big Island to Oahu, her stomach knotting every time she thought of meeting her father. She pulled the photo her aunt had given her out of her pocket.

In it her father smiled a handsome, square-jawed smile. A toddler Lei sat on his shoulders, her hands buried in his dark curly hair, her grin as big as the moon.

"I don't have anything more recent," her aunt had said. "I couldn't stand to take a picture of him in that orange jumpsuit. But he's aged, honey. Prison life hasn't been that kind."

"No, it hasn't," Lei whispered, touching his face. She slid the photo back in her pocket and looked back out the window. According to her aunt, he'd been recently transferred to Halawa from Lompoc in California, with another year on his sentence.

Her phone rang, vibrating against her side. She pulled it out, flipping it open as she looked at the plaque attached to the seat in front of her: NO CELL PHONES.

"Hello?" she whispered.

"Lei?"

"Yes? Who is this?" she flipped the phone over to see the screen ID: *Unavailable.*

"Me. Your special friend."

Lei sucked in her breath, held it. Every hair on her body stood on end. The voice was loud but muffled. She couldn't tell gender, age, anything.

"How did you get this number?"

"That doesn't matter. What you need to know is that I haven't forgotten you."

"I haven't forgotten you, either," Lei said, her whisper vibrating with rage. "I'm going to find you and make you sorry."

A long pause.

"I hope so." Then laughter, a low rumbling chuckle. "I like a challenge, Lei."

Click. Dead air.

Lei snapped the phone shut and pressed the power button to turn it off. She stood up and stepped into the aisle, scanning the people in their seats for any unusual activity. There were only a few other passengers, hunched over portable video games, or tucked dozing into corners. She walked to the back of the bus and into the closet-like restroom and locked the door.

She took some relaxation breaths. Splashed water on her face and hands. Did a nervous pee. Washed her hands again. Splashed water again. Nothing was helping to diffuse the adrenaline that had pumped into her system. She went out, scanned the seats again. No activity. She walked down the aisle, touching a few seat backs for balance as the bus swayed. She walked back and forth a few more times until her heart rate was back to normal and the trembling of her legs had calmed. She sat back in her seat and took a few more relaxation breaths, longing for the familiar weight of the Glock, which she'd left at home due to airport hassles. All she had with her was the black lava stone from Mary's memorial.

She rubbed it, and then flipped open her phone and texted Stevens:

Stalker called my cell. Can you trace my phone activity? Anything new your end?

She'd called him and Pono the night before to let them know about her plans to go to Oahu, and he hadn't had any more overtime authorized for her Saturday so she'd gone ahead with the trip. A few minutes later the phone vibrated with his phone call.

She didn't pick up, texted again: *On bus so can't use phone to talk.*

A few minutes later, he texted back.

No action here. Will put in trace paperwork. Will check records for caller number. You ok?

Shaken up but ok.

Why you on bus?

Going to Halawa to see my dad. He's in prison there, told you yesterday.

Think he knows anything about the stalker stuff?

Lei paused, looked out the window at the lushness of remote Halawa Valley rising around her in sculpted beauty. Her eyes hardly registered the scenery. *Could* her father be connected to the stalking campaign that had been going on? It didn't seem possible.

Don't think so. Unfinished business. She clicked the phone shut. It vibrated once more:

Call me when you can.

Will do, she texted back, unaccountably warmed.

She sat at the battered Formica table in the communal room, waiting for her father. It had been an ordeal getting in. She had been able to get on the schedule for a visit but only because of her police and daughter status. She hadn't known what to expect. The prison was medium security so the visiting could have been anything from plastic windows and phones to this open setting.

He must have some privileges, she thought, looking around the room. Couples and families clustered around battered tables, playing cards or talking. The spacious room was bathed in sunlight from high windows shadowed by safety wire. Lei sat facing the door, and when he came in, she knew him instantly.

He walked slowly toward her. His curly hair was shot with silver, and his face reminded her of a cigar-store Indian she had seen once, all craggy cheekbones and deep furrows. His dark, hooded eyes were wary.

"Lei," he said, looking down at her. She'd forgotten how tall he was, the rack of his shoulders seeming to block out the light. She stood up.

"Hello." Touching wasn't allowed so she did an awkward little wave. Her smile felt like a tic.

"Lei." he said again, this time his voice soft. "You came."

"Yes, I did."

They sat down at the table. Wayne took out a little spiral notebook.

"Do you have a pencil? I'm not allowed to carry one."

She dug one out of her backpack and handed it to him. She felt the round eye of the surveillance camera watching them. Wayne took the pencil and began sketching quickly, and she saw her face emerging on the little lined pad: upturned nose, square jaw, full mouth, curly tangle of hair, wide tilted eyes, sprinkle of freckles. Only when he was satisfied with his drawing, and the swift glances he stole at her to complete it, did he hand the pencil back to her.

"Helps me remember things," he said, flipping the notebook shut and slipping it back in his pocket.

"You seem to have a knack."

"Something to do with my hands."

The awkwardness choked Lei. She cleared her throat.

"I bet you wonder why you never heard from me."

"I used to."

"What do you mean?"

"I figured you had your reasons. Probably good ones." This so closely echoed her own thought about Aunty Rosario hiding the letters that she cocked her head, smiled at him.

"Until recently, I thought you forgot about me when you were taken away."

"Why?" His brow furrowed.

"I mean . . . I never knew you wrote to me." She looked down at the table, unable to bear looking at his eyes.

"I don't understand."

"Please don't be too mad at her but . . . Aunty Rosario never gave me your letters until just recently."

The silence stretched out. She sneaked a peek at him. His carved face was still.

"That explains a lot," he finally said. Lei nodded.

"Anyway. She brought them to me. And I realized what I thought was true, wasn't true."

"Which was?"

"You know. That you forgot me."

"Never," he said, leaning forward with sudden intensity. "I *never* forgot you." Lei blinked, eyes swimming.

"I wish you hadn't gone in here," she said, her voice small.

"You and me both." He set his hands on the table, as close as he could get them to hers. Lei stared at them and the tears fell, running down her cheeks like wax.

"I'm sorry," he said. "I know you've had it rough."

"Not so bad." She sniffed and dashed off her cheeks. "After Aunty took me in."

"I'm glad she took you in, but I still get some things fo' to say to my sister."

"She was nothing but good to me. She thought she was protecting me."

"From the big bad drug dealer?" Her father had been given a maximum 20 year sentence without possibility of parole for heroin and cocaine dealing in an era of severe sentencing.

"I guess."

"So you read the letters. Then you know I never meant any of this to happen."

"Nobody ever does." Once again, the long silence. Finally Lei said, "Did she tell you I'm a cop?"

"Yeah." He laughed, a rusty chuckle. "Proud of you too."

"It makes me feel good to make the streets a little safer, to help people. I've had some trouble lately, though."

"What's been happening?" He frowned, dark brows snapping together.

"Long story. I'm being stalked. Do you have any enemies in here? Anyone who knows about me? One of my cop friends thought there might be a connection somehow. Sketchy, I know."

He stared at her, eyes hard. She wasn't afraid of him but knew others could be.

"Get me up to speed."

She did, filling him in on recent events.

"He called me on the bus on the way down here."

"I have some enemies. You can't avoid it, being in here. I had to kill a guy a few years ago."

"Great, you're a murderer."

"It was self defense. His name was Terry Chang, he was a serious player in Hilo and we tangled in the game back in the day. Then he got convicted and tried to shank me in Lompoc. I ended up getting him. Added some years to my sentence."

Lei lowered her head. What do you say when your dad tells you he killed someone?

"I don't think his family's letting this go. That or his connections. I've been getting threats."

"What kind?"

"Just rumors. People saying the Changs are looking for payback."

Lei looked at her hands, squeezed the web between her forefinger and thumb. Terry Chang. The name was familiar.

"I think I know that name. Pono told me his wife is the player now."

"Healani? Wouldn't surprise me. She's one tough lady."

"Why now, and not when you first killed him?"

"Rumor has it, some new blood trying to move up by earning cred, something like that."

"Well, I'll look into this. Are you safe in here?"

"I can take care of myself. You just here for the day?"

"Yeah, just today. We're in the middle of a pretty intense investigation, and Aunty's still at my house. I have Pono keeping an eye on her, but still I can't be gone long. So . . . how much longer you going to be in?"

"I'm done with my time in six months. Before you leave, can I get your address? Sorry to say, I don't trust your aunty anymore to handle the mail."

"Can't say I blame you." Lei gave him the address and her phone number. She slipped her hand into her pocket where she'd stashed the black lava stone that morning. It felt good to rub it. He got his notebook out, did another drawing of her. This one was her as a little girl with a grin that took up her whole face. He did it quickly and passed it across to her.

"This is how I remember you."

She laughed, folding it and putting it in her pocket alongside the stone, a hard little square she could touch whenever she needed to.

"I always did have a big mouth," she said.

The buzzer sounded for the inmates to return to their cells.

"Watch your back, Dad." The word sounded foreign in her mouth.

"I always do."

She watched him walk away and the thunk of the steel door shutting behind him squeezed her breath out of her lungs with loss and again, the claustrophobia. She couldn't wait to get out.

Leaving the big square poured-concrete building with its lacy scrim of razor wire, Lei flipped open her phone and called Pono.

"Hey there, Lei."

"Hey. How's everything at the house?"

"Fine. Your auntie she cleaning. Wants to know when you getting home."

"Soon as I can." She told him about her father's threats from the Chang family as she got back on the bus.

"I hope that's nothing, Lei. Those Changs—don't have anything to do with them."

"I don't think it's good intel. I think the stalker is the guy who molested me when I was a kid," she whispered into the phone, getting "stink-eye" from the bus driver. "I'll tell you more when I get home."

Chapter 36

L ei went up the chipped cement steps of her little house in Hilo. Keiki nosed her leg, sticking close. After she'd got home, she turned right back around to take Aunty to the airport. She'd had to pry her aunt out of the house with promises of a visit to California, but she couldn't risk having her at the house with Charlie Kwon or whoever it was escalating the situation.

Didn't know I could miss it so much in a day, she thought, slipping her key in the lock and taking a deep breath of the humid Big Island air with its faint plumeria scent. She disarmed the alarm and went into the kitchen to sort the handful of mail. Keiki barked happily, sniffing all the corners, and did a quick patrol before whisking out through her dog door.

"Stevens, it's me. I'm home."

"Glad you're back. Nothing on the stalker call; the number was a disposable."

"Crap. He's been good at covering his tracks so far. Listen, you doing anything for dinner?"

She took a container of beef stew out of the freezer.

"You asking me out?"

"I guess I am. I have some food from my aunt's restaurant, and I can nuke you up some."

"No problem. I'm always up for a home-cooked meal, no matter who made it. See you soon."

She shut the phone and set about her preparations. Keiki came back in from her patrol and sat wagging her stump of tail in anticipation, her triangle ears pricked.

"Okay baby, coming right up. Don't forget I fed you first." She set the dog's food down, her stomach fluttering. She couldn't wait to see Stevens, to see if she felt that fizzy bubble when she saw him. It seemed only moments later that the doorbell rang. Lei took a moment to check the peephole before she opened it.

"Hi, Michael."

"Hey," he said. "You remembered my name."

She looked at him a long moment, taking in his height, breadth, and intensity—then they each stepped forward at the same time so they bumped awkwardly as they hugged. Lei laughed, gesturing toward the kitchen.

"Come on in and enjoy Aunty's cooking." She led him to the table where a candle burned and places were set.

"Nice. Smells good."

"You'll have to tell Aunty next time she comes," Lei said, getting the warm purple taro rolls out of the oven to go with the beef stew. They ate heartily, catching up on departmental business and the progress on the Mohuli`i/Gomes case.

"Reynolds had his arraignment and made bail. Guy has some CPA connections to real money as we had the bail set at a million. We're not making the Gomes case stick to him at all though—starting to think the cases are separate."

"Awfully coincidental in a town of forty-five thousand. You sure about that?"

"We're not sure of anything, just following the evidence. Thank God the search turned up Haunani's gold ring or we wouldn't have been able to pick him up. As it is, DA's thinking

Reynolds did the girls and the Campsite Rapist is still out there, maybe escalated to doing Gomes."

"Still want me to help out?"

"Absolutely. Just not sure how at the moment; we seem to have run out of leads."

"I've got something new on my stalker." Lei got up, fetched the note out of the freezer. He cocked an eyebrow as she took the note out. "Don't ask. It seems like a secure location and makes me feel better somehow. Anyway, this thing about the bath—only the guy who molested me could know something that personal. I've got a real lead now. His name is Charlie Kwon."

She filled him in on everything she could remember about Kwon. He tapped the letter.

"You sure there's no one else who could know about this? Seems pretty farfetched he'd come back after all this time and endanger himself by stalking you. That's pretty ballsy behavior for a pedophile, especially the opportunistic type like Kwon sounds like."

Lei stood up, paced. "There are a few people who knew his name, but it's just as unlikely they'd use the information this way."

"What about your father? Did he know?"

Lei paused midstride. Went over to the sink, gazed unseeing out the window. He probably did know, at least as much as her aunt had told him. It had never occurred to her to ask him. She cringed at the thought.

"I don't know. I'd have to ask my aunt. Anyway, probably not the details."

"But how do you know that? Wouldn't he have asked Rosario about it, wanted to get some payback?"

"I don't know. I'll have to call my aunt in the morning since she's on the plane. That reminds me, he had a lead for me too, the Chang family and their connections. Said they're threatening him because he was the one to off Terry Chang a few years ago."

"Could Kwon have a connection with the Changs?"

"I have no idea. Another good question."

Stevens whistled. "And suddenly we have a laundry list of suspects. Wish we had that many for the girls and Mary."

Lei collapsed into the chair, put her head down on her folded arms. "And to think I used to think the cases were connected somehow."

"I know, I played with that idea too. And just to add to the mix, I'm liking your friend Tom for the stalker. Means, motive, and opportunity—he's creepy enough and it would be easy for him, right down the street." Stevens gestured to the delicate orchid plant on the table.

"C'mon. He's not my friend."

"Seems like he might want to be more."

Lei stared at him. His sky eyes were on her face, dark brows lowered. She reached across the table, put her fingers on his lips.

"I don't like him that way," she said softly. "I told you."

He captured her hand in his big, rough one, and kissed the pads of her fingers. Warm breath shot tingles up her arm.

"You know who I like," he whispered, nibbling gently, drawing her forefinger into his mouth. She closed her eyes as he kissed and sucked his way across her palm and up her wrist, drawing her boneless body closer, scooting his chair around. Before she quite knew how he had done it, he had her in his lap, his arms around her.

The kiss was a conversation: a greeting, an acknowledgement, a statement of intent. Lei felt herself vibrating like a plucked string, every nerve ending coming alive. He finally lifted his head, looking down into her half-lidded eyes for a long moment.

"We've got to find this guy. I can't hold out much longer." Regret pulling his mouth down, he set her back in her chair.

"Wish you weren't so noble." She sighed, straightening her shirt. "I respect that about you. Annoying as hell, though."

"Can I spend the night? Keep an eye on you."

"No. Not if you're not in bed with me."

He groaned, pushed his hair back with both hands so it stood up in pointed tufts of distress.

"I better go then." He scrubbed his hands briskly on his jeans as if to keep from touching her.

"Thanks for all you've done. I know you're looking out for me, and I promise I won't go out tonight."

"You better not." A last kiss seared her mouth with longing. She let him out, relocking and rearming, and sighed as she did.

* * *

"The bitch is back." He watched the lights go out, and smiled, putting his camera away. He wouldn't need it again until he had her. "It's going to be worth the wait."

He watched Stevens get in the Bronco and pull out, then drive around the block. He turned on the old Pontiac he was driving, and rolled away just in time to see the lights of the Bronco come up behind where he'd been parked and pull over, going dark.

The poor lovesick bastard was going to spend the night in his car watching her house.

Not that that was going to help.

Chapter 37

Late the next day Lei went down the hall to Dispatch, checking the time she was back on the schedule.

"Hey, Irene."

"Hey!" Irene stood and flipped her headset up, immaculate in an ivory pantsuit with coconut shell buttons. She hugged Lei. "Glad to see you smiling."

"Who's this?" Lei gestured to the pretty, dark-haired girl with a chic shag who sat at the switchboard.

"My niece, Tanya." Tanya gave a little wave and smile but she was talking to a caller. "She's been helping out. Charlotte finally quit and I told the Lieutenant that Tanya would make a good backup."

"Good to have you, Tanya," Lei said, and the girl nodded and turned back to take another call.

Lei went into the central work area. Pono was at his computer with a new recruit trainee, Jenkins, seated at her desk. He'd started under Pono after she got reassigned to the Mohuli`i case. He jumped up.

"Officer Texeira!" Jenkins exclaimed. Good-looking, beefy and earnest, his high complexion deepened as he got out of her chair.

"Hi there. How's Pono treating you?"

"Good, thanks. Sorry I was sitting in your chair . . ."

"No worries. I'm off until tomorrow."

"Hey, want to tell me more about your—um, situation?" Pono wiggled his brows, clearly meaning the stalker thing but not wanting to speak in front of Jenkins.

"Call me later," she said. She greeted a few more people and pushed out through the stiff glass doors. She pulled out into the busy road and headed for her class at University of Hawaii. Driving there reminded her of Mary, and she endured the now-familiar squeeze of her heart. She wondered when it was going to stop hurting, and didn't want it to—that would mean her friend was really gone.

* * *

This was her night to come home late. She'd be tired, her guard down, and everything was ready.

Anticipation hummed in his blood. He took a shower, scrubbing himself thoroughly, using a nail brush to get under his fingernails. He'd never shaved himself, but thought it might not be a bad idea one of these days. He dressed in his special outfit: black nylon turtleneck, loose black running pants. He put the ski mask on the seat beside him, along with his hunting kit, and drove to the house. Only thing left to take care of was the dog.

Chapter 38

*L*ei got into her truck at the UH campus and drove home. Class had been interesting, and it was good to chat with her classmates, to feel like things were getting back to normal. Ray Solomon hadn't reappeared. It made her wonder if there was some connection between him and Mary. She needed to remember to call Lono Smith and tell him.

She pulled into her driveway. The headlights glared against the garage door as it rumbled up. She rolled her tired shoulders, pulling into the garage and hitting the remote to close the door. She hopped out of the truck, got her book bag out of the back, and went out of the garage into the darkness outside, noticing silence for the first time. She stopped, called:

"Keiki! Hey girl!"

There was no answering scrabble of toenails, no happy greeting bark. Panic surged through her as she dropped the book bag and unlatched the chain-link gate, running forward along the side of the house.

"Keiki, where are you, girl?" she cried. The next thing she saw was a shower of exploding white stars as her body flew forward, convulsing with electricity.

She came to slowly, waves of pain gathering into a pulsing point of agony at the back of her neck. She opened her eyes. Nothing but darkness. She swallowed, felt the rough dryness of cloth in her mouth. She tried to move and pain seared through her arms, as she realized they were cuffed behind her back. She moved her legs—they were tied too. She heard rumbling, felt vibrations beneath her: she was moving, and the metal ridges beneath her told her she was in the back of a pickup truck.

Terror surged through her. She couldn't stop herself from flailing, thrashing until the searing pain in her arms and shoulders stopped the panicked frenzy of movement. She stilled herself, sucking wheezing breaths through her nostrils. The cloth bag on her head further restricted air supply.

She closed her eyes and concentrated on breathing. One-two-three in, one-two-three out, she counted to calm herself. As she got more oxygen into her lungs, she turned her attention to her hearing, noticing the grinding of the truck downshifting. It wasn't her truck then, with its smooth, new transmission.

She berated herself—in her panic not recognizing the darkness on the side of the house for the danger it was, not realizing that of course he would take out her dog first. At that thought tears threatened. She blinked rapidly, keeping her breath steady as she turned her thoughts to escape.

She slid her hands up and down, testing the range of motion she had. The bed of the truck was the usual ridged metal. She caught her feet into one of the ridges and pushed herself forward until her head touched the side of the bed. She swung herself around again and pushed off to the other side. Her arms screamed with strain as she kept feeling for something, anything that might be useful. Nothing.

Despair washed over her. How likely was it that he'd left a weapon or the key rattling around in here? The best bet was probably to move to the back of the truck bed, try to get the tailgate down, shove out the back into the road.

Even as she began scooting herself toward the tailgate her mind screamed, *No, no, no! There has to be some other way!* She pictured falling into the road at high speed, the crunching of her bones as she hit the pavement, helpless to break her fall in any way, the possible collision with another car. Still, it was better than waiting for what he had planned. She'd die before she let him . . .

She reached the tailgate, rolled herself onto her knees and chin, reaching upward with her cuffed hands, fumbling along the metal at the top for the lever that opened the tailgate. The truck swayed around a corner and she fell sideways, feeling the crunch of her wrist against the truck bed.

She must have passed out or fainted, because she gasped as wetness hit her face. He was throwing water on her. Something was tied over her eyes now, and the gag was gone. She dragged in gulps of welcome air, stabbing needles of circulation coming back into her legs. She was lying sideways. Nausea hit her and she leaned forward, retching. Her wrist radiated a pulsing pain—probably broken.

"Goddamnit," she heard. "Get up."

A tenor voice. He sounded familiar. It was a good sign she had a blindfold on: maybe he wasn't going to kill her.

She felt him grab her feet, swing them sideways off the tailgate.

"Get up. I'm not carrying you."

She sat there, adjusting to being upright, her head swimming. She leaned forward, reaching with her feet for the ground, and would have fallen if he hadn't caught her by the arms. Her feet sank into boggy ground concealed by long grass.

"Move," he said. She stumbled across the uneven ground, impeded by the grass and mud. He grabbed her head and ducked her under a branch, yanked her arms to get her between scratching bushes. She thought of wrenching away, of running,

but he seemed to anticipate her every move, and with the
blindfold on, getting away seemed impossible.

She heard the gurgle of water and suddenly the elements
added up. She knew where they were: the Mohuli`i girls' crime
scene. She stopped, digging in her heels. He gave her a shove
from behind and she fell to her knees. He grabbed her hair,
yanking her up, forcing her to stumble forward.

"Get going, bitch. Guessed where we are by now, didn't
you? I have a lot more planned for you than those girls."

He gave her hair another yank, this time a heave. She cried
out as she flew forward, bouncing on carpet.

"Got my camp set back up," he said. "They'll never look
for you here."

That's true, she thought, getting to her knees, coiling her
strength inward.

She felt movement in front of her and hurled herself
forward, her chin tucked in, head-butting. She hit a glancing
blow to something, and heard the whoosh of exhaled breath,
but kept flying forward and landed on the ground, solidly on
her face. She didn't have time to recover before her whole
body convulsed, twitching, a thousand tiny stars lighting up
behind her closed eyes as consciousness winked out.

She woke up in steps, her brain responding to thumping
pain signals. She opened eyes gummy with dried tears. The
light was dim. The blue tarp overhead flapped a little. She
couldn't hear anything but the tinkling of the nearby stream.

An icy calm settled over her. He's going to kill me. I'll just
have to kill him first.

She was inside a cheap nylon sleeping bag, naked. Her
hands were cuffed in front. Her feet were loose, but she felt
the pinch of something on her ankle. She reached down to feel
another handcuff, this one clipped around her ankle, attached
to a steel tie-out cable threaded through the zipper of the
sleeping bag, trailing out into the bushes.

She lay in the same dilapidated shelter she'd helped clear out. The crime techs had left it there, the landowner's problem to deal with. Instead of pockmarked dirt, he'd covered the ground with a large musty-smelling carpet fragment. An ice chest was nearby and a battery-operated lantern hung from the supporting pole in the middle. Late afternoon sun slanted through the trees.

She'd been unconscious all day.

She sat up and took inventory of her injuries, feeling the welts where the Taser had hit her in the neck and back, her bruised face. Worst was the wrist, throbbing a protest with each beat of her heart.

She had to pee, and crawled out of the sleeping bag and relieved herself behind a bush. There was another welt on her thigh—probably an injection site. No other reason she would've been out all day.

Lei then explored the length of the cable tie-out. It ended looped around the sturdy trunk of a christmasberry bush. It was too short for her to move beyond the screening growth. Branches within her reach had been trimmed back with a machete so there were no dangling or handy branches, and the big pile of potentially useful trash was gone, removed in the search for evidence. There weren't even any handy rocks. The site was isolated, an empty acreage at the end of a cul-de-sac on a large, undeveloped tract of land. It was pretty smart of him to use it again, no one would anticipate that.

Her clothes were folded next to the ice chest. There was no way to get her pants back on with the cable attached to her foot, and with hands cuffed she couldn't put her bra or shirt back on either. He's done this before, she thought. He knows he has to take the clothes off before putting restraints on or he can't get them off later. The thought of Mary's ordeal chilled her, somehow made worse by this final confirmation that her stalker was the killer they'd been searching for.

Lei flipped up the lid, looking for something to use as a weapon. Inside was a bag of ice and a six-pack of water bottles. She was parched, her throat scratchy from the gag. She picked up one of the water bottles, inspecting it. It had a tiny puncture mark in the neck. She looked at the rest of them. They all did. Maybe this was how he administered the Rohypnol.

He didn't seem interested in fighting her, more in keeping her subdued.

A plan began forming. She took two of the water bottles and emptied the water out near a plant where it wouldn't show. The bag of ice was closed with a large, crimped steel staple. She had to use both hands to pull it open—difficult with her broken wrist. The thick staple wire, unfolded, could make a weapon.

Lei popped several ice cubes into her mouth, crunching them—the coolness soothing on her raw throat—and unzipped the sleeping bag off the tie-out cable to increase her mobility. She rearranged the sleeping bag the way it had been, only now with the cable pulled tighter so it looked like it went into the bottom of the bag as before, but now it came in through the top, forming a loop. She got in and set the empty water bottles beside her and chewed ice until her thirst was quenched.

She'd fallen asleep, a fitful stupor, when the growl of an engine startled her awake. The black tracery of branches against a glowing grey sky heralded nightfall. Showtime.

Lei put her cuffed hands above her head and closed her eyes, a picture of unconscious submission, the staple wire concealed between her fingers. She waited as she heard the muffled thump of the car door slam, the swish and crunch of his approaching footsteps. They slowed as he approached her.

She felt him staring down at her. She kept her breath slow and even. He prodded her with his foot. She remained limp. She felt him pick up the water bottle from beside her, heard the swish of remaining droplets as he shook it.

"Stupid bitch," he said, in that almost-familiar voice. "You were too easy. I don't know what he sees in you."

Light glowed against her eyelids as he turned on the lantern. She heard more rustling, what sounded like a paper bag. She cracked her eyes but in the dim light of the lantern she could only make out his silhouette: not too tall. He took out a sandwich and put it in the cooler. Through the screen of her lashes she watched him get a camera out of his backpack. She closed her eyes as he loomed over her, unzipping the sleeping bag, the camera clicking periodically.

It seemed like forever before she heard the rustle of his clothing coming off, the thud of his shoes as they hit the ground. Her heart beat like a drum—hollow, frantic. She controlled her breathing with difficulty, then suddenly felt herself slipping away to that other place, rising above her body to somewhere in the top of the shelter looking down. She saw the pale, muscular length of his body as he knelt beside her. His head was dark, and she realized he was wearing a ski mask.

His fingers, warm and rough at the same time, moved softly over her breast. She continued to breathe deeply, slowly as her hand palmed the wire between her fingers, curling as if in slumber.

He gently pried her legs apart. He'll see the cable, she thought, but he didn't appear to notice the shadow of the cable running beside and underneath her.

From her mental vantage point above, she watched the exploration of her body. He stroked her thighs, licking the bowl of her navel, the feathery touch of his fingers making her nipples perk involuntarily. He made a low growling noise, moving up her, tonguing and sucking, spreading her legs further apart with his knee. Every now and then, he would stop, pick up the camera and take a picture.

He leaned over, setting the camera down above her shoulder.

Now!

Arching upward she struck, aiming the wire into his eye. There was a strange popping sound as she sunk it deep, followed by her thumb. He screamed, high and thin, and she tossed the loop of cable around his neck. He tried to rear back but she pulled him in to her breast, pulling the crossed cable tighter and tighter as far as her cuffed hands could go, kicking downward on the other end attached to her ankle.

He coughed, fighting for air, and punched at her face and body. She scissored her legs around his waist, pulling him further down so he couldn't get leverage, redoubling her efforts to pull on the cable. He flailed, rearing back, and then headbutted her in the chin. Her mouth filled with blood.

He thrust forward, gaining a breath as he sank his teeth into her collarbone. Lei screamed but didn't let go. He threw himself to the side and rolled, trying to lose her, but now she was on top. She heaved backward on the cable, pulling in the slack from his movement. She pulled and kicked with the leg clipped to the cable: pulled and kicked, pulled and kicked, her hands becoming slippery.

His fingers clawed at his neck, scrabbling for a hold. He bucked and heaved, but she hung on with all she had, hearing a fierce low growling that came from her own throat.

His face was hidden behind the knit of the mask but for the wire rising out of the weeping, ruined eye. His heels drummed on the ground, his chest slippery with their shared blood. He bucked feebly. She felt the deep shudders of his dying body between her thighs.

He'd stopped moving for some time when she finally let go.

She collapsed next to him, breath heaving, body trembling and bathed in sweat. When she'd mustered enough strength, she rose on her elbow to look down into the black knit covering his face. Her wrist throbbed like a bass drum but she persisted, rolling the mask up and off his purpling, congested face. It was Jeremy Ito.

She crawled over to his backpack. His cell phone was in the side pocket and she watched herself, still floating above her body, punch in the number she had memorized.

"Jeremy, what's up?"

"This isn't Jeremy," she said. "It's Lei."

"Lei. Why are you on Jeremy's phone?"

"It's him," she said. "He did it." Her teeth began to chatter.

"Lei! What the hell's going on? You're scaring me!"

"I killed him," she said. "Come get me, please." Shivers racked her body, and her teeth clattered like castanets. "I'm at the Mohuli`i crime scene."

"On my way," Stevens said. "Hold on."

"Okay," she said, in a small voice. The phone went silent, and she closed it. The snapping sound sucked her back into her body.

Chapter 39

The dog licking her face brought her up out of a deep well of medication-induced sleep. My girl's okay, she thought. She put her arms around Keiki's big, solid body, burrowing her face into her fur, savoring the warmth and safety of her bed. Even the doggy smell was heavenly. Keiki had been found trapped in the steel gardening shed. She'd been Tased but seemed no worse for it.

"I hate to interrupt this love fest." Stevens's voice. She opened her eyes. He was at the foot of the bed on the futon, sitting up with the covers around his waist. "How're you feeling?"

"Glad to be alive," she said huskily. "Love the pain meds."

"You should've stayed in the hospital."

"I hate those places. Nothing so wrong with me that a little first aid and some sleep won't cure."

"Yeah. That's what you said last night." He jumped up with lithe grace. "I'll go make some coffee."

She stroked Keiki with her good hand, staring at the ceiling. The previous night was blurry except for a few moments— Stevens and several squad cars arriving. Stevens wrapping her in a clean blanket, taking off her restraints. The flash of crime scene photos being taken even as she was helped to the ambulance. Lying on the gurney, Stevens beside her, holding her hand.

"You should be at the crime scene," she remembered saying.

"I am," he'd replied.

The cast on her arm felt stiff and hard. Her wrist had indeed been broken. Pain throbs echoed the struggle from various points on her body. She tried not to remember it, thinking instead about giving her statement to Stevens and the other detectives.

Thank God this whole thing was finally over. She closed her eyes again, feeling tears well up. She didn't know why she was crying.

"Sit up," Stevens said, his voice brisk. He was carrying two steaming mugs of coffee. She scooched herself upright, whacking her pillow into shape behind her with her good hand. He handed her the coffee and sat in the folding chair he'd set in the space beside her outsized bed. She took a sip.

"Mmm. Strong."

"You're gonna need it," he said, reaching over to stretch a curl out, watching it spring back into the matted mass around her face. "The Lieutenant wants us to do a press conference at 11:00 AM."

"Oh my God. I can't," Lei said. Keiki stiffened and growled at the terror in her voice.

"You won't have to say much, just stand there in your dress uniform with a sling on your arm, look heroic. I'll be making a statement too."

His voice was grim, and she reached out to touch his arm. "I'm so sorry, Michael. He was your partner, your friend."

"Obviously not." He looked down. One of his hands sported bruised, scratched knuckles. "I had to punch the wall because I couldn't do it to his face. I just keep kicking myself—there were clues if you knew to see them. The photo we found on

Reynolds's hard drive, the ring. He planted both, and if I hadn't been so eager to close the case, I would have remembered that not only was he computer savvy, his hobby was photography. All along he was trying to point the investigation towards Reynolds."

She rubbed his arm, little circles. He looked down, traced the bruise on her wrist from the cuffs with the tip of his finger.

"You okay?" he asked softly.

"I don't know." The tears she'd been holding back welled, dropped on the cast she held over her stomach. "I've never killed anyone before." She sniffed loudly, wiped her nose on her sleeve. "I'm alive, and that's what counts. Alive, and not raped."

"Yeah." He put his arm around her, pulled her over in a rough hug. His voice was harsh with emotion. "I'm glad you did what you had to do. I just wish I could have done it for you. I figured you were missing when I called and your phone kept going to voicemail. I went to the house and found it in the driveway. I knew he'd just outwaited us then. I was going crazy."

She shuddered, a flash of memory making her shut her eyes. "God—I hope that was the last time I ever have to kill someone. And it's not like I got to shoot him. It was gross, so up close and personal, both of us naked . . I didn't have time or room to think about my plan not working, but it almost didn't work."

"You did what you had to do," he repeated. "And I'm proud of you." Abruptly he got up, paced back and forth. "Guy was the worst kind of scum, a police officer preying on women. It's going to take me awhile to stop wishing I could be the one to kill him." He scrubbed his hands through his hair in that familiar gesture, took a breath. "I'll be back to pick you up at ten-thirty. Oh, and after the press conference you have an appointment with Dr. Wilson."

"That was inevitable, but I'm not sure I'm ready to talk about it."

"Lieutenant's orders," he said, leaning down to give her a kiss on the forehead. "See you soon. Put your game face on." He hooked his jacket off the chair and closed the door behind him.

It seemed like only a short time later she was standing in front of the police station behind a lectern, surrounded by bristling microphones, lights shining in her eyes. It wasn't hard to look pale. She leaned on Pono for support.

"Officer Texeira was abducted two nights ago," Lieutenant Ohale started off. "She was able to overpower her assailant and he is now deceased. We then searched his home, and have found proof that he not only killed Haunani Pohakoa and Kelly Andrade, but was responsible for a series of kidnap rapes that began on Oahu and ended here with the recent kidnapping and murder of another police officer from Pahoa. The perpetrator's name is Jeremy Ito and he was a detective here in Hilo."

The crowd of reporters exploded with questions, and he raised his hands and outstretched them, Moses calming the Red Sea.

"And now if you'll settle down, Detective Stevens will take questions."

Stevens replaced him, taking questions from the crowd. Pono sheltered Lei with his bulk, and then steered her by the elbow through the reporters as the press conference ended. He pushed open the double glass doors of the station and walked her to her cubicle.

She held court for a while in her creaky office chair with the officers that stopped by. It seemed Jeremy had not been well liked, and she nodded and smiled as different staff came up to tell her "something was off about him," and how glad they were she had survived. Finally Lieutenant Ohale shooed her visitors away.

"So of course you know you're on admin leave until your investigation wraps up. Take it easy, get better. Now it's time to go see Dr. Wilson. No arguments," he said as he hoisted her up gently from her chair, giving her an affectionate pat that pushed her down the hall.

She walked to the office and seemed to fall into Dr. Wilson's arms as the psychologist opened the door.

"Thank God you're alive. Come in here and tell me all about it." And Lei did.

Chapter 40

L ei showered, letting the hot water pummel the hurts on her body, careful with the plastic bag that kept her cast dry. Getting out of the shower, she grimaced at the ragged bite on her collarbone, and swallowed one of the antibiotics the doc had sent home with a swish of water. She daubed the oozing wound with ointment and re-covered it with a big, square band-aid. It looked like it was going to leave a scar.

Her lip was puffy and split where she'd bitten it, and bruises peppered her torso where Ito had punched her during the struggle. She stripped off the plastic bag on her arm and slipped on a silky tee shirt that managed to cover all the bruises.

She wanted to look as nice as she could—Stevens was on his way over for dinner.

She was checking on a pan of reheated, roast *kalua* pork from Aunty's restaurant when the doorbell rang. She glanced at herself in the mirror next to the front door and was not reassured. After checking the peephole, she opened the door, her heart racing.

"Hi Michael. Thanks for coming."

He held up a bottle of wine. "Medicinal purposes."

"Thanks." She took it, laughed. "I'm really going to enjoy this with my Vicodin."

"You'll have a helluva hangover." He followed her into the kitchen. "Got a present for you." He set the bulky bundle he had been carrying down on the table. "New gun. Thought you should have a backup."

"Michael!" She hugged him, hard. "That's what I like about you—you bring me alcohol and a gun. I can't think of anything I want more."

"I can," he said softly, intent. He raised her arms slowly from his waist and put them around his neck, then pulled her in tight, his hands cupped around her bottom as he lowered his head to hers. She hardly noticed her bruised mouth as their lips met, asking and taking.

She'd wanted him so long, and his touch seemed to erase those other hands that had left invisible prints on her. She pressed into him, her hands filling with the springy texture of his hair, the broad column of his back.

"You're too short," he said, bending over, smoothing her body with long strokes. She felt him learning the shape and feel of her.

"You're too tall," she said, straining upward to reach his neck with her mouth. He pushed her back and lifted her up onto the counter. She wrapped her legs around his waist, rubbing against his jeans.

Hungry to feel the roughness of his chest against the curves of hers, she unbuttoned his shirt, sliding her hands in around his waist, stroking the contoured muscle. He made a low noise and whispered in her ear, kissing and nipping as he peeled her shirt off over her head, pausing to look at the bandage on her collarbone with a grimace.

He kissed the bruises on her torso gently. His tongue was a balm as he bent her back over one arm, his other hand caressing her. Lei closed her eyes and gave herself over to the waves of sensation pooling in her lower body, need stabbing almost like pain. Everywhere his mouth and hands touched felt like it was being healed, coming alive.

She sat upright again, keeping her legs tight around his waist as she trailed her fingertips and tongue over all she'd longed to touch and explore: the hollow of his throat, winged line of his collarbone, the tender whorl of his ear.

When neither could stand it any longer he carried her to the bed. The last of their clothes came off and passion made him clumsy with the condom, but when he slowly moved into her, cradled in the frame of his arms, she felt something entirely new.

Safe.

It was a long time later when she raised herself on her elbow.

"I didn't know I could do that," she said wonderingly. "Or that you could do that. Whichever."

He lay as though felled, but a rumble of laughter came up from somewhere deep.

"Told you I'd make you scream." He'd whispered it in her ear in the kitchen.

"I did not." She smacked his shoulder.

"Ask the neighbors," he said, his eyes still shut but a little smile on his mouth. She tugged a bit of chest hair but he only rolled over.

"C'mon. Dinner's ready," Lei said. The smell of her aunt's cooking had filled the house.

She washed up and pulled on her old kimono before padding back into the kitchen and dishing up the meal. Stevens appeared in the doorway, clad only in his jeans. He gave a jaw-cracking yawn.

"If I wasn't so hungry I'd have stayed in bed," he said, finding a wine key in one of the drawers. He splashed the pale liquid into a pair of jelly glasses as Lei set their full plates on the table—steaming kalua pig slow-roasted in an underground

oven, rice, and limp, overcooked green beans. He prodded
these with his fork.

"You distracted me," she said, picking up her glass. "To
my aunty's cooking."

"I'll drink to that."

"So."

With dinner over, he refilled their glasses.

"I love presents," Lei said. She pushed her dishes aside
and pulled the sturdy molded plastic gun case over.

"You were lucky. They only had one left."

She popped the clasps and opened it. Nestled in the gray
foam was the clean, matte black shape of a new Glock .40.

"Oh," she said, sighing, "so pretty."

She took it out, checked that the magazine was removed,
racked the slide a couple times to make sure the barrel was
empty, and dry-fired it, disengaging the slide and setting the
grip, slide and firing pin mechanism in a neat row.

Stevens watched, sipping his wine as she got up and
brought a small zippered carryall to the table out of one of the
drawers. She took a moleskin rag and rubbed each piece of
the gun; padded a steel rod with a cloth patch and rammed it
back and forth in the barrel; and lightly touched the top four
points of the slide track with gun oil, polishing the excess off.
She blew the interior of the grip out with compressed air. Her
movements quick and economical, she reassembled the gun,
racking the slide a couple more times just to hear the smooth
snick it made, dry firing and enjoying the fat muffled click of
the trigger. Grinning, she turned to him.

"I love this gun. Nothing works for me like a Glock."

"Works for me too," he said, hooking her neck to pull her
into a kiss that left the Glock dangling, forgotten, from her
hand. "That was the sexiest thing I've ever seen," he whispered.

The crowing of wild roosters heralded the morning. Mynah
birds squabbled in a nearby mango tree and wafting plumeria

perfume tickled her nose as Lei misted her orchids, savoring being in her little backyard and the well-being that filled her body in spite of its injuries.

The orchids were a little dry and leathery, but they looked like they would recover from the brief stint of neglect when she'd been too distracted to care for them. Keiki sniffed around the edges of the yard, checking the perimeter.

"Good morning."

She turned, mister in hand, and smiled at the sight of Stevens in the doorway, a mug of coffee in his hand and jeans riding low on his hips. It was a replay of a scene not long ago, one she'd been too distracted by Mary's death to appreciate.

She didn't realize she was still staring until he came down the steps, set the coffee on the orchid bench and kissed her thoroughly.

"You can't look at me like that without paying the price."

"Okay," she said meekly, and let herself be led back inside. It was the first time she remembered ever being meek, and it felt damn good.

Later, Stevens got out of the shower, sighing as he toweled his hair.

"I hate to go to work," he said. Lei watched him from the rumpled bed. He put on his low-key aloha shirt, chinos, a pair of tan running shoes. Threaded his belt through the loops, holstered his weapon, clipped his badge on, pocketed his cell phone and wallet.

"Duty calls," he said. "Get some rest."

She continued to watch, fascinated by the brisk, economical movements. He put his hands on his hips.

"You okay?"

"Can't remember ever watching a man get ready for work before."

"You telling me this is your first morning-after experience?"

"Yeah."

"Damn. I got to be sure to do things right then," he said, and crawled across the bed to kiss her some more. She was still smiling when the door clicked shut behind him.

Chapter 41

That afternoon, Lei held her arms straight out, the new Glock level, sighting down the barrel. Fortunately her trigger finger was on her good hand. She squeezed and shot out the center of the hanging target in a circle of neat round holes. Both the kickback and report were more than she remembered, and her broken wrist thumped a protest.

Screw physical therapy, she thought. This will strengthen my wrist just fine, and boy, do I love the practice.

She lowered the weapon, expelling the empty clip, ramming in a full one. Felt a tap on her shoulder, turned. It was Ray Solomon from class, hazel eyes crinkled in a smile behind clear safety goggles.

"Hey, there." She pried up the soundproof earmuffs, dropping them around her neck. "Howzit going, Ray?"

"Hey, yourself. Where you been, girl?" He gave her a brief hug, pointed to her cast. "Problems?"

"Long story," she said. She holstered the Glock. They exited her booth into the foyer area. "Didn't know you came here to shoot."

"Not many places besides here," Ray said. "Hilo Gun Club's the only show in town. So what's the story?"

"Tangled with a perp." Lei shrugged. "I'm on recovery leave."

"Hope he got the worst of it."

"No worries there. So what's new?"

"Not much. Still trying to get on the force. Can you put in a word for me? I've got an interview with Lieutenant Ohale next week."

"Maybe." She cocked her head. "Anything I should know about your shady past?"

"No." He laughed deprecatingly. "I got busted selling weed as a senior in high school. They decided to make an example of me, sent me to juvie for 6 months."

"That's too bad. Learned your lesson, did you?"

"Of course."

"So where you been? Haven't seen you at class lately."

"Family problems. Had to work some things out." She wished she could see his eyes, but it was hard to tell behind the safety goggles. "Hey, I'm about done. Want to get something to eat?"

"Thanks," Lei said, "but I just put in another clip. I've got to get in at least an hour. I'm so rusty."

"Some other time." He swung his equipment bag up onto his muscular shoulder. "See you around."

"Bye."

She watched him go, frowning a little as he brushed out through the double doors of the firing range and crossed the parking lot, heading toward a charcoal-dark Toyota Tacoma.

No way. Another dark Toyota truck?

Her heart slammed against her bruised ribs. Oh yeah, she'd killed the guy, and it wasn't Ray Solomon.

He looked back as he climbed into the cab and she quickly bent over, pretending to be tying her shoelace. She then ran to the window and looked at the license plate as the truck pulled out, memorizing it and taking her cell phone out of her windbreaker pocket.

"Pono. You at your desk?"

"Yeah. What's up?"

"Can you run a plate for me? HLMGH44."

"Just a minute." She heard keys clicking. "Ray Solomon, age twenty-six. High school record for dealing in California—nothing current."

"Would that keep him off the force if he tried to become a police officer?"

"Probably. It's a felony conviction at age seventeen. Looks like they gave him maximum sentence. What's this about?"

"Not sure. Ran into him here at the firing range." She put her finger in her ear against the muffled thump of shots from the soundproofed booths. "He's in my Criminal Justice class. He's asked me out a couple times, and he's just—a little off."

"You got the stalker though. Not every guy in a dark Tacoma is a criminal, sister. Sure you don't need to go see Dr. Wilson again?"

"Already did. Never mind." She shut the phone abruptly. Her gut was out to lunch on this one. She went back in to use up her ammo.

She put Keiki on her leash and set off on an afternoon walk, her cast stabilized in the sling the doctor had sent home. The straps from the sling and the holster rubbed uncomfortably and her stride was slow as she made her way down the block, keeping her casted arm clamped over the gun and handling the leash with her good hand. Leaving the gun home had somehow seemed like a bad idea.

The prevailing wind that usually blew Kilauea Volcano's belching smoke out to sea had changed direction today, and thick 'vog' had settled over the town, a gauzy haze that softened the edges of everything.

She went along her favorite route beside the Bay, watching the mynahs hopping on the grass of the park. The light breeze clattered through the leaves of the coconut palms, a soothing harmony with the hushing of waves against the rocks. She found a place to sit on the jetty, perched on a boulder. Keiki gave a sigh and settled her big square head on her paws, watching the restless, turquoise water.

Her phone buzzed in her pocket and she dug it out with her good hand. It was an unfamiliar number.

"Hello?"

"Lei? It's Wayne. Your dad."

"Oh, hi." Long pause. She remembered she had given him her number. She stared, unseeing, at the foaming surf. It was weird hearing his voice after so long, weird that he could just call her—and yet not unwelcome.

"What happened with the Changs?"

"Oh yeah." She'd forgotten about that. "The stalker was somebody else. He came after me, and . . . I killed him."

"What, seriously? Are you okay?"

"Few bumps and bruises. Broken wrist. But he got the worst of it." She squeezed her eyes shut to block out the memory of Jeremy Ito's ruined eye, the wire rising out of it.

"Thank God you're all right. Well, I guess that was a dead end then."

"Yeah."

Awkward silence. Finally he said, "I'm glad nothing I did had anything to do with you getting hurt. I was really worried about it. Those Changs are bad news."

She nodded. Remembered he couldn't hear that and tried to speak but nothing came out.

"Well I just thought I'd follow up. I don't expect you to say anything. Just know I—miss you." He hung up.

A criminal, flawed, he was still her dad. He missed her. That felt good.

That reminded her to call Aunty Rosario, whose exclamations and machine-gun questions took up the whole walk home. Love and family. Sometimes it was just a pain in the ass.

"Hey Lei!" Tom Watanabe came up his driveway toward her, his brow furrowed.

"Hey, Tom."

"What happened to your arm?"

"Tangled with a perp." She was beginning to like her brush-off line.

"I'm worried about you. Can you come in for a minute and talk?"

"Okay. Just for a minute." It was time to get this over with anyway, she thought with an inward sigh.

"I'm sorry, maybe I forgot to mention it, but I have a cat. She'll freak if Keiki comes in."

"Okay," Lei said, and made the big Rottweiler sit. She tied the leash around the railing of the porch. She went in through the minimalist gloss of his front room, following him into the kitchen. He ran a glass of water from the refrigerator filter and handed it to her.

"It seems like there's a lot of drama going on. You sure you're okay?"

She set the water down on the granite island without drinking it.

"The stalker thing is over, so yeah, I'm okay. Just need to recover. Listen, I don't think I've been fair to you."

He smiled, a baring of teeth.

"Oh, here it comes. The part where you tell me, 'let's just be friends.'"

"I guess. I like you, just not . . . that way."

She reached for the glass of water.

"Sure I can't change your mind?"

"I'm sorry. I'm just not interested." Lei set the glass down with finality.

"It's too bad, you know," he said conversationally.

"What do you mean?"

"That you won't give me another chance. I could've helped you."

"Helped me? I don't need help."

"Really? The way you lock yourself in, like that'll keep you safe? The way you run like you could get away? The way you carry a gun just to go for a walk?" He gestured to the bulge under the thin windbreaker. "It's pathetic. All your efforts, and you couldn't catch someone who might be just trying to show you how vulnerable you are, that you need somebody."

Lei pushed away from the counter. He was blocking the door of the kitchen.

"I don't have to listen to this." Her heart thudded as she put her hand on the Glock. "Let me out. Now."

"Your loss," he said. He took one step to the side. She edged past him, backing out through the house, but he didn't follow as she went down the steps and untied the dog. Her cell rang, a jarring vibration as she jogged toward her house. She transferred the leash to the hand with the cast and dug it out of her pocket.

"Hello?"

"You sound out of breath." Stevens.

"Running," she huffed.

"Sure you should be doing that with your bruised ribs and all?" His voice was sharp. The question made her realize there was indeed a stabbing pain in her side, one she had been ignoring since she'd left her house. She slowed to a walk.

"Probably not."

"Thought we could go on a real date tonight."

"Okay."

"Such enthusiasm. I'll pick you up at seven. Wear something nice."

"I'll see what I've got." She closed the phone and concentrated on getting home and locking the door behind her.

Chapter 42

They sat at a corner table of the Banyan Tree, Hilo's finest dining restaurant. The oceanfront view reflected gleaming torches on the water. Stevens raised his glass of expensive chardonnay.

"To new beginnings and a real date."

Lei clinked her glass against his. She sipped the crisp wine. It still hurt to smile, and her ribs ached from running. Her thoughts spun like confetti.

"You look beautiful."

"That's what you said when you picked me up." She'd anchored her hair on top of her head, leaving curls dangling. Her ears were heavy with the unfamiliar weight of glowing Tahitian pearls, Aunty's graduation present. She wore her only dress, a tropical print wrap that hugged her lean curves and managed to cover the bandage on her collarbone.

He reached for her good hand, stroked the back of it.

"Something's wrong."

"No." She pulled her hand away. "Everything's wonderful. Thanks for doing this."

"Cut the crap, Texeira. What's up?"

"I'm sorry. I don't want to ruin our first date." He watched as she took a fortifying gulp of wine. "Some stuff happened today," she said.

"Like what?"

"Had the 'let's be friends' talk with Tom Watanabe, and he didn't like it."

"Nobody ever does."

"No, but he said some things that made me think . . . maybe he's been up to something. I'm probably just being paranoid." She fiddled with her napkin, smoothing it, avoiding his eyes.

The waiter came and gave them a pause as they ordered. The minute he left, Stevens turned to her again.

"What did he say?"

"He said maybe someone was just trying to show me I needed help, needed someone to look out for me."

"Asshole."

Lei sneaked a glance over at Stevens' bunched jaw and tight fingers on the stem of his wineglass.

"I also met a guy from class at the gun range. He was a little off too." She pulled on a curl and it wrapped around her finger. "I'm sure Dr. Wilson would say I've got some post trauma stress or something."

"You went for a run and to the gun range two days after an attack that should have put you in the hospital? I thought you'd be home in bed like any sane human."

A long silence.

Lei looked out at the ocean. The sunset had faded and the moon trailed silver footprints over the ruffled water.

"This is going to be hard, if you won't take a little bit of care of yourself," he said.

"I'm fine. I need to get back on the horse, get back to work."

"What you need to do is chill out. If you're going to keep doing whatever you think of without caring about your safety .

. . it's going to be hard." He sat back, picked up his wineglass. "It already is hard."

"I am who I am," Lei said, in a small voice.

"Do you have any idea what it was like for me to ride in that ambulance with you, to see what he did to you, how close you came to being raped, even murdered? Disappear on me, fly to see your dad in prison . . . God knows what kind of characters he associates with . . . Run around town with all these injuries . . ."

Lei looked at her hands. She felt herself detaching, flying away, her vision dimming to a pinprick. She grabbed her arm above the cast, digging her nails in, trying to stay present.

He's not going to hurt me, she told herself. No matter how angry he is, he won't hurt me.

Her vision expanded. She breathed, slow breaths in and out. He was still saying something.

"It's because I care. I know you've got issues, and just getting through this situation has taken all you've got—let alone worrying about how I'm dealing with it. I know that. But . . . I can't help it. I want you to remember me, too, and include me. I need you to, or this thing," he said, gesturing between them, "isn't going to last."

"I'm just not used to having to include someone else." Lei firmed her chin. "I don't like you being mad at me, but sometimes I'm gonna do what I need to do—and I'm sure you're going to be pissed off. But I'll try to be more careful and keep you in the loop."

"Okay, I said my piece." He sighed, sat back. "Can't help my caveman instincts, I want to kick the crap out of anyone who threatens my woman. Gotta remember she can do her own ass-kicking." He raised his glass. "To you, Lei."

Lei sipped uneasily, but he didn't seem to be making fun of her. She reached across with her good hand to touch his. As usual the right words wouldn't come.

"You know what?" His mouth turned up on one side, a rueful smile. "Can't say I wasn't warned."

This time she was the one to take his hand.

"I'll try to make it up to you."

Stevens kissed her goodnight at the door when he dropped her off, insisting she go to bed early. She watched him drive away and remembered she'd forgotten the mail. She took the letters out, rifled through them—a few bills and the now-familiar plain white envelope with **LEI TEXIERA** on it.

"Impossible," she said aloud, going up the dark stairs. "He's dead."

She ripped the envelope open. Her eyes scanning the street, she looked briefly down at the sheet of computer paper she'd unfolded.

This note was different.

She went up the porch and into the house, relocking and rearming the door. Keiki greeted her, whuffling and bumping with her head, but Lei ignored the dog. She flicked on the light, sat down at the little kitchen table and opened the folded paper.

Her own childhood face looked up at her—a photocopy of the school snapshot from third grade, the year she was nine. An aureole of curly hair framed an olive-skinned, lightly freckled face with tilted almond eyes and a too-wide smile. The note, all in caps, glared up at her from beneath.

YOU ARE DAMAGED GOODS AND ALWAYS WILL BE. SEE YOU SOON.

Lei barely made it to the bathroom before throwing up. She clung to the toilet, heaving well past when anything was left, and then sat back, her head resting on the cool porcelain of the tub. She crawled over and locked the door, then curled up on the bath mat, clutching her abused ribs, rubbing her aching stomach, a keening in her throat echoed by Keiki's whining outside the door.

Damaged Goods. That's what he'd called her. D.G. for short. He had even called her that in front of her mother, telling Maylene it meant Dear Girl.

Memories roiled up, images that she had stuffed down past knowing. She'd remembered that first time, the struggle even though he'd doped her with cold medicine, and the pain of things never meant for someone so small. That blank space in her memory had kept her from knowing anything more until now. It all crashed back on her with the simple phrase he'd used as he used her.

She longed to escape to that other place, but this time it didn't work. Like a broken film clip the memories ran. When she realized there was no way to stop him, she'd cooperated— and on some level she'd secretly liked the attention he gave her, the little presents, the protection from her mother . . . and when he left, she'd cried and missed him.

He'd said he loved her, and she believed it.

Damaged Goods. That was what she was. Shame and self-loathing swamped her and Lei retched some more, and went to bed.

Keiki barking, the deep bellow she reserved for intruders, penetrated the darkness of her dreams. She got out of bed and padded to the bathroom yelling, "Just a minute!"

Pale morning light did bad things to her complexion in the mirror and she couldn't meet her own eyes as she splashed water on her face and rinsed out her mouth. She went to the front door, put her eye to the peephole.

Michael Stevens stood there. He was holding a bouquet of flowers.

She turned and ran back to the bathroom, stomach heaving as she fell to her knees. Keiki ran back and forth, confused and whimpering.

"Lei! What's wrong?" She heard Stevens pounding on the door. She raised her head, yelled.

"Go away! I'm sick!"

The pounding stopped. She rested her head on the tub again, tears welling as she thought about Stevens, about the feelings she'd had before she knew what she really was.

Damaged Goods. That's my name. My destiny.

"Lei? You sure you're okay? Can I come in, help you or something?"

"No! Seriously, I'm just really sick. Please go away."

Keiki was staring at the front door, her ears cocked in anticipation. She gave a little greeting bark, recognizing his voice. First time she's ever done that, Lei thought, and it'll be the last.

She heard his footsteps walk back and forth on the porch, and then her cell rang, buzzing on the side table where she'd dropped it.

"Lei pick up!" he called. "Let me talk to you."

"No. Goddamn it, just go away, and let me be sick in peace!"

This heart-cry took the last of her strength, and she slammed the bathroom door and curled up on the mat, sobbing into a towel until no more tears came. It was just all too damn much.

She eventually got up, brushed her teeth, opened the bathroom door. The silence told her Stevens was gone. She knelt, gave Keiki a chest rub.She fed the dog and looked at the table. The unfolded paper seemed alive, a burning, pulsing wound. She put it in a Ziploc bag and stuck it in the freezer. She opened the front door to make sure Stevens was gone. The bouquet of flowers lay wilting on the welcome mat. She slammed the door, armed the house, and went to bed with a handful of Vicodin.

They'd been so sure Jeremy was the stalker! They'd found pictures of her on his phone—and her house at all hours of the day and night, as he tracked her routine. How he'd known about the bath thing she'd still wondered, and now she knew.

He wasn't the only guy stalking her.

Chapter 43

*P*ono finally got her to open the door a day later. He held up the browning flowers.

"These yours?"

She snatched them out of his hand.

"You look like shit," he said, following her into the kitchen.

"Thanks. I feel like shit."

"So what's up? Flu? Food poisoning?"

She stuffed the flowers into the overflowing trash can.

"I can't see Stevens anymore."

"That's some flu you got." Pono sat down, rubbed his lips thoughtfully with his finger. "Want to tell me what's really going on?"

"Only if you swear not to tell Stevens and you promise to keep this confidential. It's my case and I don't want him on it anymore."

"That's going to be tough. Man deserves an explanation. He can tell something's up, something worse than the flu."

"I'll deal with him—but you need to keep this confidential." She dug in the freezer, pulled out the Ziploc bag. Took the letter out, unfolded it.

"Nice smile." Pono sat forward. He touched the photo. "Who is this sick bastard? This the reason you have an alarm on your house and a Glock under your pillow?"

"The Glock's where it should be—in the holster hanging on the headboard." She took a deep breath, tapped the letter. "This sick bastard is Charlie Kwon. He was my mother's boyfriend when I was nine. He raped and molested me for 6 months. He broke up with my mom and she overdosed. That's when I went to live with Aunty Rosario."

"He calls you damaged goods. Bullshit—if you were damaged it's because he did it to you. No little kid signs on for that."

"It's complicated." Lei picked at her cast. "What this has done is made me realize I'm not fit to be in a relationship. That and I'm probably gonna meet up with this guy and kill him sometime soon. It's what I do. And frankly at this point I don't care if I go to jail for it."

"So do you think he's the one who's been stalking you?"

"I think there was Jeremy Ito. The notes, the panties—have been Charlie Kwon."

"So you were being stalked by two guys at the same time." Pono whistled. "Popular, you."

"Yeah, popular. What's wrong with me that I get all the sickos?"

"Stevens likes you."

"He's as sick as the others if he does. I'm damaged goods. Always have been."

"Shut up. All I know is, you been a good partner." He patted her shoulder.

Lei got a paper towel off the roll and honked her nose. "Thanks."

"We got to tell the Lieutenant about this. We thought your case was closed when you took Ito down."

Lei just shook her head, closing her eyes. Her brain didn't seem to be functioning.

"Got a beer?" Pono asked. "It's five o'clock somewhere." She got up and uncapped two, set one in front of him and took a long pull off the other. He put the letter away in the bag and now he tucked it inside his jacket.

"Going to sign this into evidence," he said, patting his pocket. "Need to lay the foundation for your defense in a future murder case."

She wished she could smile at his ironic tone but couldn't.

"I wish you didn't have to—that I could just burn the damn thing," Lei said.

"I'll also put out a BOLO on him. Bet he's using another name. Got a physical description?"

"I remember him as medium tall, wiry build, a good-looking mixed Chinese Filipino in his thirties. He had dark hair. Used to wear a goatee. He'd be fifteen years older now."

"Do you want to work with a sketch artist?"

His pupils seemed to loom up in front of her, expanding into darkness as she tried to picture his face.

"No. Not now. See what you can find on him in the computer first."

"Going to do a Temporary Restraining Order?"

"Would that keep me from assaulting him?"

"Works both ways," Pono smiled a bit. "But it would establish the stalking as pre-existing harassment when we do catch him. Then you can press charges for the sexual abuse."

"I don't plan to do that. Too hard to prove and it would ruin my rep in the department. But I guess I better do the TRO."

"I think you should press charges on the old stuff too. Think about it anyway. I'll start the paperwork when I get back to the station."

She nodded, sighed. "Do you miss me down there?"

"God, yes. That Jenkins is so 'Fresh Off The Plane' I can hardly stand being seen with him. Guy gets sunburned riding in the Crown Vic. I didn't know that was possible."

She laughed, more of a watery snort, took a sip of beer.

"You need to get back on the job," Pono said, leaning forward. "Chase some taggers, bang some heads. You'll feel better for it."

"You're probably right. Think the Lieutenant will let me come back early?"

"I've been following your case and it looks like it's wrapping up, though there's quite the media shitstorm because Ito was in the department. Just don't watch the news, it's better not to. Did you complete all the counseling?"

"No. Got two more sessions." She dreaded telling Dr. Wilson about this latest development, the complicated horror of her Damaged Goods past. Maybe she could bluff her way through the sessions. . . . She flinched, remembering blue eyes that always saw too much.

"I'll stop in the Lieutenant's office tomorrow, tell him you'd be better off on-duty. It'd help if you call him and request it."

"Will do." She pushed a sealed envelope toward him. "Can you give this to Stevens?"

"No way." Pono held his hands up, refusing to touch it. "You know the saying, 'shoot the messenger'? Well, that man is armed."

"Chicken." She pulled the envelope back. "I thought you had the stones to hand a guy a Dear John letter."

"I wouldn't do that for my sister back in eighth grade, and I'm not going to do it for you. Do your own dirty work." He stood up. "Okay. I'm taking this in and I'm going to try and get you back on active duty. I can't take one more day with Jenkins, so don't let me down."

"Thanks. I'll call you tomorrow." She followed him outside to his huge lifted truck, pulled up on the sidewalk.

She took the mail out of the box. He waited silently to see if there was anything new while she flipped through the slim pile. Nothing. She waved him off and he hopped up into the truck. Lei didn't feel safe even after she got back into the house.

Back in the kitchen, she cleared the beer bottles away into the recycling bag. Pono's bottle cap had been left on the table. She picked it up, put it in her pocket. Sat down and took out her phone, speed-dialed Stevens. She put her hand in her pocket and played with the cap as his phone rang.

"Lei. How you feeling?"

"Better, thanks. Listen, I have something to tell you."

"I don't like the sound of that. Let me come over, we'll talk in person."

"No. This is fine. I need to just say it." She took a deep breath, squeezed the bottle cap in her hand so the sharp crimped metal bit into her fingers. "I can't be with you. This was a mistake."

Silence.

"What's going on?" His voice was soft, kind. Easy tears welled in her eyes and she squeezed the cap harder. She felt one of the tiny ridges break the skin and she welcomed the pain.

"Nothing. I'm just not ready to be in a relationship. This has all been too much and I need you to leave me alone."

"Okay. I understand that." His voice was cautious now. "We can take all the time you need. In fact, I was thinking we needed to go back to the beginning a bit—that's why I brought flowers."

The tears spilled down her cheeks. She held her breath so she wouldn't sob, feeling blood welling into the palm clutching the bottlecap.

"No. No. I am just not right for you, Stevens. Leave me alone, I'm telling you. It's over."

She closed the phone with a snap, couldn't help throwing it away from her even as she cried out in dismay. It skittered across the table and crashed to the floor in two pieces.

She took her hand out of her pocket, went to the sink. The bottlecap had cut her palm. She held her hand under the sink, watching the blood well and disappear for a long moment. Then she took the bottlecap in the hand with the cast and dug it deliberately into the meat of her arm just below the elbow, dragging it downward.

The roar of pain washed over her, a burning that felt like absolution. She did it a few more times until all she could think about was the hot throbbing of her arm. She watched the blood trickle off her elbow into the sink, a hypnotizing watercolor of pinkening droplets as it melted into running water.

This crazy shit was the kind of thing you did when you were Damaged Goods.

The calm that follows pain came to her at last.

She blotted the cuts with a paper towel and striped them with antibiotic ointment in the bathroom, covered them with a band-aid. She also took care of the nasty bite on her collarbone, changing the bandage by looking in the mirror. She never once looked at her own eyes.

Lei changed into running clothes, went back into the kitchen and put the phone back together, anchoring the pieces with a strip of duct tape. Fortunately it still worked. She slipped the bottlecap into the pocket of her running shorts as she called the station and requested Lieutenant Ohale.

"Hey Lieutenant. Lei here. I'd like to request to come back on active duty."

"Yeah, Pono came by to see me already." She heard the creaking of his overworked office chair. "Good to hear from you. How's the wrist?"

"Getting stronger every day," she said with forced cheerfulness. "I did an hour of target practice yesterday and it held up fine." She looked at the wrist, ignoring the dull ache it gave her back.

"So what about those counseling sessions? And I wanted you to have that extra post-trauma debriefing after the incident with Ito."

"All done," she lied. She knew Dr. Wilson had turned in the evaluation paper in good faith, and guilt stabbed her before she ruthlessly quashed it. She couldn't afford to let the psychologist know what was going on. Her only chance to get back to normal was to get back to work and find Charlie Kwon herself.

"A few more days, okay? The investigation is wrapping up. When you do come back I want you to wear a sling. Last thing I need is some workmen's comp claim years from now."

"Deal," Lei said. "Thanks, Lieutenant." She closed the phone, snapped her fingers for Keiki, and took the truck out onto the road toward Volcano Park.

She couldn't be home when Stevens came by—he'd never accept just a phone call to break things off.

Chapter 44

Lei ran down the narrow path along the crater, Keiki
ahead of her, the dog's ears laid back. She'd chosen the
lush side of the park where massive fern trees arched
over the trail winding along the cliff's edge. The north side
of the volcano caught rain, and a primordial jungle of ohia
trees, wild ginger, and hundreds of ferns blanketed the slopes
while the south side stretched away in miles of raw black lava.
Knobbed guava roots reached up to tangle her feet, and off to
the right the caldera steamed gently, a vast black moonscape
hundreds of feet below the path.

The sheer scope of the scenery failed to distract her today.

The brittle calm from cutting herself had evaporated halfway
to the Park. Her mind churned with nauseating memories she
couldn't stifle. Over and over again Kwon's face loomed, his
pupils darkening her vision as she remembered and felt again
all the ways he'd raped her.

The drop off the massive cliff she ran along seemed to pull
at her, an almost magnetic tug. Her agony of self loathing, her
rage, her dim future as Damaged Goods could be over. How
easy would it be to just take a running leap out into space? She
pictured a cartwheeling fall, the vast distance to the bottom of

the crater more than high enough to make sure the jump was fatal. Her mind played the jump again and again as her body ran on autopilot.

Lei increased her speed, having to concentrate fully on the treacherous ground, the emptiness of total effort finally extinguishing the fantasies. She ran all out, oblivious to the exotic beauty of the setting.

God, help me. I can't take much more of this, she thought. The prayer echoed in her pulse. *God help me, God help me.*

Keiki began to lag, her tongue lolling. Lei pulled up at a vista area bordered by the service road, resting her hands on her knees as she caught her breath, looking out over the drop behind the low steel safety barrier, but no longer feeling that murderous pull so strongly toward the edge. With a pang of guilt, she wondered what would happen to her dog if she were gone. Keiki quested through the long grass for moisture, lapping at dewdrops.

"Sorry, baby," Lei panted. "I have a drink for you." She took a water bottle out of the pocket of her windbreaker, now tied around her waist. She poured water into her palm, holding it for the big dog to drink.

The shoulder holster was hot and itchy. She unbuckled it and laid it on a picnic table, sat on the table with her feet on the bench and let the wind off the caldera cool her face.

She noticed the sweet piercing song of the *apapane* at last, the rare, red honeycreeper that called the park home. She looked across the vast expanse of the volcano to the distant rim. A steam vent exhaled vapor that blew off the edge in a falling cloud. The sky arched overhead, a dome of soothing blue. All was right with the world.

She let go of Keiki's leash, letting the dog nose through the grass and flop down to rest after a good roll. She lay down on the picnic table, covering her eyes with her good arm. The vigorous exercise had finally broken through the turmoil of her mind.

A different memory came to her, a line from the Bible that she had read over and over in the dingy hotel rooms of her life with her mother, as if repetition would help her understand: *In the beginning was the Word, and the Word was with God, and the Word was God . . . And the light shines in the darkness, and the darkness does not comprehend it.*

Did that mean she was in darkness, because she didn't understand? But I think God is helping me anyway. I have to remember exercising works better than cutting myself . . . She sat up, sighing. Maybe it was time to make a new card that would help her remember.

A charcoal Toyota truck with heavily tinted windows rolled toward them, cruising slowly along the narrow blacktopped road. Lei sat up, reaching for the leash as Keiki stood, her ears pricked. The truck drew abreast of them, stopped. She tensed as the mirrored window rolled down.

This couldn't be good.

She saw a muted gleam of sunlight off a matte black metal surface, and launched herself off the table onto the ground.

"Keiki! Down!"

Lei saw the muzzle flash, heard the blast, and her dog yelped, twisting in the air as she fell.

"No!" Lei screamed. "Keiki, no!" Her ears rang from the shot, a jolt of terror and shock blasting through her system.

She reached up and caught the dangling strap of the holster, yanked it down into the grass beside her. The vehicle's door opened, a leg stepped out. She pulled her gun, and hunkered down in a slight depression beneath the picnic table. The wide crossbar blocked her view.

"Lei, come out." He knew her name.

She sighted around the crossbar and fired, hitting the jeans-clad leg. The man shrieked, falling back into the truck. She crawled forward, braced her elbows on the ground for another shot. The shooter's curses were cut off as he slammed the door. The engine revved, and the Toyota began to pull away.

She surged up from the grass, aiming for the front and side tires. They blew out with a satisfying boom. The truck ground into a turn. She heard the thunder of more shots fired back at her, but stood square, aiming for the other back tire. She blew it.

The Toyota kept going. She aimed for where the driver's head would be. The reflective back windshield broke inward, a grapefruit-sized hole, and the vehicle jerked to a halt.

She dropped flat again, belly-crawling to Keiki. The dog raised her head and whimpered. A bloody hole showed where the bullet had entered her upper chest and blown out the shattered shoulder in a much bigger crater, leaving a long oozing score down her side. Blood welled from the exit wound.

"It's okay, girl. I think you're gonna make it if we can get out of here," Lei whispered, laying her windbreaker over the wound and leaning on it. Keiki writhed but lay still as Lei brought her gun up again, sighting on the stalled vehicle.

"Drop your weapon and come out with your hands up," she bellowed, "and I promise I won't kill you."

"Screw you, bitch!" came from the truck, followed by more shots fired in her direction.

She crawled backward behind the picnic table, dragging Keiki by the hind legs. The dog let her, only whining a little as Lei situated them in the slight decline in the ground beneath the table. In one quick heave she stood up and flipped the table on its side facing the car. Shots fired, and this time splinters gouged Lei's shoulder as a bullet buried itself in the wood inches away.

She bit her lip to keep from crying out. She turned her head to look and felt her stomach lurch at the same time as pain hit like a red-hot poker. A spray of splinters stuck up like porcupine quills from her left shoulder.

She sucked a few breaths, getting the pain under control, and peeked around the table. She looked at the spot on the wood where the bullet had gone in. It hadn't made it all the way through the thick timber. The benches' angle threw the tabletop forward, but she was still hidden behind it.

She hunkered back down, putting pressure on Keiki's wound again. They'd be safe for the moment. She dug the cell phone out of the blood-soaked windbreaker. Thumbed it open and dialed 911. Reception was always iffy in the park, but the bars lit up. She identified herself, called for backup and an ambulance.

"Sorry, Officer Texeira, help's about ten minutes away," the operator said. "We'll notify the park service and maybe they can get there sooner. Take cover and we'll be there as soon as we can."

"Keiki, we're okay," she whispered in the dog's ear, closing the phone on the operator's protests to keep the line open. "Hang in there, baby."

The Toyota started up again. She stood up in a squat behind the table, trying to see what he was doing, her weapon out. There was only one operational tire left, but he could still get far enough away on the rims to escape on foot. The truck rolled forward, the blown tires rumbling and flapping against the road.

He wasn't going to shoot her dog and get away with it—it was that simple. She'd only used up five of the Glock's fifteen rounds.

She jumped up and dodged out from behind the table, running bent over, weaving. A wild shot blew up gravel that stung her legs as the Toyota rumbled away. She shot out the remaining tire but it kept going, picking up speed. She followed in an all-out run now and blasted the rest of the clip into the back of the cab.

This time when the truck stopped, the horn sounded, one long mournful blast.

She crouched, came along the driver's side. Grabbed the handle, popped the door.

"Come out with your hands up and I won't shoot!"

The driver was slumped against the door and, as it opened, he tipped out, falling out of the truck facedown. She recognized the back of his head, sleek as an otter's pelt. A bullet wound bled from the center of his spine.

She hauled him all the way out into the road by his armpits. He was alive, and blinked up at her, hazel eyes confused.

Ray Solomon.

Nothing surprised her anymore.

"Lei. I can't feel anything. I can't move my legs."

"Goddamn it Ray, I thought you were a friend!" She sat down next to him. He looked bad, his complexion gray and greasy, his body limp.

"Am I dying? I heard you feel cold when you're dying. I don't feel cold. I can't feel anything."

"You might be dying, I don't know. What the hell is going on?"

"We're Changs," he said. "Your old man killed our old man, and me and Anela thought we'd get him back, prove ourselves to Healani and the captains. I was never going to qualify for the police department. . ." His voice trailed off as the sound of sirens got louder.

"Wake up. Who else was in on this? Who is 'Anela'? Come on, confession of a dying man and all that." She slapped his cheek.

He'd passed out. She kicked away his Glock, fallen beside him, and got up and hurried back to Keiki. She was leaning on the wound when the park service, followed by response vehicles, rolled up.

She waved and yelled, "Priority first aid over here!"

The paramedics ran over with their bags. When they saw the fallen was a dog, they turned to leave. Lei pulled the empty Glock.

"Help my dog. *Now.*"

Detective Ross, getting out of his unmarked Bronco and responding to one of her emergencies yet again, waved one of the paramedics away and directed the other.

"Texeira's in shock. She didn't mean it. Help the dog, please. Lei, put the gun away, for crying out loud."

The paramedic did first aid as best he could, and when the ambulances loaded up, they were carrying two stretchers.

Stevens pulled up with Pono in the next wave of responders. He ran over to where Lei sat on the righted picnic table talking to Ross and Nagata, who'd put the two Glocks into evidence bags for Ballistics.

"Lei!" he scooped her into a hug, blood and all. She winced at the pain from the splinters in her shoulder and pushed him away.

"I'm okay." She saw the blood drain out of his face as he stepped back, obviously remembering she'd broken up with him.

"I was coming to talk to you at your house when I heard about it on the radio. How did this happen?"

"Remember I told you about the guy from my class and the gun range acting weird? He just rolled up on us and started shooting."

He tried to get Lei to look at him, moving to stand in her sightline—she wouldn't.

"I'm thinking he's been in on the stalking, maybe from the beginning." She noticed the alert gaze of Detective Ross and turned away. "Leave me alone."

"I need to take you in for an interview," Ross said. "Come this way."

The lanky detective gave her some support under the elbow as she staggered, exhausted. He let her sit up front in the Bronco as they headed out. She watched Stevens getting smaller in the rearview mirror as they drove away.

Chapter 45

L ei gave her statement in one of the interrogation rooms, accompanied by her union rep, a Budda-like Indian named Vishka. After a strenuous hour or two Ross and Nagata dismissed her to go speak to Lieutenant Ohale.

"He's been observing," Ross said in an aside as she left. He gave her good shoulder a kindly pat. "Hang in there. We're going to wrap this up soon."

Lieutenant Ohale was pacing his office. She didn't remember seeing him move that fast before. He pulled her in and shut the door.

"I've been pestered by your partner and Stevens every ten minutes. Thank God Ross and Nagata are done interviewing you so they can give their statements."

"Sorry for all the hassles," Lei said. "Can I sit down? I don't feel too good."

A fine trembling wracked her extremities. She'd only let the paramedics remove the splinters after she was sure Keiki was cared for, and their extraction had been excruciating. She was still in clammy running clothes, splattered with blood from various sources. Ohale gestured to one of the padded plastic chairs in front of his desk and she fell into it, wrapping arms around herself.

"So why didn't you come to me with this Chang conspiracy thing?" he said, still pacing. "The Changs are a big problem we've been trying to get a grip on for years, and there might have been something in your case we could use to nail them."

"To be honest, Lieutenant, I didn't take my dad's tip seriously." Plus, I was too busy having a nervous breakdown to think straight.

"Dammit, this situation deserves the full attention of the department. You helped crack the Mohuli'i case at considerable personal expense, and I appreciate the way you've got yourself out of some deep *shibai*. Taking down some Chang connections might also help with the bad PR we've had from the Ito mess."

"Something new happened with the last two stalker letters." She took a deep breath and told him about Charlie Kwon, and the only 'Anela' she knew, the waitress working for her aunt's restaurant. "Someone knows a lot more about me than just my cell phone number. Can I call my aunt? She's the only other person that knows about the molester, and I haven't heard from her since she went back to California."

She took a few minutes to call Aunty Rosario, verifying that she didn't know anything about Charlie Kwon's whereabouts and that Anela Ka'awai still worked at the restaurant. Rosario hadn't talked to anyone about Lei's sexual abuse except the social services worker and the therapists she sent Lei to, and no names had been mentioned.

"But I told you Momi knows, though," Aunty finally said. "I don't know, she might have told someone. Now put that police Lieutenant on cuz I like talk to him."

Lieutenant Ohale got on the line. He closed his eyes and pinched the bridge of his nose as Rosario gave him a piece of her mind in pidgin. When he was able to get a word in he told her that it looked like they were finally going to be able to solve Lei's stalking case and the full resources of the department were behind the investigation.

"I see where you get your fighting spirit," he said, handing her the phone at last. "Stevens is going to take you home."

"Okay," Lei said, and decided not to push her luck by asking for someone other than Stevens. Lieutenant Ohale walked her out to the SUV, which Stevens had idling in the parking lot. She got in and they sat in awkward silence for the drive across town.

"Can you turn off the AC?" Shivering, she plucked the stiffening, bloody shirt away from her body. "I can't wait to get a shower."

Stevens didn't try to talk to her; just turned on the heater full blast.

They pulled into her driveway and Lei ran in, punched in the code and hurried to the bathroom. She showered until her fingertips were pruney and the hot water was running cold.

She eventually had to come out, toweling her hair and wrapped in the old kimono.

"Thanks for giving me a ride home." She'd put the clothes she'd been wearing into a couple of Ziploc bags for the crime techs and she set those by the door.

"No problem." He was putting some food away in the fridge. She went to the couch and wrapped herself in the crocheted afghan Aunty Rosario had made. She wondered if she'd ever feel warm again.

"Did you hear about Ray Solomon?" she asked. Nagata had told her he was paralyzed, his spinal cord severed.

"Yeah."

"I wonder if he would rather have died," she said thoughtfully. "I think I would."

"He should have known better. If he'd surrendered when you told him to he'd still be able to wiggle his toes. I'm making some soup—want some?"

"Yes, please." Her stomach rumbled, as if hearing the conversation. She relaxed a little. It seemed like he wasn't going to talk about their breakup. "Has anyone figured out what Ray's relationship is with the Changs? He told me he was a Chang."

He stirred the soup on the stove. It smelled delicious and her stomach rumbled again.

"Yeah. Soon as you told them that Ross and Nagata started digging. Ross told me he's the illegitimate son of Terry "Hatchet" Chang. He was raised by his mother's relatives and took their name in California."

"I knew he grew up in California with relatives. No wonder he never wanted to talk about it."

"Chang was quite the ladies' man. He had four children with Healani, who are all grown and up to no good here in Hawaii, but scattered around California are several children by other women, including someone you put the Lieutenant onto." He put down the spoon, consulted a spiral notepad. "Anela Ka'awai."

"Anela!" Lei exclaimed. "She works at Aunty Rosario's restaurant—she's a waitress there. She must be the connection to Charlie Kwon—she must've got his name out of Rosario or Momi somehow, been spying on me. I bet she's the one who sent the panties, too, since Aunty gave them to me for Christmas."

"Sounds likely." Stevens reached for his phone. "I'll check with Ross and we'll have her picked up for questioning."

He made the call while stirring the soup and dishing it up. Lei listened with half an ear to the discussion as she spooned up the tasty chicken noodle, getting up and serving herself seconds. Eventually he closed the phone, spooned up his own soup.

"Not as good as Aunty's," he said.

"Good enough. I was hungry." She sat back, eating a cracker from the pile he had served with the soup. "What a long, god-awful day."

"Glad you're still here to bitch about it. That was some gunfight."

"I don't like you being on my case." She got up, cleared her bowl to the sink. "I don't mean to be rude, but I don't want you involved. It's a conflict of interest."

"Tell the Lieutenant, then," he said evenly. He opened a file on the table. She realized he hadn't looked at her all evening, and seemed to be holding himself in check with an effort. "He assigned me as backup for Ross and Nagata."

"Shit." She could hardly stand to look at him the pull toward him was so strong—and yet, she was so wrong for him.

"You know what?" He slammed the folder shut. "You seem to think you get to be the only one who has anything to say about this relationship. You seem to think that because some pedophile called you "damaged goods" and did a number on you, you're going to be ruined forever. What a load of crap. You think you're the only one who knows about pain and dysfunction?" He put his hands on his hips and finally looked at her, and when he did his Viking blue eyes were blazing. "I'm not buying that old shit. I know what we had, what we could have, and you're not getting rid of me that easily. That's what I came to tell you this afternoon while you were out trying to get shot in the park."

She couldn't think of a thing to say, and found herself scuttling to her room and locking the door.

"I'm going to be around whether you like it or not," he said through the closed door. "You're damaged. I'm damaged. So what. Now get some rest."

She climbed into bed, exhaustion and the safety he brought making it possible for her to snuggle deep into her silky sheets, relaxing. She closed her eyes, a smile curving her mouth. He might just be even more of a glutton for punishment than she was.

Chapter 46

Lei sat on the floor of the kennel the next day and stroked Keiki's big square head. The dog's eyes looked up at her trustingly as she played with the light-brown eyebrow patches, stroked her satiny ears. Keiki lay on her good side, a big white cone around her neck to keep her from biting at her bandages or the veterinary staff.

"She's looking good," Dr. Westfall said, pocketing the stethoscope he'd used to listen to her lungs. "The bullet came in through her chest but missed any organs, and exited the shoulder as you can see. The biggest concern right now is blood loss and infection. I've got her on a fluid drip of antibiotics. If we can keep her sedated and resting a few more days I think she'll be out of the woods. Later on, our concern will be the mobility she will have through that shoulder."

"Thanks, doc," Lei said, resting her cheek against Keiki's. The dog stuck her tongue out, trying to lick her, and she laughed blearily. "You have no idea how much this means."

"You'd be surprised," he said. "Animals can be closer than family."

"This one is family."

She didn't notice when he left the kennel, closing the door softly.

Nagata was waiting for her on the worn little porch when she drove up. She hurried to join him on the top step.

"So far your story is checking out about what went down in Volcano Park. Lieutenant wants you on admin leave until this whole thing gets sorted out."

"That sucks. I'm going to go nuts with that much time on my hands. What's happening with the Chang thing?" Lei rubbed the black stone in her pocket as she talked with the detective.

"We've had Anela picked up in California. Ross is flying back there to interview her. The local PD in San Rafael don't know enough about the situation to get us what we need. Ray Solomon's stable in the hospital and has admitted to doing the stalking campaign."

She'd thought as much, but it was good to have it confirmed.

"Anyone been able to find out anything about Kwon?"

"Yeah. He's in Lompoc Federal Prison for molesting some kids."

Lei rocked back as she absorbed this, standing on her porch. The weak sunlight of an overcast day gilded the tilted aluminum pole of her mailbox, the chipped cement steps, little rag of lawn. She was disappointed Kwon was out of reach. Part of her had fantasized pointing her Glock at his crotch and pulling the trigger.

"We still don't know how much the other Changs are involved in this and if Healani Chang has authorized any further action against you. Lieutenant would like you to come to the county safe house," Nagata said, adjusting his dapper button-down shirt as he went down the steps.

"No. They're sending Keiki home tomorrow, and she needs to be in familiar surroundings," Lei said, adjusting her sling as she walked down to the sidewalk beside him.

"Yeah, we know how you feel about that dog," Nagata said with a twinkle, as he got in the unmarked Bronco. "Okay. We're sending a uniform out to do sweeps by your house."

"Thanks."

She watched him drive away with a tremendous feeling of relief. She was almost sure whoever was left in the Chang conspiracy would think twice about messing with her now that she'd shot Ray. Lei hurried up the stairs into her cottage as Nagata drove away, punched in the code and re-activated it behind her.

Sighing, she went to the kitchen and ran herself a glass of water, drank it at the sink, then went and took a shower. Feeling a little better, she sat down at the little Formica kitchen table wrapped in her robe.

It was taking a lot of showers to feel like the blood had finally been washed off.

Stevens had left behind the file he had been studying last night. It was full of photocopied records on various members of the Chang crime family. She perused the records on the patriarch, Terence "Hatchet" Chang.

His rap sheet had close to fifty different drug, racketeering, and trafficking charges, many of which had been dismissed. Eventually he'd been convicted of felony drug trafficking and second-degree murder. His cause of death three years ago was listed as homicide.

No assailant name was listed on the criminal report, but Lei knew that name was Wayne Texeira and so did the Changs. She looked at the next of kin—Healani Chang, 221 Olomua Avenue in Hilo—the crime boss was guardian of the teenage boys she and Pono had brought in for tagging, and their neighborhood wasn't that far from hers.

I wonder what would happen if I just went there and talked to her, checked up on the boys. . . Send her a message I'm on to them. I might be able to clear this whole drama up myself.

Hiding out at the house was just not Lei's style.

Galvanized, she changed into running clothes, strapping on the shoulder holster with the old Glock since her new one was at Ballistics. She filled the pockets of the windbreaker with handcuffs, cell phone, and badge. Not that she was investigating or anything . . .

Lei got in the truck, feeling the hum of adrenaline in her veins as she turned the key. She remembered Stevens' lecture at the restaurant about taking care of herself, and felt a stab of guilt or maybe apprehension—none of the team working her case would think this was a good idea. But if she could just talk to Healani, maybe it could all be cleared up.

Lei threw the truck into reverse and pulled out before she could change her mind.

Chapter 47

The Chang house was in an older, poorly-maintained neighborhood. It was a dilapidated plantation style that had been added onto until it sprawled in all directions, filling a large corner lot. Several expensive cars were parked on the strip of dry, weedy grass, and a pit bull in the side yard barked ferociously as she pulled over onto the curb in front.

"Hey!" A dark figure appeared at the iron latticework security door as Lei got out. Her hand settled on the Glock. "What you doing in our neighborhood?"

She faced the house. Several other shadowy figures had clustered around the one addressing her.

"You talking to me?" Lei put cop in her voice.

"I said, what you doing here?" A reedy timbre—one of the teenagers.

"Coming to talk to Healani Chang. You got a problem with that?"

The door opened. It was the lanky kid she had run down in the alley. He was wearing a red do-rag on his head, gang colors.

"This is harassment," he said. Three other teens came out, ranging behind him, their arms folded over their chests as they tried on attitude.

"Chill out." Lei took her hand off her gun, opened her arms. "I just want to talk to your grandma. Is she home?"

"What you like with her?"

"Nothing. Just saying hi, and hope you boys are staying out of trouble."

Her nonaggressive stance and calm voice were working.

One of the boys turned and yelled back into the house, "*Tutu*! Get one cop out here like talk to you!"

A few seconds passed and the screen door creaked shut behind an older woman in a scarlet muumuu, frowning as she wiped her hands on a dishcloth. She made shooing motions.

"What you boys doing? Get back in the house!"

The teenagers scattered, only Do-rag pausing to give Lei the finger behind his grandmother's back.

Lei waited as the Chang matriarch came down the steps and stood a few feet away. She reminded Lei of a beautiful warship's figurehead after it had been through some long campaigns. She folded arms on an impressive chest and gave a good staredown.

"You Wayne's girl," she said. Healani Chang knew exactly who Lei was.

"Yes."

A long moment passed.

"Someone been making trouble for me. I like you make it stop," Lei said.

"You think I care?" Healani Chang laughed, a rusty cough. Lei stared into the woman's rich, chocolate-brown eyes.

"Please." She softened her voice. "I just want it to end. I got no beef with you. The cops will be all over you folks if they aren't already."

Healani said nothing, staring at her unblinking.

Lei turned away at last. It had been worth a try.

"Wait." The older woman's voice was husky, as if from smoking or yelling at the teenagers. "It was Ray, and that other girl Anela in the Mainland.Thought if they made trouble to you, took you out, I'd recognize them and give 'em a part in the family business. It was never going to happen. I told Ray if he kills a cop he brings trouble for all of us."

"Glad you see it that way," Lei said. Her ironic tone was lost on Healani.

"I was never going give nothing to Terry's bastards," Healani spat. "No matter what they did."

"The cops took Anela into custody and Ray will have trouble ever shooting anyone again. Know anything about Charlie Kwon? Any way he was involved?"

"Charlie, he my cousin." Healani nodded as Lei's eyes widened. "Sick pedophile who deserves to be in Lompoc and I hope he stays there a long time, but he still family. He always had it in for Wayne from going against him on the street, and he tol' us back in the day what he did to you and Maylene— getting her more hooked by the day until he broke her. From prison he gave Anela information she wen' pass on to Ray." Her flat eyes reminded Lei of a moray eel as she shrugged. "They thought they'd impress me with that? I play the game, but I play straight up. So I telling you I had no part in going after you, nor any of my children."

Lei struggled to assimilate this. Apparently Charlie'd got her mother deep into her addiction on purpose, and raping Lei had been a nice perk along the way. Her vision dimmed, but she dug her nails fiercely into her palm to anchor herself.

She'd deal with Kwon someday. It was a promise.

"So it's over."

"It was over when you shot Ray. Stupid bastard." The way the older woman said the word Lei knew she meant its literal meaning.

"All right, Mrs. Chang." She couldn't bring herself to call the older woman 'auntie' as would be customary. "Goodbye then."

Healani didn't answer, just looking at her with that basilisk stare as Lei walked toward the truck.

Her scalp prickled, a feeling like a thousand fire ants crawling over it. She always knew when someone had a gun on her, and as she glanced up into the doorway she could see Do-Rag waving a massive silver .357 Magnum at her. Talk about overcompensating. She walked away and got in the truck, pulling away sedately, ignoring the tingling at the back of her head.

She gunned the engine when she reached the end of the block and thumbed open her phone to call Nagata with the details. She'd taken a risk and for once it'd paid off.

Chapter 48

*E*verything was in its place: the paintings, the Japanese sand garden, the doctor in her lounger. This felt good to Lei and she breathed a little easier as she sat back on the couch in Dr. Wilson's office.

"Are you okay?"

"I don't think so."

"Where do you want to begin?"

"I don't know."

They sat in silence for a while. Lei took the black stone from Mary's memorial out of her pocket and rubbed it in both hands. It felt substantial enough to anchor her, a tiny black bit of the earth's blood that would always remind her of her lost friend.

"Okay then. Why don't you begin at the beginning. Tell me about child Lei."

"Why? What's that got to do with trauma debriefing, which is what I'm here for?" The old defensiveness raised its voice. Lei wished it would shut up.

"Everything has to do with everything else—you know that by now. So begin at the beginning, and it will lead to the end."

So Lei told about losing her father to a drug bust. About how that loss led her mother Maylene further into addiction, how Charlie Kwon came into their lives. What Charlie did and how he'd made her Damaged Goods.

Now she remembered everything, and couldn't dissociate anymore, even when she wanted to. In the midst of all that, she had been stalked by a rapist and murderer. A man who saw himself as an artist. A man who had betrayed all their trust, whom she'd killed with her bare hands.

She described how she'd been with and broken up with Stevens. She told about an illegitimate son named Ray who desperately wanted to prove himself worthy of inclusion in a powerful crime family. Ray recruited his half sister Anela into a revenge plot against their father's killer and his daughter.

Anela sent the panties and hair, and gleaned information about Lei's sexual abuse from Kwon in prison. Ray had masterminded the stalking campaign, and when that wasn't enough to impress Healani, he'd tried to kill Lei.

"I'm still missing some pieces. Where do the chases with the black truck come in?" Dr. Wilson asked. Lei dragged the tiny rake through the sand garden on the low table and set her stone in it, making a scene of simple beauty.

"I think the first time it was Ito. He was scoping out Mary or me, had taken his crime vehicle out to do that. The second time it was Ray."

"Too many dark Toyotas in this town," Dr. Wilson said. "Wow."

"Wow is right." Lei looked down at her hands. The right one was still in a cast, the webbing across her palm peeling and grubby, the left relatively unharmed. Her good hand—one of the only parts of her body that wasn't bruised, scratched, bitten, or broken.

"They're calling me Hurricane Lei in the station," she said. "Funny nickname."

"I heard."

"It seems to fit."

"It may not, anymore. That part is up to you now."

"I just want to . . . get back to normal. I feel like I am always going to be covered with blood." Lei shut her mouth, tightening her lips into a thin line. She saw Ito's ruined eye, Mary's bruises, or the faces of two drowned girls every time she closed her eyes. She pinched the web of her hand between her thumb and forefinger but it didn't help.

"You've had more than your share, that's for sure. Everyone is accounted for who needs to be, right?"

"I guess. Ross and Nagata interviewed Healani Chang. She's claiming that Ray and Anela acted on their own. I think we just have to accept that though I wouldn't be surprised if Healani instigated the whole thing." She fiddled with the cast. "I'd love to find Charlie Kwon someday and kick his ass, but yeah, I guess things are pretty sewed up . . . I just can't relax. I can't take enough showers to feel clean."

"That's an understandable post-traumatic stress reaction. Be patient with yourself. Let's talk every day until the flashbacks get better. It also might help to have your partner or Stevens stay with you for a little while."

"Stevens—I don't know what I'm going to do about him. I broke up with him and I don't know why I don't feel better about that."

"Ambivalence maybe?"

"I guess."

"Huh."

"I don't like the sound of that," Lei said with a little smile. "It's not a good sign when you say 'huh.'"

"Really? Well, I go back to my original thought—sounds like you're ambivalent about breaking up. Why did you?"

"Oh, damn." Lei looked at the time on her cell phone. "Looks like our time is up, Dr. Wilson. Catch you tomorrow." She got up and left with a little wave, pretending not to see the psychologist's ironic smile.

Lei pulled into her driveway and got out of her truck, walking around to the passenger side. She opened the extended cab door.

Keiki lifted her head. She was lying in the back passenger seat, the white funnel collar still in place, her side bulky with strapping. Lei lifted the big dog and struggled toward the front porch.

Just then Tom ran up, sweaty in his running clothes.

"Oh my God, let me help!" he exclaimed.

"Be careful," Lei cautioned, and Tom scooped Keiki into his arms. He carried her up the cement steps onto the porch, peering awkwardly over the big collar. Lei fumbled the key into the lock and they went inside.

"Holy crap, she's big." Tom panted as Lei punched in the deactivation code.

He carried Keiki into the living room and then knelt, lowering the Rottweiler onto the bed Lei had prepared for her, the futon covered with Keiki's favorite ratty old blanket. Lei settled the dog, patting and stroking her. Keiki tried to rise again and Lei pushed her back.

"Just rest, baby. Everything's going to be okay," she soothed.

"I'm sorry about the other day," Tom said in a low voice. "I was an ass."

He was still kneeling beside Lei as he patted Keiki's shining back. Lei had to grope to remember what he could be talking about. Ah, the confrontation in his kitchen.

"It's okay." She stood up. "Thanks for the help."

"What happened?" He stood up as well, dark eyes concerned.

"She got shot."

"Oh my God. Wow. Shit just keeps happening to you, doesn't it?"

"Yeah, I guess so."

"Well, let me know if I can help with anything."

"You sure showed up at a good time. Thanks for that." She followed him and closed the door behind him as he left. The unsettled feeling she'd had about him was gone—he was just an awkward guy.

Lei went into the kitchen, sighed as she looked at the blood orchid's fallen petals on the kitchen table. She picked up the neglected plant and the spotted one Tom had given her.

"Maybe now that the child molesters, stalkers, and rapists are out of the way I can go shopping," Lei said over her shoulder. "Order pizza on me, okay Keiki?"

She went out into the backyard. The last of day was dying out of the sky in a conflagration to the west as she walked across the fallen white pinwheels of plumeria to her orchid bench. She misted the plants and picked a branch of the fragrant plumeria flowers, careful to avoid the sticky white sap, put the flowers in a vase and called for pizza. She and Keiki deserved a treat.

The doorbell rang as Lei sat beside Keiki with the TV on. She got up and put her eye to the peephole. Stevens stood there, holding an orchid plant. Her heart picked up speed.

"Hi."

"Hey Lei. Heard a friend just got out of the hospital."

Lei laughed nervously and reached for the plant, but Stevens put the orchid behind his back. He went around her and into the house, kneeling by Keiki on her pallet. The big dog lifted her head. He put the plant down beside her.

"Brought you something," he said. The vivid spray of dendrobium looked like a flock of tiny yellow butterflies arcing over the dog. Keiki looked at him soulfully, then closed her eyes in bliss as he sat beside her, rubbing between her ears.

Lei ducked her head as she went into the kitchen. He'd told her he wasn't accepting their breakup, and it was hard to hold out against an underhanded tactic like bringing her dog an orchid. She had to smile as she opened Stevens a beer, brought it to him as he sat beside Keiki on the floor.

"She sure is happy to see you." The dog had fallen asleep with her head on his leg.

The doorbell rang again. Lei paid the pizza guy and brought the box over to the coffee table beside Stevens.

"Want some?" She opened the box.

"My timing is impeccable," he said. "We bachelors have a way of dropping by about six P.M. and getting invited to dinner. Pono's family gave me laulau last night."

"Hmm, never thought of that. Bachelor timing—I should try it sometime." Lei bit into a gooey slice, handing Stevens one on a paper towel.

A silence descended. A frisson of awareness of his nearness lifted the hair on the back of her neck, translated into an exquisite hyperfocus on the details of the room, the textures in her mouth, the muted movement of the TV screen. Lei wished she could get up and make herself an emergency vodka shot, maybe two.

They finished the pizza. Lei drank a glass of water instead and kept her eyes anywhere but on Stevens.

"So," he said.

"So."

"Did you hear the latest on Ray?"

"No. What's the story?"

"He's going to lockup soon as he leaves the hospital. Don't think he can make bail and the Changs don't appear to be picking up the tab." Stevens leaned back against the couch, sipped his beer. "Healani Chang is sending us a message by leaving him in there."

"I wish I hadn't liked him. I guess I feel bad he's paralyzed."

"You kidding me? The guy kept asking you out. What do you think he meant to do to you once he had you alone?"

Lei thought back to the gun range, the strange expression in those changeable hazel eyes behind the plastic safety goggles as he asked her out for the last time. Good thing she'd been so determined to use up her ammo.

"Shit."

"No shit," Stevens answered. He took a sip of his beer. "Just like Ito. You did what had to be done."

"Not really. I could have let him get away. He almost did."

"After trying to kill you? After shooting Keiki?" Incredulity in his tone. They both looked at the big Rottweiler, snoring softly in her funnel collar, her head pillowed on Stevens' thigh.

"You're right. Letting him get away wasn't an option." She felt something dark unknotting inside of her. She hadn't even realized she felt guilty.

Stevens put his hand over her good one where it rested on the trunk table.

"I don't know what I would have done if something had happened to you."

Lei looked down at the big hand covering hers.

He lifted it an inch, hovering above her hand. She could still feel faint heat, a magnetic tingling. She turned her palm up, reached up with her fingertip to the palm of his hand, drew it lightly down to his fingertip, and swiveled their hands so they were facing each other, palms touching upright.

She saw the hairs rise on his forearm, and he made a tiny sound.

She couldn't look at him because she knew what she'd see—a longing that matched her own. Their fingers played together, dancing, saying all that couldn't be said, and finally her hand curled up, resting cupped in his. He held it gently, lowered it to the tabletop. Warmth enfolded her through his fingers.

"Remember when I said we should wait to be together?" Stevens asked.

She nodded. Remembered that long-ago evening when he'd tried to set some rules.

"I told you I was messed up. I still am," Lei said.

"I told you something then. It's still true."

"What?"

"That if you could work on trusting me, I could work on waiting. I'll wait as long as it takes."

"Okay." She looked down at her curled hand resting in the cup of his. "But don't say I didn't warn you. They don't call me Hurricane Lei for nothing."

Acknowledgments

This book would not have been possible without the help of many people: Cheri LaSota, my first editor, who whipped me and the MS into shape enough to attract an agent. Irene Webb, my tough and hardworking agent, led me to Kristen Weber—my second editor. Kristen, an expert in crime/mystery genre, helped me take this manuscript, and the ones that follow, to the next level.

J.L., a busy Texas detective, is my awesome crime consultant and has selflessly and ruthlessly read all my books for police authenticity. A writer himself, J.L.'s critique has been invaluable and his corrections of my butchered cop lingo and wrong procedure have been particularly helpful. He even offered links and examples of gear and technology law enforcement use.

Jamie Winfrey, local Molokai police sergeant, also read, gave her stamp of approval and answered questions about being a female officer in a male-dominated field, Hawaii police protocol, and the Glock .40 pistol. (She walks like a cop, even out of uniform. I saw it firsthand.)

My family must be acknowledged for putting up with me through the rollercoaster of this process: my daughter for reading many early drafts in spite of it Not Being Her Genre; my long suffering spouse and son who continued to root for me and promise to read it "when it's in print." Sister Bonny gave early and important feedback, and sister-in-law Linda became one of my most supportive "fans" and beta readers. Knowing you guys believe in Lei's story has kept me going through sleepless nights and grumpy days.

Thanks also to my writing groups. You have been witnesses and torchbearers and assured me I wasn't alone in the obsessions and passions of being a writer.

Most of all, thanks be to God, who deserves all the glory.

About the Author

Toby Neal was raised on Kauai in Hawaii and makes the Islands home after living elsewhere for "stretches of exile" to pursue education. Toby enjoys outdoor activities including bodyboarding, scuba diving, photography and hiking as well as writing. A mental health therapist, she credits that career with adding depth to the characters in the Lei Crime Series.

Find Toby online at: http://www.tobyneal.net/

Watch for these titles

Lei Crime Series:
Blood Orchids (book 1)
Torch Ginger (book 2)
Black Jasmine (book 3)
Broken Ferns (book 4)
Twisted Vine (book 5)
Shattered Palms (book 6)
Dark Lava (book 7)

Companion Series:
Stolen in Paradise:
a Lei Crime Companion Novel (Marcella Scott)
Wired in Paradise:
a Lei Crime Companion Novel (Sophie Ang)

Middle Grade/Young Adult:
Island Fire

Contemporary Fiction/Romance:
Somewhere on Maui, an Accidental Matchmaker Novel
Somewhere on Kaua`i, an Accidental Matchmaker Novel
Unsound: a novel (Dr. Caprice Wilson)

For more information, visit:

TobyNeal.net